Yellow

Jeanne Charters

ISBN: 978-1-62420-504-0

Credits
Cover Art: Designs by Ms G
Editor: Sherry Derr-Will

Dedication

To the Free Press

One

Friday afternoon, New York City

1986

Thwack! As Sylvia Reynolds walked from the sofa to scan the Manhattan skyline, a huge black crow slammed into the window. She clamped her eyes shut, then opened them to see it begin its somersault down thirty-seven stories. One black feather stuck in a small patch of fluid remained on the glass.

"My God, Austin," she said, her voice nearly a squeal. "Did you see that?"

Austin Montgomery laughed, rose from the sofa, and ambled across the carpeted floor. He pushed a button on his desk. Gossamer curtains glided together to cover the floor-to-ceiling windows. "It happens during migration season." He gestured for Sylvia to sit down again and slid into the chair behind his desk. "The window washers will clean it."

She willed her eyes away from the feather, still visible through the sheer curtains. Sitting, she looked down at her white hands clenched over the black Hermès suit bought for this meeting. Consciously, she relaxed them and thought, *I belong in this office and today will bring me one step closer.* She held her breath. The room seemed to pulse in electric silence.

"Sylvia," he said. "I'd like you to take over as general manager at WABN." She exhaled and jumped to her feet to shake his hand. But he continued, "Provided you can follow a few critical directives."

Directives? Odd word. It struck her, as it often did, how affected Austin was—this spare man in one of his ever-present Versace suits. He even resembled Gianni Versace. Same shock of silver hair, same perpetual tan, same blinding white teeth.

Sylvia inclined her head. "Certainly. You're the chairman. Your word is law."

He looked pleased. "Good. Because there's someone at the station I need you to keep an eye on."

"Who is he?"

"She, actually. Finley Smith, the news director."

"I've met her." *That corporate party in the Bahamas. Long hair, longer legs. Gorgeous. Hated her on sight.*

"Everyone's heard of Finn," he said. "She's won every award in the business. She's a powerhouse. Her ratings are through the roof."

"Then why do you need me to watch her?"

Manicured fingers raked the white mane, "Finley's ethics are a bit—umm, lofty for my purposes."

"Your purposes?" *For Christ's sake, get to the point so I can get out of here and celebrate with a martini.*

Austin's hands lowered to the arms of his glove-leather chair. "Let's just say it's important to Prescott Broadcasting that Governor Morgan is reelected."

Sylvia's brow creased. She softened it, not wanting to appear perplexed. "Does Finley dislike Morgan's politics?"

He waved his hand in dismissal. A diamond ring flashed. "She's something of a crusader, one of those liberal journalists for whom truth trumps profit. That's all well and good if you're a saint, but let's be candid here, saints don't belong in this business." He stood, walked to the mahogany side table, and extended the silver coffee carafe toward Sylvia. She shook her head.

"Morgan has relationships with many of our most important clients." Austin refilled his cup. "They make big donations to his campaigns. And give our stations the largest share of their ad buys. It benefits those companies if, on occasion, the biggest TV station in Pennsylvania..." he cleared his throat, "looks the other way."

"Oh," Sylvia said. "You want Finley to play nice with Morgan's supporters?"

"Exactly. I'm tied to this office, so I can't be in Philadelphia to keep an eye on her."

"Why don't you just fire her?"

"That would be complicated—and suspect. Her reputation is big and growing. And, bottom line, nobody produces ratings like Finley. You see the position that puts me in, don't you?"

Sylvia adjusted the strap on her slingback shoe, waiting for a reaction that didn't come. *Curious he didn't stare,* she thought. *Men like my legs.* She gave a mental shrug. *Whatever.*

She focused back on her goal. Austin was in his mid-fifties. In ten years, she'd be forty-six. And the first female chairperson of Prescott Broadcasting.

"Rest assured." She crossed her legs again. Still no reaction. "I'll take care of Ms. Smith."

"Good. I figured if anyone could..." His laugh was cold. "Do you know people call you 'the barracuda?'"

Sylvia bristled then relaxed. *Not a bad reputation to have in this business.*

"Besides Finley, you'll need to handle the other duties of a general manager, of course. Same stuff you've done before. Raise profits, cut staff, the usual."

"No problem." Her voice sounded bitter—even to herself. "That's the fun part."

"That's what I like about you, Sylvia. You think like a man."

Yes, like a man. Like the son my father wanted. The old bastard.

She willed herself not to glance at the black feather again. "When do I start?"

Two

Friday afternoon, Philadelphia

The newsroom vibrated with deadline urgency. Only thirty minutes till the six. Weekend crews checking assignment sheets collided with reporters. Reporters screamed instructions to producers. Stringers huddled over phones in cubicles. Editors furiously punched camera directions into scripts. An intern typed text into a Teleprompter.

Finley Smith pulled long auburn hair out of her eyes and tied it into a knot on top of her head.

Emily Sanders, the weekend anchor, sitting at the same table, drew a red line through a script. Finley jumped in disbelief.

"Emily, you marked an edit through a story we agreed was set for the six. What are you thinking?"

"Sorry," the younger woman said. "Just a mistake."

Finley rose to her full five feet, ten inches. "You don't make mistakes like that."

Emily shook her head.

Finley's usual good humor was fraying fast. She had agreed to meet Meadow Marx at the gym at seven before heading over to Meadow's condo for wine and Chinese takeout.

When Emily wrote an impossible camera direction on another script, Finley led Emily by the elbow into her office and closed the door. "What's wrong with you?" Finley asked, hands clenched behind her back.

Emily sat down. Finley perched on the edge of her desk, arms crossed over her white silk blouse.

"I'm sorry," Emily said. "You're right. I'm not with it today. I can't stop thinking about rumors this morning from our stringers in Harrisburg. About the Governor."

Finley snapped to high alert. "Morgan? What rumors?"

Emily lowered her voice to a whisper. "That he signed with Cavaleri Construction to rebuild a bridge near Pittsburgh. A no-bid contract."

"Cavaleri?" Finley tried to recall why the name sounded familiar. "Weren't they the ones accused of something or other by a hospital last year?"

"Exactly. The hospital was in Pittston. Vince Cavaleri wasn't convicted, but his company has drawn complaints from across the state. The research knocked my socks off. Shopping centers, municipal buildings, even an orphanage in Scranton. Cavaleri's been charged with cutting corners for years. Unfortunately, no one's ever nailed him."

Finley put a red edit pencil into her mouth and gnawed on it. *God, I wish I still smoked*. Emily continued.

"My sources say Cavaleri's in the mob, and that Morgan is playing ball with him to get their campaign contributions. He has an election coming up, you know."

"Of course, I know." Finley took the pencil out of her mouth, looked at it in disgust, and tossed it on her desk. "Can you prove any of this?"

"Not yet. But if Cavaleri's been cutting corners like I hear, I'd think twice about crossing that Pittsburgh bridge once it's finished." Emily stared into Finley's eyes. "This whole thing stinks and we need to investigate it."

Finley had been the top investigative reporter at the station before becoming News Director three years earlier. Nothing escaped her. Now, tied to an office and Nielsen ratings, she envied Emily's freedom to travel the state and uncover real stories.

"Finn, please tell me you'll agree—to a probe," Emily begged.

Finley grabbed the pencil off her desk and started chewing again as she paced the office. After a moment, she stopped in front of Emily and stuck the pencil behind her ear. "This is tough to admit, but I'm nervous about doing another investigation right now. Austin's still furious about the story we did on that coal mine in Ravine hiring kids. He's warned me more than once to stop crusading."

Emily's mouth fell open. "You can't let corporate dictate our news coverage. Good God, this is America, home of the First Amendment, remember?"

I remember, Finley thought, angry. *I do not need a rookie anchor to lecture me about the First Amendment—even if the rookie is right. Austin Montgomery be damned.*

Finley planted her feet in front of Emily's chair. "All right. Start the investigation on Cavaleri. Go back ten years. Interview the people at the hospital and shopping center—everywhere there's been a problem. If the rumors are true, we will report it."

Emily stood to leave. "I can't tell you how relieved I am to hear you say that, boss."

"Hold it." Finley stopped Emily with a hand on her shoulder. "Keep this assignment confidential. I do not want word to get back to corporate until you know all the facts. They'd squash the story."

Emily grinned, gave Finley a thumbs up and raced out of the office.

Three

The same Friday evening, Philadelphia

Soft music drifted over the gym as lithe bodies flowed from posture to posture. Finley, though, was edgy and couldn't be silent another minute.

"I want to tell you something, but it can't be repeated, okay?" Finley whispered to Meadow as they lowered from downward dog to child pose.

Meadow Marx turned her head toward her and zipped her lips with her thumb and forefinger.

"Emily thinks Morgan cut a crooked deal with Cavaleri Construction," Finley murmured.

Meadow, reclining into corpse pose, jumped to sitting. "Huh?" The word reverberated against the soft strains of flutes and harps filtering through the room.

"Ladies, please. We're going into relaxation," Amelia, the yoga instructor, said gently.

"Sorry," Finley whispered. "We have to leave early. See you next time." She and Meadow gathered up yoga mats and blankets and tiptoed gingerly over the reclining figures on the floor of the room.

They remained silent until they were out on the street, duffle bags in tow, ready to drive to Meadow's condo.

"So, what's the deal with Morgan?" Meadow said.

"I'm hungry. Tell you over wine," Finley climbed into her car. "Pour mine and I'll stop at Wok Shop and pick up dinner. Be at your place in a jiff."

~ * ~

Twenty minutes later, Finley pulled white-socked feet up onto Meadow's couch and tilted her glass of Pinot Noir. "To Fridays."

"Amen to that." Meadow raised her own glass and gulped a swallow. "So, what's the story with Morgan and uh—who was it?"

"Cavaleri Construction."

Meadow bit her lip and lifted her eyes skyward. "Sounds familiar—oh, I remember. They booked an image campaign with the station a couple of years ago. They needed the P.R. after some fiasco with one of their clients." Meadow was the sales manager at WABN. She had started in sales shortly before Finley left the magazine she was working for to become a television reporter.

"Really?" I don't remember that."

"I could probably still dig out the commercials if you want them."

"Maybe. Emily's heard rumors that Morgan contracted with them for the repair of a bridge in Pittsburgh. It's all very hush-hush."

"Morgan's a slime," Meadow took another sip of wine. "Everybody knows it except the voters. So, what will you do?"

"I told Emily to pull out the stops on an investigative piece—and to keep it confidential from everyone. I don't want it to get back to Austin. So, like I said, Meadow—not a word."

Meadow crossed her heart. "Promise." Her bright eyes clouded. "Austin's a prick, and I know he's up to something. He's loading our commercial inventory with politicals and pharmaceuticals. I can hardly squeeze in regular clients. My account executives are bitching our rates are so high that local advertisers can't afford us. But Austin's buddies are willing to pay top dollar."

"Since when does the chairman place ad buys?" Finley said. "That never happened when John Prescott was running things."

"Right. And it's never happened at any other station I've worked at. Sales managers manage sales, but not now. I don't get it." Meadow scowled. "Austin's a slime. He'd never have that job if he hadn't married Regina Prescott."

Finley nodded. "What in God's name did she see in him? He's such a weasel."

"Hmm, more a ferret, I'd say." Meadow reached for a fortune cookie. "I reserve the term 'weasel' for my useless ex—who, by the way, has gone to court again for more alimony."

"I cannot believe you still pay him. That's nuts. He's a grown man."

Meadow popped the fortune cookie into her mouth, sliding the paper fortune into her fingers. "It's never enough. He must have a spy in accounting and knows every time I get a bonus. His radar is impeccable." She looked at her fortune. "Holy shit, this says great wealth is coming my way. Don't tell my ex."

Finley peered down into her wine glass. "I don't have that problem with David. He's stuck by his child support to the dollar." After a year and a half, the divorce still stung.

Meadow put a light hand on Finley's shoulder. "Why don't you two give it another try? You know you still love him, and I think he feels the same way."

"He says I'm addicted to news." Finley chuckled grimly. "Calls it my drug of choice—that I have no time for a family." She lowered her eyes. "And, let's face it. He's right."

Meadow shook her head. "It's lousy. When guys work hard, people call them ambitious. If we do it, we're neglecting hearth and home." She nibbled at the cookie. "Randy spends every waking moment at the station. And his wife loves it—as long as she can max out her Bloomie's charge." Randy was the general manager at WABN. "Yum! This is good," She speared a pork dumpling with a chopstick and closed her white box. "But I'd better watch it. Once you hit forty, the pounds stick like super glue."

"Like Randy...pretty porky lately, don't you think?"

"It's all the entertaining. The man never met a drink or a piece of meat he didn't like. It's a shame. He was gorgeous when he came in as general manager."

"Meadow," Finley said, turning her body as she crossed her legs Indian-style on the couch. "I have to ask. Did you ever *do* him?"

Meadow's head jerked. "Pardon me?"

Finley raised a hand in mock defense. "I'm not prying, girlfriend, but let's face it. You two took lots of trips together. I wouldn't blame you if something happened. Randy was gorgeous back then."

Meadow's eyes danced with mischief. "No, nothing heavy ever happened. We flirted and fooled around once after too many drinks at the d'Orsay bar, but I got off the elevator on my floor, not his. Horny as a half-fucked fox, but still chaste." She fluttered her eyelashes innocently. "Don't forget. Randy's quite married. Corporate would blame the woman."

Finley reached over and patted Meadow on the hand. "Glad to hear reason prevailed, sister. I'm proud of you."

Meadow high-fived Finley. "I can't believe I used to worry you'd be my competition for station hotshot. And here you are, my very best friend in the world."

"I could never compete with you. You're too crazy." Finley started to dig in her purse. "I'm looking for that card you had printed." She gave up the search. "Remember?"

It had circulated right after Meadow was named corporate salesperson of the year. It read *Meadow Marx...a piece of tail with every sale.*

When a male client tried to collect, Meadow had said, "Oh, I didn't mean mine. I meant Finley's. You'll have to negotiate that with her."

"Where did I put those cards?" Meadow said. "Maybe if I start passing them around again, I'll get lucky. It's been a long dry spell."

The ringing phone made Meadow jump. She grabbed the receiver from the side table. "I'd better take this. Might be Mikey. He's in finals and is freaking out that he won't keep his scholarship." She stood and walked into the kitchen.

Finley heard Meadow soothing and reassuring her son. *Meadow's a great mom,* she thought. *I wish I could get that close to Caroline. Now that she's almost ready for college, will I ever?*

Finley put down her glass and walked over to the large picture window. She looked out from the sixth story at the darkening April sky. Lights flicked on in buildings across the street. Cars stopped below for a light. Twilight deepened over Meadow's uptown neighborhood.

"That boy," Meadow said, picking up her glass and returning to the couch. "He gets straight As but is still scared shitless of slipping. How'd I ever end up with an anal kid? I squeaked by on bullshit my entire college life. That and my supreme sexual chemistry." She threw her head back and laughed.

Meadow's cat, Chester, jumped onto the couch and circled Finley's lap until he found his perfect spot. Then he plopped down in a heap of yellow contentment and fell asleep, purring. She caressed his head and ears.

"You should get a cat, Finn," Meadow said.

"I want to be alone for a while. See how I do after Caroline heads to college in September. I need to be happy by myself."

"Okay, but that little fur ball makes mighty good company. He doesn't care how I look or if I'm crying my eyes out onto his back. His motor calms me like nothing else, except maybe an orgasm. And I doubt I'll be having one of those very soon, at least not in mixed company."

Finley lifted the sleeping cat. His claws extended to grasp her shirt. Gently, she put him beside her on the couch. She stretched her legs, finished her wine and stood up. "Gotta go. I want to catch Caroline before she heads out for the night." She bent over to stretch out her back. "Stay put. I know my way."

She tied her gym shoes, grabbed the Nike bag from beside the couch and carried her empty takeout box to the kitchen. Then, she put on her jacket. "Bye, love." As she opened the front door, she glanced back to see Meadow pick up the remote.

"Another night with my good friend, *J.R.*," Meadow called out. "Ciao."

Finley hurried down the hall on the plush carpet toward the elevator. She pushed the down button and heard the reassuring machinery of the rising car. Her car keys were in her hand when the door opened.

"Finley," a deep voice said, surprise plastered on his voice.

She couldn't believe her eyes. "Randy," she answered. "What're you doing here?"

"Need to talk to Meadow. I'm hearing some rumors. Want to see if she knows anything."

"What rumors?"

He hesitated, "Uhhh, it's probably nothing."

Finley nodded. As the elevator door closed, her mind tumbled with possibilities. *Why didn't he just call? Could Meadow have lied about never doing Randy? Could that have been him on the phone? No, Meadow wouldn't fib to me.*

She paid the parking attendant and started navigating home.

But one question still puzzled her. *What kind of rumors would bring Randy to Meadow's apartment unannounced on a Friday night?*

Four

Friday night, New York

"Hi boss," his housekeeper yelled when Austin opened the door to his apartment.

"Hello, Zee." He hung his jacket in the hall closet. A small terrier ran to him and jumped up on his leg. "Hey there, Magnus. How are you?" He bent down to scratch behind the dog's ears. "Whew, your breath still stinks. We need to talk to Dr. Jameson about that."

A short woman with a neat grey bun at the back of her head bustled into the hall, drying her hands on an apron. "That bad mutt peed on your couch again." Zee planted her fists on stocky hips. Zee was from Warsaw—having come to New York three years earlier with her husband and four children.

"Did you give him his afternoon walk?" Austin asked.

"No time, boss," she said, scurrying around the room, plumping the pillows. "That damn phone been ringing off the hook. Those guys calling from New Jersey. Say you owe them money. You been gambling again?"

Austin's face paled under the tan. "That's not your business, Zee. Don't stick your nose in places it doesn't belong."

"It belongs there as long as I work for you, boss. I worry about you. I don't like the way they sound, these men. They mean as cat dirt. Especially that one called Sal. He say something on the phone about concrete. What that mean?"

Austin moved toward his bedroom with the dog close at his heels. "Not your concern. I'm going to change clothes and take Magnus for his walk."

Zee was right. Sal Dominici was a very mean man, and that last trip to Atlantic City had left Austin in bad shape with the greasy bastard. He had to put his hands on some money—and soon. Better call him back tonight.

Zee took off her apron and shook her head. "Okay, okay then. I go home now. Dinner in fridge. Nuke five minutes."

"Thank you," he said. "You're the best." And she was. Austin knew Zee was the only person on earth who cared if he lived or died. Most people wished he would die. But not Zee. She kept this apartment immaculate and cooked to his specifications, balancing protein, carbs and calories. Though she always said he was crazy when he rejected her rich sauces.

"Night, boss," she yelled from the front door.

"Night, Zee. See you tomorrow."

He walked into the bedroom, Magnus still shadowing every step with excited squeals. "All right, Magnus. Give me a few minutes and we'll go out."

The dog's ears pointed up at the last word and he jumped onto the bed. Austin picked up the phone and punched in the numbers.

"Hi Sal. I know I owe you money." He listened as Sal ranted on the line. "Yes, yes, Sal. Please give me a little more time. I have a plan to pay you off in full." He listened again. "Yes, very soon. You'll get your money and interest, I promise." He closed his eyes as Sal yelled and threatened him. Finally, he said, "Thanks Sal. You won't be sorry." He hung up.

Austin changed into Gucci loafers, dark-washed jeans and a tight black turtleneck. He looked at his side reflection in the full-length mirror, checking for any bulge in his abdomen. There was none. Good, still trim as a boy.

He scanned the messages Zee had scrawled on the tablet on his desk. The last one brought bile up into his throat. It said: *Dominici called. Wants to know your shoe size.*

Austin trembled despite the warmth of his apartment.

He pulled the black lambskin jacket from its hanger. He thought again that it was worth every dollar it had cost. He never wore it without getting lucky.

"Okay, Magnus." He picked up the dog's leash from the hall table.

"Let's go."

The doorman opened the front door with a flourish, and Austin thanked him with a five-dollar bill. He turned right onto East 53rd with Magnus stopping at each fire hydrant and lamp post along the way.

Magnus pulled left on Lexington. Austin chuckled as he watched the plumed tail swishing before him. If someday this little mutt gets lost, I'll know exactly where to find him.

On the crowded street, people stopped, trying to pet the scampering dog. But Magnus was relentless in his determination and would not stop for them.

They turned down a dark side street and Magnus started running, his nails clicking on the sidewalk. When they arrived at the unmarked doorway beneath the purple awning, the dog scampered up the steps to the door and sat. Austin followed him and knocked twice.

A voice came through the door. "Friend or foe?"

"Foe, fie, fee, fun," Austin answered. The door opened in seconds. A huge black man dressed in blue harem pants and a lavender turban stood there. His chest was bare.

"Interesting outfit, James," Austin said. "You must introduce me to your tailor."

"Austin, you devil. Get in here. Hi, Magnus. Want a cookie?"

Five

Monday morning

"We have now reached our cruising altitude of thirty-five thousand feet," the pilot's voice resonated. "You may now feel free to move about the cabin. We'll be in Philadelphia in ninety minutes. Sit back and have a nice flight."

Sylvia Reynolds slipped off her Ferragamos.

I should always fly first class. And from now on, most definitely will. I deserve it. When corporate needs to improve the bottom line, they know who to call. Sweet little me, that's who.

"Would you like a drink, miss?" The stewardess's proximity startled Sylvia.

"Yes, actually, I would," Sylvia replied, exaggerating her drawl. "Grey Goose martini. Straight up."

When the stewardess placed the icy glass on her tray table, Sylvia ran crimson-tipped fingers around it, savoring the anticipation of that first sip. She stirred the drink with the toothpick and popped the olive into her mouth. It was soaked perfectly with vodka. Her lips pursed from the salty tang.

Sylvia relished every part of taking over a station. On her first such assignment five years ago, the staff at KTVH in Santa Fe had greeted her with enthusiasm. They had a party to welcome their new general manager and raved about her sophisticated clothes and adorable Southern accent.

"Where did you get that suit, Ms. Reynolds?" Billy Mendoza, the effete production director, had asked as he touched the sleeve of her jacket. When she jerked away from his hand, his eyes turned panicky, and he excused himself. Sylvia saw his fear and smiled as she remembered his discomfort.

Her appearance often took people off guard. She liked that. Who could fear a dainty blonde with a Southern drawl and big green eyes? No one noticed the set of the jaw until it was too late.

As she sipped her martini, she scanned the roster of WABN managers and account executives. Each name was followed by the person's tenure, salary, and generated revenues. Her practiced eye flitted down the list, focusing on those whose longevity had resulted in a high salary level. Methodically, she placed check marks next to three names.

Marty Sax…Chris Andrews…Meadow Marx. When her pen poised over Randy Thompson's name, she smiled. He already knows I'm coming to town. Wait'll I tell him why.

She thought back to the company awards dinner in the Bahamas. She was there representing KTVH but already had her eye on WABN, the crown jewel of the three-station Prescott chain.

The awards banquet had ended with WABN winning most of the trophies, as usual. People clustered around Randy patting him on the back for a job well done. He was flushed with compliments and scotch.

Sylvia moved in. "Congratulations, Randy."

"Thanks, Sylvia, but I don't deserve much of the credit. My only talent is that I hire good people."

She had scanned the room. Randy's wife was occupied with Chris Andrews, WABN's ancient anchorman, and his silly young girlfriend. "I need some air," she said. "Join me for a walk?"

He looked surprised and checked the crowd, settling on his wife's back on the other side of the ballroom. Sylvia could almost see his addled brain trying to make the decision. Finally, he answered. "Sure. Last night in paradise, right?"

They walked out to the balcony and down the stairs toward the sand. She slipped out of her sandals and raised her arms to welcome the cool evening breeze. The move caused her strapless dress to fall slightly. "Take off your shoes, Randy. Feel the night. Tomorrow, it's back to reality."

Looking awkward, he removed his shoes and black socks. As they strolled down the beach toward the water, they were soon away from the lights of the resort. About fifty yards from the hotel where they could scarcely hear the music from the orchestra, she said, "Let's sit down for a minute. It's beautiful here."

"I don't know, Sylvia," he said. "They might be looking for us."

"Oh, come on. We only live once. How often will we find ourselves in such a beautiful place? Besides, the awards part of the evening is over. "

At first, he hesitated, but finally, looking down at his taupe linen slacks, he dropped down on the sand, as she knew he would. She sat facing him, her bare legs tucked under her, aware that her dress had crept down to reveal more of her breasts. She started to filter sand through her fingers onto his feet and leaned forward to give him a better look. His eyes darted left to right as he seemed to shrink smaller into the night while staring fixedly at her breasts.

"Don't be an old scaredy cat." She touched his cheek.

He pulled back, then made his move, taking her face into his hands and plunging his scotch-laced tongue into her mouth.

"Randy," she hissed into his open mouth, then pulled back. "How dare you!"

He looked like a bad boy caught raiding a forbidden cookie jar. "Sorry, Sylvia, just the booze. Don't know what came over me. Won't happen again."

You bet it won't, she thought, unless it suits my purposes.

Now she had him exactly where she wanted him. They hurried back toward the resort, him babbling apologies like an adolescent fool. Sylvia remained silent as a stone. Her plan was in place.

Grinning at the memory, Sylvia went back to the WABN roster. She hit Finley Smith's name. Her pencil stopped. High salary—but untouchable for now. She'd make Ms. Smith get those ratings even higher. More tabloid stuff would do it. It worked at every station she'd managed. But eventually, she would get rid of Finley. Sylvia didn't want her around

She continued checking the list. Though Finley was off limits per Austin's orders, others weren't. Sylvia knew plenty of sales managers, production directors and account executives who would kill for a chance to come to a large market like Philadelphia. For less money than these people were earning.

The stewardess removed her glass and Sylvia declined a second drink. She took a compact from her purse and snapped it open.

The mirror reflected the eyes of her father, the legendary Michael Reynolds. Like Sylvia's, his eyes were green—the color of money—and they could calculate a return on investment quicker than anyone in the business. He had headed up Reynolds, Simpson and Schwartzman for twenty-five years, the top advertising agency in Manhattan. Everyone said her daddy was a shark. She smiled. Wonder who'd win in the fight between a shark and a barracuda?

No one, including her father, knew of the dark, mysterious men in airport cocktail lounges across the country. Men whose pasts or futures were of no concern. She used aliases, Miriam or Anne or Avery, with surnames picked from phonebooks. It was a fun game. She even had business cards printed with her fake identities.

Her eyes would connect with the man over the rim of her cocktail glass then lower with feigned shyness. That was usually enough.

"Excuse me, miss. Do we know each other?"

She'd investigate his features. "I'm not sure. I'm Miriam (or Anne or Avery)." He'd respond with a name and a card and the cat-and-mouse game would begin. If they were flying to the same town, they would have another drink upon arrival and she'd make her decision. She could change reservations to wherever he was staying, if he was worth it.

She never knew if any of them tried to contact the woman whose name was on the business card. She smiled, visualizing their faces as they learned that no such phone number, company or person existed.

Sylvia only remembered one of them with any clarity. It was at O'Hare in February, and the airport had closed during one of those blizzards that often cripple the Midwest. After two hours of canceled flights, she resigned herself that she wouldn't be getting out that night. Frustrated, she booked a room at the airport Marriott and arrived there around ten. A bellman took her luggage and coat to her room and Sylvia headed for the hotel bar. It was packed with travelers drowning their grumbles. She spied an available seat and grabbed it, nearly knocking an elderly man over in her haste. The harried woman behind the bar didn't see her immediately.

Finally, the bartender stopped in front of her. "Would you like a drink, miss?"

"My God, yes, I'd like a drink. I thought I was invisible."

"Sorry...we're so busy."

"Johnnie Walker, blue, and hurry."

As the bartender turned to pour Sylvia's drink, a deep voice beside her said, "You know, sugar, you'd catch more flies with honey than vinegar."

She swiveled her stool in his direction, poised for a fight. Then she saw his face, a handsome face, the face of a shark. The corners of his dark eyes creased. He was laughing. Sylvia started to tell him she had no interest in catching flies, but then he touched her hand.

"Soft," he said. She saw the white ring mark on the tanned left hand but ignored it. *That's his wife's problem—not mine.*

He told Sylvia he had been heading home from a conference in New York, before this God-awful blizzard trapped him in Chicago. He gave her a card that identified him as Daniel Brower of Coswell, Brower and Mittner, a law firm in Denver. By the time they started a second drink, she knew. He would come to her room, and she'd invite him in.

This man, this night, was different. Daniel Brower seemed to have all the time in the world and nothing on his mind but Sylvia. His hands were slow as they unbuttoned, unhooked and slid clothes from her body so gradually she scarcely noticed them falling away. All she could do was feel—feel her nipples pucker as they lifted to him, hungry for his mouth—feel her groin pushing urgently against his hardness. When his hands lowered and found her wet, she was suddenly embarrassed. How could she open herself so eagerly to a total stranger? Her need for him frightened her. Sylvia, always in charge, was losing control to a man she'd met only an hour earlier.

But all fear disappeared when he groaned appreciatively and lifted himself to his elbows. "Ooohhh," he said. "So soft, so wet." He slipped on a condom without Sylvia knowing where he'd gotten it and entered her deeper than she'd ever been penetrated before.

He slowed, rising above her and staring into her eyes. He lifted her hands and placed them on her breasts. "Pinch your nipples, baby. It'll feel good." His hand rose to his mouth and he moistened his fingers, then lowered them to just above where he was thrusting. The fingers started to squeeze and pulsate. At first, Sylvia tried to stop him, fearing she would lose her mind. Then she stopped caring if she did. Her mind didn't matter— nothing mattered but the torrent of ecstasy sweeping through her. Whatever she lost, whatever she never regained was worth it.

When the kaleidoscope of stars faded from behind her clamped eyes, she opened them to see him propped on one elbow, grinning down at her. "My turn," he said.

She awoke the next morning to a note. "Had to run back to the airport. Thanks for a magical night. D."

With Daniel Brower, for perhaps the first time in her life, Sylvia imagined herself cherished. Tried the feeling on for size and found it to her liking. She wrote Sylvia Brower on her notepad to see how it looked, then scratched through it, embarrassed at her silliness.

Two days later, she tried the number on his card.

"The number you have called has been disconnected," the recorded voice droned in her ear. "We have no further information on this number."

She called the Bar Association and was told that no Daniel Brower practiced in the state of Colorado. Slowly, a painful realization dawned on her. He had played her game better than she. She wondered if he ever tried to contact Avery Nordstrom at the number on the card she'd given him and sadly realized he probably had not. Sylvia'd been beaten at her own sport, and it hurt like hell.

"Please return to your seats and fasten your seatbelts. We'll be landing in twenty minutes." Sylvia forced the memory of Daniel Brower or whoever he was out of her mind and fastened her seatbelt. Randy Thompson would be waiting to drive her to the station. Sucking up to her, perhaps a little scared, but not yet suspecting that Sylvia was there to take away his job.

Sylvia deplaned and headed toward baggage claim. She saw Randy at the carousel before he spotted her.

"Hello there," she said to the broad back.

His head snapped around at the sound of her voice. "Sylvia, good to see you again." He pumped her hand. "Can't wait to hear what brings you to WABN."

As he hoisted her Gucci bag onto his shoulder, she turned her back to him and smiled. "You'll learn my purpose for being here soon, Randy. Very soon."

Six

"Caroline," Finley yelled up the staircase. "Get up. You're going to be late for school."

She waited, pushing back her cuticles and mentally counted. *Eight potato...nine potato...ten potato.* "Caroline! Now!"

Feet hit the upstairs floor hard. Next came the sound of a flushing toilet. Seconds later, the shower spurted.

"Good," she muttered to herself as she returned to the kitchen. "The princess has arisen." She whisked eggs in a mixing bowl. The action of the metal whisk whipping through the eggs and smacking against the ceramic of the bowl soothed her. And Finley was much in need of soothing this morning.

The entire weekend had been a nightmare of screaming followed by a distant quiet after Caroline broke curfew Friday night and came home reeking of alcohol. Caroline's words were slurred. "Fuck off and die, mommy dearest."

At that moment, Finley remembered the news stories about the crazy mothers who drowned kids in bathtubs or drove them into lakes or laced their oatmeal with rat poison. She'd been horrified when she'd reported on them. Now she almost understood. If there was some way she could get away from this monster her daughter had turned into since the divorce, she'd take it.

She'd call David tomorrow. He'd be back from his conference in Buffalo then. Maybe she'd suggest Caroline go live with him for a while—at least until the hatred abated—if it ever did. Caroline had threatened often enough to go live with her daddy. Okay, maybe it was time to call her bluff.

Finley heard the hair dryer switch off upstairs. She sprayed the small skillet and started scrambling the eggs. Her timing was perfect. Just as they hit Caroline's necessary degree of fluffiness, the girl stomped into the kitchen.

Finley slid the plate of eggs to Caroline's place and pushed the pitcher of orange juice toward her. Caroline poured a glass of juice and downed it quickly. No "thank you."

Finley turned her back to the table and started scouring the skillet. Anything to keep busy. Anything to avoid looking at the sullen look on the face shoving eggs into her mouth and then standing up to stomp away from the table. The door slammed and Finley heard Caroline's car accelerate.

I'll take that damned car away from her, Finley resolved as she scraped leftover eggs into the compost pot on the sink. *But then I'd have to drive her to school every day and pick her up after and that's not going to happen. I can't leave the office.*

Hurrying to finish the dishes before work, she slammed the plate against the faucet and it shattered. Looking at the shards of glass in the sink, Finley's eyes blurred. She tried to be careful picking them up, but one sharp edge pierced her forefinger and blood flowed over the broken glass. It was a deep cut. *Where did I put the antiseptic spray and Bandaids?* Her mind was as muddled as her kitchen looked in that moment. She wrapped a paper towel around the finger.

~ * ~

Finley arrived at the station, pushed the start button on the coffeemaker, sat down at her desk and exhaled. All the papers were exactly as she'd left them on Friday. She sharpened an edit pencil and enjoyed the sound. Her stapler, paper clips and telephone were perfectly arranged on the desk top. She centered the wooden block with the gold plate that read "Finley Smith, Director of News" at the front of her desk.

Satisfied, she poured a cup of black coffee and began to read the weekend newspapers she'd found stacked outside her office. By the time she'd finished studying them and had downed a second cup of coffee, an hour had passed.

The Monday morning sales meeting would be over. She wanted to talk to Meadow. She needed a sounding board about Caroline, and she also wanted to know why Randy had come to Meadow's condo Friday night.

Her mouth tasted sour from the coffee. She grabbed breath spray from her purse, ran her fingers through her hair and walked out of her office.

Meadow's secretary looked up from the computer, pushed her glasses up from the tip of her nose and smiled.

"Hi, Heather. She available yet?" Finley asked.

"She's not coming in today, Ms. Smith. Went to New York unexpectedly. Told me to clear her calendar. Even canceled the sales meeting." The girl shrugged her shoulders as if confused.

Finley kept her face impassive. "No problem. I had a quick question about a story that could affect sales. I'll catch her tomorrow." Meadow went to New York? Without mentioning it? Finley hadn't called her all weekend because of her upset state of mind over Caroline, but Meadow usually checked in at least once. Especially if she was leaving town. What was going on?

She hurried back to her office, dodging a reporter who tried to sto p her. "Catch me later, Sue, okay? Something I need to attend to right away." She shut her door and picked up her phone. At the message, she said, "Hey Meadow. You didn't tell me you were going to the city today. What's up?"

Minutes later, her phone rang. Finley recognized the number. "Hey, Meadow."

The voice was hushed. "Finn, I was sitting in Marquand's office when you called. You know, the guy with the fake hair?"

"Yes, I know who you mean."

"Randy asked me to corner him today and see if the rumors he's heard are true."

"What rumors?"

"That Austin's sending a hatchet man to the station."

"Who?"

"I don't know yet. Marquand's playing it cute. Acted dumb. I can't get in to see Austin. He's in closed-door meetings all day, according to his gargoyle gate keeper."

"So, what are you going to do?"

"I have to catch the train back before six. I have meetings scheduled all day tomorrow. So I may come up empty on this whole trip."

"If you find out, Meadow, call me."

"Promise." Click.

~ * ~

Finley was trying to fit *Pet Connection* into the Noon News format when Chris Andrews, the six o'clock anchor, walked into her office. His perfect face looked worried.

"Why are you in so early, Chris?"

He paced to her window, turned his left side toward her—the side the camera loved best. Then he walked back and slouched into the chair opposite her desk. "Just wanted to get an early grip on the day." He began to run a hand through the grey-templed black hair, and stopped, as if remembering it had just been sprayed to perfection.

"So," he said, examining his nails. "Heard any news?"

"What kind of news?" Oh no, she thought. The gossip mill is running. Something must be going on.

"Oh, I don't know," he said.

"Yes, you do, Chris. Please tell me what you're talking about."

"Rumors are some hatchet woman is going to replace Randy."

Woman? Who?

"Chris, don't believe that stuff," she waved her hand in dismissal. "Randy's doing a great job. We're top in the market."

Chris shifted in the chair. "Maybe you're right. But just in case, I'm sending my resume to a headhunter. I might be ready for a bigger market. I don't need a hassle from some corporate bitch at this stage of my career."

Finley moved behind him. She started kneading the tight muscles beneath his impeccably tailored jacket. Years of experience had taught her how to deal with insecure anchors, and she didn't want Chris to get hurt. They'd been friends since the day she came to the station. He'd supported her through all the years since. A headhunter would be quick to let him

26

know he was way past his L.A. or New York City days.

He turned his head and raised anxious eyes to Finley. Needing assurance, she thought. Pity and concern welled up in her. She had to find the right words. "You're the number one anchor in Philadelphia, Chris," she purred. This at least was true. "Everybody loves you." Even as she said it, she flinched, remembering his "Q" score in the last focus group. "Don't worry. It'll be okay." His shoulders eased into the kneading of her fingers. She avoided disturbing his hair.

He picked up the picture from her desk. "How's Caroline? Pretty girl."

Finley's forehead creased. "Oh, she's okay. Usual teenage stuff."

"How's she dealing with the divorce?"

"Pretty good," she lied.

"That's good. My kids won't even speak to me. Their mother's poisoned them against me. Since we split, she's been on a mission to make me look bad, not just to the kids, but to any tabloid that wants to smear me."

Finley smoothed the fabric of his jacket and returned to her chair. She was worried about Chris, whose only talent lay in addressing a Teleprompter and turning to camera on cue. He still liked to boast that he never read a newspaper. Ten years ago, viewers thought that was funny, but time and tension had diluted the humor. Competition was just too tough.

Behind closed doors, people at the station joked about the night he had tried for an ad lib and said, "Good news, Philadelphia. Inflation is up."

When they were off air, Tom Boyle, a field reporter, had taken him aside. "Hey Chris, you know, inflation isn't really good news."

"Fuck you, Boyle," Chris had exploded. "Who died and made you guru?"

If the rumors were true, Chris Andrews' days at WABN could be numbered. And after all his years here, Finley feared he couldn't take the slap in the face that could be ahead. Who was this hatchet woman?

Seven

Monday morning, Philadelphia

With Sylvia's luggage stashed in his trunk, Randy maneuvered through dense traffic toward the station. Sylvia sat quietly as he chattered away like a nervous school boy. Had he somehow gotten wind of something? She smiled in anticipation of an interesting day.

"Nice car, Randy," she said, and observed with amusement his pride at her compliment. It was a beauty—a brand-new Lexus that purred along like a sleek black panther.

"Thanks, Sylvia. Just got it. My reward to myself for a great first quarter." He patted the dashboard.

Sylvia crossed her legs and saw his eyes dart to the right at the soft murmur of silk. She waited for him to change the subject and stayed silent. Randy was not the kind to remain quiet for long.

He jolted his gaze back to the highway. "How's your dad doing anyway?" he asked. "Enjoying retirement?"

"He's busier than when he was at the agency." She stretched her hands over her head and saw his eyes swivel to her outthrust breasts. She smiled. "Serves on just about every important board in New York now, even Prescott Broadcasting's. He could never retire...too much energy."

"Great guy, but tough," he chuckled. "I remember how he intimidated me when he was the media buyer and I was his new account executive. The first time I called him, he told me I had the timing of a turd."

"Sounds like Daddy," Sylvia said. "Come to think of it, he was right on about your timing. Remember that night in the Bahamas?" She watched him now, knowing her question would make him squirm.

His hands whitened on the steering wheel. "Now Sylvia, that was the Scotch talking. I've said I'm sorry in eight hundred ways. I hope by now you know I mean it."

"Sure, Randy." She savored his discomfort.

He pulled the car up to the side of WABN and parked in the spot marked General Manager. He led Sylvia into the lobby and introduced her to Stephanie, the receptionist, who stood, extended her hand and smiled. "Happy Monday."

When the elevator door opened on the third floor, Sylvia saw the prototypical TV sales department. Tiny cubicles, sectioned by Plexiglas walls, each inhabited by an earnest young man or woman talking into a phone or hunched over a Daytimer. Randy waved to them as he directed Sylvia to the right and into his office.

The room covered nearly one quarter of the third floor. A wall of windows displayed the panorama of downtown Philadelphia. In the distance, she saw the Philadelphia Museum of Art and the Delaware River. It was a decent downtown and Sylvia hoped to find an apartment close to all the shops and cafes nearby.

"Nice town." She turned from the window and took a seat on the plush red couch that, along with a few red-matted black and white photographs provided the only color in the dramatic black and white office. *He used a decorator*, she mused.

He lowered himself behind the lacquered desk and ruffled papers nervously. "So how long will you be visiting us, Sylvia?"

She remained silent and watched beads of perspiration form on his broad forehead.

Finally, she spoke. "Actually, I won't be leaving. You will. Austin thought it best that I be the one to tell you. You'll finish up by close of business today, and I'll replace you as general manager."

She paused, letting the yeast of her words rise in his consciousness. When she crossed her legs this time, the move didn't register on his flushed face.

"But why?" he stammered as his high forehead began to visibly shine.

Maybe I should take out my compact and offer to powder him a bit.

She smiled.

"Our numbers are good," he continued. "Revenues are up. Why would they replace me?"

Sylvia waved a dismissive hand in the air. "Oh, you know how corporate is. Sometimes, they like to shake things up to see if profits can be increased. They think I'm best prepared to do that. You've been here seventeen years, a little stuck in a rut, they say. It's time for a change. I make changes. Corporate knows it."

Randy jumped to his feet, then seemed confused to find himself standing. He wandered to the window and stared down at the street. "I'll sue. That's what I'll do. They can't get away with this. Not after all I've done for this company."

Sylvia stood and walked to a mirror on the side wall. Fluffing her hair, she said, "Now, Randy, you won't sue. You'll get a decent severance if you don't make a fuss. But if you cause problems..." She formed a zero with her thumb and forefinger. "You know the drill. If another company learns that you've sued Prescott and, of course, they all will, you'll be dead in the industry. So, don't blow smoke.

"Besides, if you tried anything like that, I'd have to tell the company lawyers about that night you tried to stick your tongue down my throat. Remember? Austin was terribly shocked when I told him how violated I felt. He thinks we should just keep it quiet—for now. But if you cause trouble, I won't have any recourse but to sue you for sexual harassment. I wonder how your chubby little wife would like that."

Sylvia sat back down on the couch and watched him quietly.

His mouth hung open. "You told Austin?"

"Well, of course I told him. I was so hurt and confused I didn't know what else to do."

He started to storm around the office in what looked like panicked disbelief. Then, she saw reality set in. He returned to his desk and adjusted his stapler.

He jumped when his phone started ringing. "Yes," he answered, sitting erect. "Oh hi, honey." The struggle to control his voice was pitiful. He slumped in his chair and pulled at his hair as he listened. "That's great news, babe. Princeton, huh? So, he doesn't want to go to Penn State any longer?"

Sylvia could hear the woman's voice on the line as it accelerated and rose.

"Of course, I'm excited, sweetie. It's just that Princeton is so expensive."

The woman's voice grew even louder.

"I know, I know. Don't worry. I won't spoil it for him. Give him my congratulations and tell him he can pick the restaurant for a celebration this weekend. Tell him to invite his friends. Give him the book of station trades."

He hung up and sank back in his chair.

Sylvia spoke. "Randy, you know perfectly well restaurant trades are only for client entertainment. You use them for personal matters?"

His laugh had the hollow ring of a gallows. "What the fuck does it matter now, Sylvia? What're you gonna do, fire me?"

~ * ~

By that afternoon, the news had spread across the station. Finley headed for Randy's office as soon as she heard. *Damn. Of all the bosses I've worked with, Randy was the best*

She stuck her head in his door. "Is it true?"

No answer was necessary. An embarrassed-looking man in uniform stood guard as Randy packed boxes with his personal belongings. "Jesus Christ," Randy railed. "What's she think I'm gonna do, lift the files? They put this goon on me to make sure I don't steal the fucking paper clips."

Finley looked at the security guard who shook his head sadly.

"Severance?" Finley asked, sitting down.

"Yeah, something, but I haven't had a chance to tell my attorney to check it out with corporate."

"Randy, that should be the first thing you do." She kept her voice gentle.

"I know. Of course, I know that, Finn. But this shit has knocked me to my knees. Can't seem to navigate my brain. Haven't told Phyllis. Pete got accepted at Princeton, and she's on cloud nine. I was praying for Penn State, but now..."

Finley knew Phyllis. A nice-enough woman with very expensive tastes. She and Randy had three kids, and Pete was the eldest, Phyllis's pride and joy.

Finley continued softly. "You'd better talk to her about that. Penn State is nothing to be sneezed at. His tuition will be a fraction of Princeton's."

Randy shook his head as if to push away the shock. Finley's heart ached for the big man sitting opposite her. After seventeen years, he deserved better. *But the brutal business of local television didn't often play fair.*

"Steve," Finley said to the security guard. "Could we have a few private minutes?"

The man nodded and left the room.

"Let's take this one step at a time," she said. "First, sit down. You can finish packing this stuff later. Call your lawyer and ask him to contact corporate. See what they're offering. Tell your attorney to negotiate up. Next, start making a list of your friends in the business. I'll help you with that. They're all over the country. You'll land on your feet."

Like an automaton, he picked up the phone. When he had finished his conversation with the lawyer, he buried his face into his hands. "I'm fifty-two years old."

"What?"

"You know what that means. Over the hill. Too expensive. They can buy two twenty-five -year-olds for less than I make. I know this business. From here on, it's downhill for me."

Finley remained silent. She couldn't argue against the truth. Maybe Randy could get a job in cable or in a smaller town, but his big-market network days were over, and they both knew it.

They sat together watching the sun as it crept behind the Philadelphia skyline.

"God, Finn, what am I gonna tell Phyllis? You know how she is."

"The truth. Maybe she'll surprise you." The words hollow even as she said them. Phyllis was a high-maintenance wife, much like Finley's own mother had been. But Finley's dad had left his family well situated when he died. His money was old and well invested, so there'd never been a problem. Randy and Phyllis were different. Their money was new, and they both liked to spend it on toys like cars, jewelry and member ships in the best country club in town.

A sharp rap at his door stopped her reverie. Phyllis walked in. "Randy, did you forget?"

Finley cringed. Phyllis had stuffed her ample figure into a tight purple cocktail dress and was wearing false lashes.

"We're meeting the Martinsons at the Club in one hour." Phyllis turned to Finley with a *deliver me* expression. "Men," she continued. "I knew he'd forget, so I brought him a fresh shirt. I don't know what he'd do if he didn't have me around to dress him."

Phyllis turned her attention back to Randy, "You can change in the car. We'll just make it."

How odd—she didn't even notice the packing boxes, Finley thought. "Phyllis, great news about Pete. You must be so proud." Finley said.

"Proud? I'm over the moon. I was hoping for Ivy League, but was prepared for Penn State, just in case." She pulled Randy to his feet. "Wish we could stay and chat, Finley, but I have to get this big lug presentable while we're in the car or we'll be late for our dinner date. See you soon, I hope."

Randy scanned the packed boxes with panic in his eyes. Finn said, "Don't worry about them. I'll have them sent over." He nodded, then walked toward the elevator as though a hangman awaited him there. Well, one sort of does, Finley thought, as she headed to her own office, heavy with sadness. She flipped on the plasma TV to watch the six o'clock broadcast.

The familiar blue and red graphics swirled across the screen as the music built to its customary crescendo and the call letters WABN came full screen.

"Good evening," Chris Andrews spoke from a two-shot next to Emily Sanders. "The latest report on casualties from last November's volcanic eruption in Columbia has reached twenty-five thousand people. Scientists question whether the increase in natural disasters around the world could be related to the discovery of the first hole in the earth's ozone layer."

The footage of destruction on the television dissolved to a full-screen shot of a handsome American actor. "Doctors have now confirmed that Rock Hudson's death last October was the result of AIDS."

Oh no, Finley mused. *He really must have been gay. Unbelievable. That's why he was so thin.* She closed her eyes and leaned her head back against the couch.

She opened them again at the sound of Emily's hopeful voice. "There's good news in the fight against breast cancer. With us is Dr. Angela Goodwin, WABN's health editor, to bring us up-to-date." Dr. Goodwin spoke of promising results of MRI research on breast cancer that could reduce the number of deaths in the future.

When the screen dissolved to commercials, Finley flipped off the set just as Meadow stormed into her office, eyes blazing. "Did you hear?" she said. "That drawling bitch is replacing Randy."

"Yes," Finley answered, weariness invading every bone of her body. "I left his office twenty minutes ago."

"How is he?"

"How do you think? He's wrecked. Trying to figure out how to tell Phyllis." Finley sat back down behind her desk. "I wonder who'll be next."

The two women stared at each other until Meadow stood and said, "Screw 'em. I'm going home."

Eight

Tuesday afternoon

Finley's head throbbed as she waited for the phone to connect. She was so tired. The changes at the station coupled with a still-sullen Caroline had kept her mind buzzing until the alarm rang at six this morning. She had no choice—she had to call David.

Finally, the female voice answered the phone. "Good afternoon, Dr. Smith's office. How can I help you?"

"Hi Nancy, it's Finley. How've you been?"

"Finley, I'm so glad to hear your voice. I've missed you."

"Thanks, Nancy. That's good to hear. Is he in?"

"Yes, he's with a patient right now, but the time's almost up. Can you hold for a second?"

"Yes, I will...and, Nancy—it's great to hear your voice again, too."

The familiar music kicked in and Finley leaned back in her chair. She rubbed her right temple and hoped the sounds of Celtic strings would soothe her nerves.

The refrain ended. "Hi, Finn. What's up?" His voice was deep and to the point. *Must he be so abrupt?*

She pushed aside the hurt. "It's Caroline. She broke curfew Friday night and had been drinking. When I try to talk to her, she treats me like a Neanderthal." Her throat caught. "I think she despises me."

"Damn," he said. "Should we sit down with her?"

"She won't even stay in the same room with me. I'm lost on this one."

There was a long pause. "Then it's best if I talk to her alone. I'll try

35

to see what's going on and, if necessary, refer her to Jim Templeton. He's the best in town for teen stuff." He paused and lowered his voice. "I know the divorce is bothering her."

Without warning, Finley's temper flared. "So, this is my fault?"

His sigh sounded defeated. "I didn't say that. It's no one's fault. Kids have to grow up and rebellion's part of the process. I guess there's no good time for a girl to adjust to the fact that her parents have split."

Finley steadied herself. "Maybe I should have tried harder, David." She closed her eyes, willing him to reassure her that it wasn't too late.

"Hell, I suppose we both should have. We've been through this a hundred times, and nothing's changed. I blame your crazy job, and you say I don't understand. It's a classic problem. You're an addict to the news biz, and I still don't think the boob tube quite equates to brain surgery gravitas."

For a second, her anger flared. *I make more money than you do, buddy.* Finley forced her voice to a cheerful tone. It wasn't easy. "Okay, David. When can you see Caroline?"

"I'll call tonight and see if she can have dinner with me tomorrow. We'll make it around six so that she can get her homework done before I pick her up. Fair?"

"Fair. Bye, David. Thanks." She hung up and lowered her head to her desk.

She jumped to attention when Tom Bucci, the assignment editor, charged into her office. "Hey Finley," he said. "Bad accident at Penn's Landing. Two cars involved...and injuries. Need to get a producer and cameraman over there quick so we can hit the five with the story."

Finley's throat tightened in momentary panic. Caroline's school was at Penn's Landing. No, she reasoned—Caroline would be home by now. Her classes ended early on Tuesday.

"Take Johnny and Angela. She's our fastest producer."

"Right," he said, racing from her office.

~ * ~

At three fifteen that afternoon, Angela Zarobsky entered Finley's office without knocking.

Angela's hands trembled as she sat down across from Finley. "Finn, listen, love." She hesitated. "There was a girl involved in the accident at Penn's Landing. We don't have positive identification on her yet, but the injuries were bad. We'll run the disclaimer about not mentioning names until family notification. I have the footage ready to roll." Angela looked ready to cry. She stopped talking.

"Angela, what are you not telling me?" Finley said.

Angela shuffled her feet and lowered her eyes. "Someone said the girl goes to Pennbrook."

Finley tried to reason her panic away. No, it wouldn't be Caroline. Lots of the girls at Pennbrook had cars. It could be any of them. But she had to find out.

She dialed Caroline's home number. The cheerful voice delivered its usual message. "Caroline here. No talkie right now. Leave your digits. Hope you're having fun. Buh bye."

Finley raced into the newsroom. "Emily," she said handing the girl the format sheet. "Can you finish this up?"

"Of course." Emily stood. "We're set for the five." She looked worried. Angela had obviously told Emily about the Pennbrook girl.

Finley dialed the school. A recorded voice answered. "No one is available at Pennbrook School to speak to you at the moment. Please leave your..." Finley slammed the phone down, cursing at the innocuous, invisible voice.

She raced to the elevator, yelling instructions to her secretary as she pulled on her jacket. In seconds, the door opened.

Sylvia Reynolds stood in front of her. "Well, hi there, Finley. Just the person I wanted to see. Got a minute?"

Nine

"The hell with her," Finley muttered. She put the car into drive. Sylvia's face, impassive at Finley's hurried excuse, had hardened into a scowl. *Fuck her,* Finley thought, racing toward Penn's Landing. Her nerves screamed at each stop sign and traffic light until she thought the top of her head might explode. Finally, she came to the intersection, and there her breathing stopped.

They were attaching Caroline's little Honda to the tow truck—the car she and David gave her for her sixteenth birthday. The twisted red metal and shattered windows sent Finley out of control. "No-o-o-o," she screamed.

An SUV loomed like an elephant next to the Honda, its fender stained red from impact. A sobbing woman stood next to it, babbling to a police officer.

"Where did they take the injured?" Finley screamed out her car window to the driver of the tow truck, hysteria threatening her speech.

"Over to Wills Eye Hospital on Walnut," the cop answered over his shoulder.

As she turned her car toward Walnut, she pulled over and ran to a pay phone. With trembling hands, she called David's office. Again, an answering machine.

When she pulled into the Emergency Room parking area, his car was already there. *How did he get here so quickly? Who told him? He must have broken every speed limit in the city. Thank God he's here.*

She ran in the door and frantically looked around the crowded waiting room. She didn't see David. She hurried to the receptionist.

The woman had dyed red hair and wore purple eyeliner. Her flowered dress was cut low enough to reveal large, freckled breasts. She laughed into the phone. "You're kidding. He said that? What a jerk."

"Excuse me, please," Finley interrupted, nearly screaming. "My daughter may be here. Her car was involved in an accident at Penn's Landing."

The receptionist's eyes widened. She said into the phone, "Call you later, doll." Her eyes scanned Finley's contorted face. "What's your daughter's name?"

"Caroline Smith. She's only seventeen. I saw her car at the accident site."

The woman rifled through the cards on her desk. "Yes, ma'am." Her voice softened which frightened Finley still more. *Why is she being nice now?* "Your daughter is being treated in the E.R. Your husband is with her. The nurse will take you in."

Finley followed a white-masked woman through the closed door and focused on the cheerful print of her jacket. Flowers and balloons blurred before her eyes in a myriad of pastel colors. When they arrived at the treatment room, the nurse put her arm around Finley's waist and opened the door.

David was standing back from the examining table, his hands clenched behind his back. When he saw Finley, he came to her and took her in his arms.

"Is she?" she stammered.

"She's alive, Finn, but badly hurt. Unconscious. We can't talk to her. The best thing we can do is let the doctors help her and stay out of their way."

"Can I see her?"

The nurse led her gently to the examining table. Finley gasped. The mummy creature lying on the gurney did not resemble her beautiful daughter in any way. The eyes were closed, bruised. Her forehead was stitched. Tubes and wires cascaded from her body and connected to beeping machines with constantly changing graphs on monitoring screens.

The nurse turned to her and said in a gentle voice, "Please stay calm, ma'am. We'll take real good care of her."

Blackness descended. Just before Finley hit the floor, David's arms caught her and brought her back to her feet. "Take it easy, honey. She's tough. She'll make it," he said.

Would she? As darkness clouded Finley's vision again as she thought *he called me honey*.

~ * ~

The intensive care room was cramped. David and Finley sat in the two uncomfortable chairs as nurses and technicians buzzed in and out, checking monitors. Caroline remained unconscious all of Wednesday. "She's stable," one young man said. *Was he a doctor?* Finley supposed so.

After a sleepless night for Finley and David, Caroline was moved to a hospital room which was marginally larger than the last one with slightly more comfortable chairs. Finley's eyes were nearly closed when Caroline's slight moans wakened her. A man in white was examining her. "Finn, this is Doctor Thompson. He's a hospital surgeon," David said.

Caroline's pitiful whimpers were the only sounds in the room as the doctor examined broken bones and stitched wounds. Finley and David never left the room and as time passed, took turns resting in the uncomfortable sleep chair the hospital provided.

David canceled all patient consultations, making one exception when his secretary called, concerned about a fragile woman with a history of attempted suicide. "It'll take me an hour, Finn, so I'll be back here by four. You going to be okay?"

"Yes, David," she answered wearily. "She seems okay now. If anything changes, I'll call your office. Go take care of your patient."

Finley did not call Sylvia. Rumblings of the woman's displeasure at her news director's absence were filtered through Meadow's gentle humor, but Finley kept the news running from the hospital with a pay phone and her staff's assistance. WABN seemed far away.

Two days passed with no change. Meadow brought dinner each night, and though David and Finley protested that she was doing too much, in truth, the food and Meadow's cheerful company sustained Finn through the hours of waiting for a transformation that didn't come.

"Meadow, you needn't do this. I know how busy you are. But thanks," Finley said as she finished the chicken parmesan and ziti from Rosetta's Italian Garden. She stood to prepare the sleep chair for the uncomfortable night ahead.

"Can't have you subsisting on hospital food, Finn. You'll get so skinny you'll make me look fat."

David left Caroline's bedside for a moment to give Meadow a hug. "You're the best, Meadow. I'm glad Finley has you in her corner."

"Hey, Finn...think he's trying to get in my skivvies? He's mighty cute." Meadow lowered her eyes at David and sauntered across the room, hips swaying. David smiled, shook his head, and returned to Caroline.

Finley knew that Meadow was trying to relieve the tension with her usual humor, but nothing could seem funny as long as Caroline remained unconscious.

"Have to get home now. See you guys tomorrow," Meadow said, hugging Finley as though she'd never let go. Finley saw tears in her eyes as she left the room.

David stood and stretched. "I'll head home, too, Finley. I'll take the night shift tomorrow." His big shoulders hunched as he kissed Caroline good night.

After he left, Finley tried to contort her body into a comfortable position in the chair beside the bed. She caressed her daughter's battered face and let the tears come. "Oh, Caroline, honey, please get better. I love you so much. I never meant any of the mean stuff I said to you."

As she lay there staring at the inert form of her only child, her thoughts dreamily drifted back to when Caroline was little.

~ * ~

It had been a long drive to Ohio to visit David's parents. Seven-year-old Caroline was antsy, and it was getting on Finley's nerves. *If she asks "are we there yet?" one more time, I'm going to lose my mind. Maybe I'm not equipped to be mother. I'd much rather be editing a story right now.*

David said, "What do we want for lunch?"

"McDonald's," Caroline answered.

"Nah, let's try something different...how about a road kill sandwich?"

Caroline grabbed her throat in mock gagging. "You're kidding, Daddy, right? Road kill?"

"Not kidding...I mean it. We need to decide whether we want possum, squirrel, or maybe skunk. I've heard that skunks taste really good once you get past the smell."

Caroline was immediately caught up in the game. "Do you mean it, Daddy? You've gotta be kidding. You can't be serious." The banter continued for the next half hour with David enlisting his daughter's aid in spotting road kill by the side of the highway. It didn't stop until they pulled into a Subway in a strip mall East of Dayton.

~ * ~

David was magic with kids, silly to a point they adored, yet grounded, dependable and safe. Remembering, Finley buried her wet face in the arm of the sleep chair and let the familiar regret sweep over her.

Two years later, she still wondered why they'd divorced. If she couldn't make marriage work with David Smith, she'd never be able to do it with anyone. David was the best thing that had ever happened to her.

Finally, exhaustion overcame fear and she fell into a restless sleep. Her father's face materialized, hazy in her dream. If he were still alive, he'd be here. She could see him clearly now, tall and rangy, hair a little too long, dressed in the plaid flannel shirts and chinos his wife detested.

"Remember, Finny girl, nothing is as important as your integrity," he'd said to her. "You have many gifts. Use them well and be careful what you wish for. You'll probably get it."

Finley's memory shifted sharply, hearing her mother's voice, "Edward, we're expected at the Crabills. Please comb your hair. You forgot to get it cut again." As her mother swept from the room, her father had turned to Finley and crossed his eyes.

"Daddy, Daddy, come back," Finley cried out in her sleep and jolted upward in the chair. She looked over at Caroline, motionless in the hospital bed, and knew she would not sleep again this night.

~ * ~

Meadow's parents, Arlene and Stan, came to the hospital Thursday morning. Finley had loved these two from their first meeting in Meadow's apartment. Arlene was the mother Finley wished she had. She immediately grabbed Finley into her arms. "Oh, Finn, what an awful thing. What can we do?"

Though Finley was a head taller than Arlene, she bent forward and buried her face into the ample shoulder covered by soft cotton flannel and sobbed out her fear. She inhaled the scents of lavender and what she could only call love from Arlene.

"Caroline's going to be okay, Finley," Stan assured her as he encircled her and his wife with his arms. "She'll come out of this soon. I know she will."

Staring at her unconscious daughter, Finley thought, *Please God, let him be right.*

That evening when Chris Andrews and Emily Sanders came to the room after the six o'clock news, Chris looked ready to cry. He led a reluctant Finley out to the settee in the hall and they sat down. He held her hand. Emily remained with David in the room next to Caroline's bed.

In spite of herself, Finley was curious about the station. She felt guilty but still asked, "How are things going, Chris? What do you think of Sylvia Reynolds?"

He hesitated for a moment then gave in to his obvious need to vent. "She marches into the News Room like a little blonde general. Treats me like a peon. I have an appointment with her next week, and I plan to give her some advice on the care and feeding of anchors."

Emily, walking into the hall, shot Finley a nervous look.

Chris stood. "I'll keep David company."

When he was safely out of earshot, Finley asked Emily, What's the look for?"

"Sylvia's been bitching about Chris's 'Q' scores to anyone who'll listen. I'm worried. Not sure how he'll handle it if they don't renew his contract."

A band of pain constricted Finley's head. Emily touched her shoulder. "Oh, sweetie, I'm sorry for bringing that up. Don't worry about Chris now. You have enough on your plate. Maybe I'm wrong about Sylvia, borrowing trouble where none exists."

Finley doubted that. Emily was smart, and her instincts for news and for life were usually solid. "Thanks for the heads up, Emily. If I am to do battle with little Ms. Reynolds, it's best I know up front what I'm dealing with. Any progress on the Cavaleri investigation?"

"Some, but not enough to talk about it yet."

Suddenly, Chris's laugh bellowed from the room, and Finley hurried back in, hoping something had happened. To her dismay, nothing had changed—Caroline was still unconscious.

"Chris, keep it down," Emily chided him softly. "This is a hospital, after all."

He looked stricken. "Sorry...I forgot myself for a moment. We'll be on our way now. Let us know of anything you need, okay?"

When Finley returned to Caroline's bedside, David said, "He's really a nice guy. Chris, I mean." He leaned down and tucked the teddy bear into Caroline's inert arm. "A little pompous for my taste, but he has a good heart." He sat on the bed and took Caroline's hand in his. "Sweetheart, it's Daddy. Come on now, it's time to wake up."

As Finley watched him staring down at the bandaged face of their child, tears brimmed in her eyes. She stuffed them back; she would cry alone. David was in enough pain. He didn't need to worry about her.

"Could you use a cup of coffee, David?" she asked, rising from her chair. "I need a break."

David stood, took his wallet from his jacket pocket, and followed Finley out of the room and toward the elevator.

As they settled into the uncomfortable cafeteria chair, he started pouring cream into his coffee.

She smiled as he continued to pour. "Want some coffee with your cream, David?" It had been their private joke for years.

He grinned and began to stir. "You seemed worried with Emily and

Chris. Something going on at the station?"

"Oh Lord, with all the worry about Caroline, I forgot to tell you. Randy got fired—replaced by Sylvia Reynolds, a corporate type with a reputation for sharpening the bottom line."

"Shit, what a nasty business you're in, baby." She felt the familiar warmth low in her stomach at hearing him call her the pet name. She'd always loved it when he called her baby, especially as he held her, whispering hoarsely into her ear after they'd made love.

She started to explain about Randy and Sylvia when a nurse unexpectedly materialized next to them. Finley jumped to her feet, spilling coffee on the table, braced for bad news.

"Dr. and Mrs. Smith...she woke up."

Ten

Thursday evening

Racing back to Caroline's room, everything seemed to move in slow motion. Finley noticed the noises and scents of the hospital. Muted equipment sounds buzzed. Smells of sickness and antiseptics filled the corridors. Her senses seemed to have awakened at the same moment as her daughter.

Rounding the corner into the room, little appeared to have changed. The wires and monitors delivered their constant messages. Tubes still surrounded the small form on the bed. Only one thing was different—Caroline's eyes. They were open and flickered at seeing her parents.

Finley rushed to one side of the bed, David to the other. "Caroline honey, you're back," she whispered. "You were in a bad accident. Do you remember?" The eyes blinked twice.

David took Caroline's hand into his own and kissed it. Finley knew it was all he could find that was not covered in bandages. "Carrie, my girl," he murmured over and over again, tears running down his cheeks.

Although she did not respond, her eyes were fixed on them with comprehension. After a time, Caroline fell back into sleep. David and Finley stayed in the room all night keeping watch.

Dr. Epstein arrived at five thirty the next morning. He approached the bed. "Hello, young lady. Tell me your name, please."

"Caroline Smith," she answered, her voice hoarse.

Both parents exhaled a sigh of relief.

"Good," he said. "Now I want to test your reflexes. I'll try not to hurt you."

Finley and David exchanged joy-filled glances, then met at the foot of the bed and, without thinking, joined hands. The doctor focused a light into both of Caroline's eyes, asked her to squeeze his hands, tapped gently on her arms and legs, expertly navigating the equipment as he moved around her. He asked her to lift her right wrist followed by her left, advising her not to move her left shoulder too much.

"Caroline, your left collar bone is fractured," he said. "I know it hurts, but it will heal." He prodded her rib cage, stopping when she winced, and listened to her heart and lungs.

"Looks good," he said, rising above her. "You're a fortunate girl. I don't think you've suffered any permanent neurological damage." He nodded to her parents. "The coma was a normal response to protect her from the trauma she experienced." He turned back to the bed. "Now it's time for you to get lots of rest so that you can recuperate."

The doctor nodded Finley into the hall. "A nurse will get her on her feet later this morning," he said.

David returned to his daughter's bedside while Finley followed the physician out the door. "Do you really think she'll be okay, Dr. Epstein?" she asked. "She still looks so bad."

"Let's sit down for a minute," he answered, indicating the small sofa outside the door. "She still has some bones that need to heal. They were set while she was unconscious. Her vitals are all good. I see no neurological damage. I'd say your daughter dodged a major bullet, but we will need a few more days to be sure. At her age, even if there has been minor brain damage, therapy can return her to normal. I believe she'll be all right, in time."

Relief loosened Finley's nerves. Things could have been so different, so tragic. *Thank you, God, thank you.*

As the doctor walked away, Finley ran to the pay phone in the hall. Meadow would still be asleep but would check messages as soon as she woke up and Finley needed to share her joy. "Meadow, she's awake. I think she's going to be okay. Spread the word around the station, will you? And don't forget to call your folks and let them know."

She returned to the hospital room and collapsed into the chair beside her sleeping daughter's bed. David dozed in another chair, and in minutes,

Finley's eyes closed in exhaustion.

She was still sleeping at ten o'clock but wakened when she heard a rustle at the door. She looked up to see her mother standing there. As always, Marion was impeccably dressed and groomed, her eyes alert and unlined. *Thanks to the best plastic surgeon on Fifth Avenue,* Finley thought, then dismissed the catty notion as she pulled her contorted body out of the sleep chair.

David opened his eyes and closed them quickly.

"Mother," she said, leading her into the room. "Caroline's wakened. Isn't that wonderful?" She took her mother's elbow, noticing its sharpness, and led her toward the hospital bed.

The woman pulled her arm away. She edged around the perimeter of the hospital room, avoiding contact with her granddaughter. Her hands, manicured and narrow, opened and closed in nervous spasms. "Yes, that's good, but all those bandages on her face. Do they know yet whether she'll be scarred?"

Finally, she walked to the bedside and spoke, "Hello, Caroline. It's Grandmother Marion. Do you know me?"

The eyes blinked twice.

"That means 'yes,' Mother."

"Oh good. Well, that's fine, now isn't it? Hello, David. How have you been?"

He raised red-streaked eyes to look at his former mother-in-law. "Hello Marion. You look good."

Finley appraised her mother closely, "Yes, Mother, wonderful, but thin. Have you been dieting again?"

Marion preened, relishing the compliments. "Well, you know, you can't be too thin or too rich." She turned to Finley, "By the way, a dash of lipstick wouldn't hurt. I know you've been worried, but one must keep up appearances after all."

Finley opened her purse, took out a tube and applied it to her mouth. Realizing what she'd done, she began to laugh maniacally. Her mother looked at her, puzzled, excused herself and scurried out of the room. "Well, I'm off."

David slapped his thigh in shared mirth and said, "Old habits die hard, right, Finn?"

Eleven

Monday morning, a hastily scheduled staff meeting

Sylvia perched stiffly at the head of the long cherry table. Her face contained no expression watching her staff file into the conference room. Their nervousness as they adjusted ties, removed glasses, and forced tight smiles amused her.

Meadow Marx arrived first, curls still damp from a morning shower. She sat midway down the table and opened her briefcase. "Good morning."

Chris Andrews' eyes looked tired "Hello, Sylvia, good to see you again,".

I'll bet that old codger hasn't been up this early in years.

Others filed in, heads down, and seated themselves around the table.

Sylvia stood in her four-inch stilettos, turned, and closed the door. "Well, hi y'all." she began, arms crossed over her chest. "I'm sure you know by now I've replaced Randy Thompson."

The hush in the room was followed by nodding heads and a soft buzz as several people turned to the person next to them and whispered.

Sylvia interrupted the conversations, her drawl soft. "Now, now…if you have comments, say them to me, please. I don't much like gossiping behind my back. The quicker you know that, the better we'll get along." She looked at the faces ringing the table, pleased to see many had noticeably paled.

"Questions?" She sat, still as a statue.

Eyes darted. People shifted in chairs. Mouths opened to speak, then closed. Confusion jumped from face to face. Sylvia, a smile frozen on her lips, waited.

Meadow raised her hand. "Do you want us to call you Sylvia or Ms. Reynolds?"

"Ms. Reynolds will do nicely. Southern manners suit me."

"All right, Ms. Reynolds," Meadow continued. "Do you anticipate changes in operations or personnel?"

"Certainly." Sylvia answered firmly. "For one thing, I'll handle negotiations with the national agencies."

"What?" Meadow exclaimed, shock widening her eyes. The veins in her neck protruded prominently.

"Corporate feels that we can get a bigger slice of that pie than you're currently generating, Meadow," Sylvia continued. "Insurance and pharmaceuticals are booming. So is the oil industry. We need to know how to play ball with them, and I do. There will be other changes, but I'm not going to talk about that yet."

When Meadow finally spoke again, her voice was modulated. "We're the top-rated station in Philadelphia, Ms. Reynolds. Our revenues reflect that. If we're not broken, why fix us?" She stared straight into Sylvia's eyes, not flinching.

Sylvia didn't like that. "That's not your job to decide, now is it, Meadow dear?"

The condescending *dear* curdled Meadow's stomach.

Sylvia spoke again. "There's always room for improvement in the bottom line, and if you disagree with my methods, it's fair that you understand one thing. Insubordination will not be tolerated."

Meadow started to chew on her cuticle.

Good, Sylvia thought.

"Other questions?" Sylvia glanced around the table. "None? All right then, everyone scurry on back to work. I'll be calling each of you in for a private meeting very soon. Just can't wait to get to know y'all better." She stood to leave, then remembering, said, "By the way, where is Finley Smith?"

"At the hospital," Emily Sanders responded. "Her daughter was in an auto accident. The girl's in serious condition."

Sylvia planted her hands on the edge of the table, then opened the black leather portfolio in front of her, and made a notation. "That's too bad. Who will tell Finley that I'd like to see her at eight-thirty tomorrow morning?"

Meadow jolted in her chair and Emily put a hand on her arm.

"I'll tell her," Emily said. "I'm sure she'll be here if she's able."

"Able?" Sylvia's eyes drilled into Emily's. "I'm sorry to hear she's having family problems, of course, but I have a television station to run; and I can't very well do that without a News Director, now can I?

"Now, all of you...back to work, and don't let me hear any of you complaining behind my back." She waggled her index finger. Her warning was clear.

~ * ~

Meadow collapsed into the chair behind her desk. Her thoughts bounced in her brain like toxic mothballs. *Who the hell does she think she is? I feel like I just took a sucker punch from Scarlett O'Hara. What's the deal with her managing national sales? That's my job, and the bitch knows it.*

Footsteps pounded outside. Chris Andrews stormed into her office and pulled the door shut behind him. "I hate that woman. Treating us like children. And that horseshit about Finn! Her kid could be dying, for Christ's sake. Monday morning meeting, my ass. Up hers!"

Meadow glanced around the office as though she feared her walls might have grown ears. "Settle down, Chris, and lower your voice. Who knows who might be outside that door? Be cool, please."

Chris paced the room, picked up a pillow from her sofa, threw it at a wall, snatched it up again and tossed it back in its place on the couch. Meadow had heard cracking joints as he bent his knees to get it off the floor. Lacing his hands behind his back, he planted himself in the chair in front of her desk.

"You're right," he said. "We have to keep our heads and watch our butts. I needed to blow off steam before I call Finn again." He lowered his voice to a whisper. "But I'm telling you right now, that bitch wants me out of here. I know it."

Meadow closed her eyes, willing the headache away. "Chris, please don't worry Finn with this. You know she'll do everything in her power for you. So will I. You're a legend in this town. No rookie can maintain your ratings. Just play this smart, okay?"

Hurt etched lines into his bronzed face. Now he looked older than his sixty-three years, but Meadow would have cut out her tongue before she'd let him know that. The man sitting before her was vulnerable in every way she could think of. Mostly because he was aging in a youth-obsessed business.

"When I talk to her, should I tell Finn about the command performance tomorrow?" he asked.

"No. Just tell her how much we love her. Emily will tell her. Deal?"

He stood and walked around her desk, then bent to put his arms around her shoulders.

Without a knock, the door opened. "Aw, isn't this sweet?" Sylvia purred, her drawl exaggerated. "An interoffice hug fest." She went on. "Is it too much to ask that you check in with the assignment editor, Chris? Seems there's a silly old bomb threat at the Liberty Bell. Last I heard you were the anchorman here."

~ * ~

That afternoon, Emily stopped in at the hospital. Finley was happy to see her and joyous at Caroline's continued progress. David, though, still held his daughter's hand. He seemed cautious about too much optimism.

"She's doing so well, Emily," Finley said, embracing her friend and co-worker.

"Thank God," Emily hugged her back.

Emily sat in the bedside chair, and Finley perched on the side of the bed. "So, how are things at the station?"

"Sure, you want to know?"

Finley nodded.

Emily started a rant that Finley could scarcely follow. Snatches of phrases. "She's so nasty, so cold. Hateful. She's awful—even worse than I expected. Oh, and by the way, she wants you in her office tomorrow at eight-thirty. If you're not up to it, I'll make some excuse with the bitch."

Instantly remorseful, Emily turned to Caroline's wide eyes. "Sorry, honey, I didn't mean to use that kind of language in front of you."

A faint chuckle came through the bandages.

~ * ~

That evening, David encouraged Finley to make the meeting. "I know how much your career matters to you. We're fine here. I'll stay tonight. Go home and get some rest. Tomorrow morning, do your thing."

Touched by his understanding, Finley edged around the hospital bed and embraced David. "Thank you."

At her touch, he stood and held her close. It felt so good, so natural, and his familiar scent and encircling arms reminded her of how much she had missed this man in her life.

Tears welled up in Caroline's eyes. "You're hugging Daddy."

It was the first complete sentence she had spoken since the accident.

Twelve

Tuesday morning

Finley's knuckles were white as she drove to the station. She composed her thoughts as she prepared herself for what she feared would be a difficult encounter.

Stephanie spotted her the minute she entered the lobby door and said into the phone, "Could you hold for a sec, please? I'll be right back." She punched a button on the switchboard and came around the desk to grab Finley. Though Finley was tall, Stephanie was taller and oak-tree solid. Finley relaxed into Stephanie's embrace, inhaling the other woman's strength into her own aching body. Stephanie smelled of musk and lemons and a very good hair conditioner.

"How you doing, cupcake?" Stephanie asked, looking directly into Finley's eyes. "Monster of a time, huh? Your baby better?"

The bond between the two women was natural, instinctual to both of them. The first time Stephanie laid eyes on Finley, she had asked, "You a Scorpio?"

Finley had been confounded. "How'd you know that?"

"I just know things. I'm a Libra, and I've always had a natural affinity with Scorpios. My mama's a Scorpio. So's my boyfriend, Anthony. We're going to be friends, okay?"

They did become friends and frequent lunch buddies, along with Meadow, whom Stephanie liked even though she thought her crazy. The first time Meadow chanted 'fuck a duck, fuck a duck, fuck a duck' as a calming mantra, Stephanie's eyes grew wide with disbelief.

"Girl, you have a mouth worse than Anthony's," she said to

Meadow as Finley laughed. Anthony Jones, a halfback with the Philadelphia Eagles, was Stephanie's boyfriend. "But I like you anyway," she continued. "Down deep, I think you're as good as any God-fearing Baptist I know. You can't fool me with your foul mouth."

This morning, Finley reluctantly pulled herself from the warmth of Stephanie's embrace. "I have a meeting with Sylvia Reynolds in fifteen minutes," she said. "What do you think of her?"

"Well, I don't like to jump to conclusions on people too quickly. I think you'd better remember to breathe nice and deep. Just keep in mind how much I love you, girl. It might not be pretty."

Finley stood before Sylvia's closed door. Randy's plaque had been replaced by a gold bar saying, **Sylvia Reynolds, General Manager**. *Wow, she moves fast*, Finley thought. In the past, this door had never been closed. Finley knocked.

"Come in," drawled the voice from inside.

Entering the office, Finley noticed that only the person behind the ebony desk had changed. "Good morning, Ms. Reynolds. Finley Smith, your News Director."

"Ah yes, I remember you, Finley. Have a seat." Sylvia gestured toward the chair across from her desk.

Finley waited for Sylvia to ask about Caroline's condition. She knew the woman was aware of the accident. No question came. She put the thought away from her mind and said, "Congratulations on your new position."

"Thank you. Corporate expects a lot from me."

"I'll help in any way I can." *As long as it's ethical.*

"Good. First thing, we need to talk about Chris Andrews."

Finley took the deep, steady breath prescribed by Stephanie. "All right. What about him? What are you thinking?"

"I'm thinking it's time for him to go, that's what I'm thinking. Do you agree?"

Remembering Stephanie, Finley inhaled again. "No, I don't, Ms. Reynolds. Chris has been here for sixteen years, and Philadelphia is loyal to local anchors. People love him."

Sylvia stared at Finley, her left eyebrow cocked into an incredulous arch. "Love him? I hear he's the joke of the News community. Consultants say he's years behind the times, and his 'Q' scores are trending down. Focus groups have found him appealing in a grandfatherly way, but is that really the direction we want to take our news? I want to build on the twenty-five to forty-nine demo."

"Consultants don't always understand a local market," Finley responded cautiously. "Sometimes they take a good product and, while trying to improve it, drop the ratings into the cellar. That happened last May in Atlanta when they fired that African-American co-anchor to bring in a right-wing blonde girl whom the consultants said was precisely what the station needed. Frankly, I don't put a lot of faith in consultants."

Finley was certain that this was not what Sylvia wanted to hear.

Sylvia's grim expression confirmed Finley's instinct. "I'm sorry to hear that, Finley," she said. "I'd hoped that you and I would agree on the direction I want to take WABN. You're a very good News Director, but times are changing." She pulled the Nielsen report from the top drawer and slapped it on the desk. "Politically conservative news is hot all across the country. And people love sensationalism. Even on radio. Since right-wing commentators and shock jocks have taken over, their ratings are skyrocketing."

Finley knew the Nielsen trends as well as anybody in the business and resented this lesson in what was "hot" from a market newcomer like Sylvia. The popularity of the WABN News demonstrated what worked in Philadelphia, and she resented anyone threating to turning her fine newscast into a tabloid.

Finley focused on the memory of Stephanie's dark arms embracing her, their strength, their warmth, and the scents that had calmed her. She took a deep breath and spoke again. "This market expects unbiased reporting from WABN It's our niche in Philadelphia and has given this station the top ratings in the state. To surrender that position to yellow journalism would be a bad mistake, Ms. Reynolds."

Sylvia's pert face remained cool. She stood, walked to the window and looked out on the city. When she turned back, the difference in her countenance shocked Finley. She looked hard as marble, and her mouth had tightened into a narrow scarlet slash.

"I disagree," Sylvia said. "And we will need to come to agreement." She crossed her arms over her chest. "The bottom line, Finley, is this. I am the General Manager of this station."

As suddenly as before, her face changed yet again and her drawl softened. "I'm sure we'll figure this out. After all, we both want the same thing, now don't we? Even better ratings. Maybe we should have this discussion next week, when things have settled down a bit."

Confounded by Sylvia's abrupt shift and her honeyed tone, Finley came to a realization. *This woman would be a wily adversary.*

Sylvia sat down and opened her top desk drawer. "Silly me—I nearly forgot—corporate sent me a Beta by someone named Richard Stone. He's from L.A. and is producing taped political segments for local news stations. I haven't had a chance to look at this. Let me know what you think. We're scheduled to meet with him next week."

Finley stood and took the tape from Sylvia's extended hand. As she left the office, Sylvia's cheery voice trilled after her. "Oh, by the way, good luck with your daughter."

Thirteen

Wednesday evening

An exhausted Finley was preparing Caroline for sleep in her hospital bed. She and David had supported the girl for a labored last walk through the sterile corridors and then he had collapsed in a chair. As Finley washed Caroline's face and pulled the covers up to her chin, Meadow, Chris and Emily walked into the room.

Meadow went straight to the bedside. "How're you doing tonight, honey?" Meadow tucked a teddy bear into Caroline's arms.

"Really good, Aunt Meadow," Caroline answered, cuddling the soft bear to her cheek. "Thank you."

Emily and Chris took turns caressing the girl, careful not to touch any injured places. Their relief at seeing her so improved shone from their faces.

Soon, Caroline nodded off, and Finley turned to them, waiting for the other reason for their visit. "So, I bet you want to know about my Sylvia meeting, right?" she asked.

Immediately, they started peppering her with questions.

"What's she planning to do?" Meadow was first.

"Did she mention me?" Chris asked.

"Or me?" echoed Emily.

"Let's take this conversation to the cafeteria," Finley answered. "David, okay with you if I take a break?"

He nodded, his eyes tired but smiling. He'd already heard the basics of the meeting with Sylvia. "Sure, Finn. Bring me a ham and cheese on rye, okay?"

She nodded, kissed her daughter's forehead, and led the others to the elevator.

The cafeteria was nearly empty. Only three women sat at one of the white plastic tables drinking coffee. As they passed the women, one looked up at them, recognized Chris, and whispered to the others.

As they settled in with sandwiches and coffee, Finley decided to level with them—within limits. "Sylvia wants change."

All three erupted in a jumbled cacophony of words. "What change? In what department? Why does she want to mess with something that's working so well?"

Finley took a page from Stephanie's book. "I want you all to take a deep breath and calm down."

When they seemed more relaxed, she continued. "She wants more sensationalism in our news and a lean to the right. I'm afraid *objective* may no longer be a term to accurately describe our product." She paused before speaking slowly. "Because of that, I don't know if I'll stay at WABN."

"You might not stay?" Emily looked alarmed

"You can't go anywhere, Finn," Chris interjected. "We all depend on you, you know that."

Meadow was quiet.

"Look, I'm not saying I'm leaving right away. Unfortunately, my take on running a news operation is miles apart from Sylvia's. My dad would turn over in his grave if I caved on a matter of journalistic ethics— a news slanted to the right, or left. I intend to give it some time and see if I can reason with her."

Chris Andrews's foot was bouncing so fast that coffee spilled on the table. "Do you think she plans personnel changes?" His voice had the practiced, casual tone of a professional anchor, but his hands were trembling.

To avoid an outright lie, Finley said, "I don't know yet, Chris. If she goes after anyone we have on air, I'll fight her. But she is the G.M. Please don't anticipate anything and overreact. Give me time to develop a strategy. Maybe she's the type to come in with guns blazing and then eventually settle down." Even as she said the words, Finley didn't believe them. Sylvia would not settle down. Her agenda would be met, no matter how many lives she wrecked in the process.

"I'm contacting a head hunter," Chris said, rising to leave.

"Not yet, Chris," Finley said, her hand on his sleeve gentling him back to his seat. She feared that, at his age, he'd find getting a new job more difficult than he thought. "Give me two weeks to let things settled—agreed?"

After a moment, he nodded and stood, hands hanging limply at his sides. He was the picture of impatience. "Okay, Finley, two weeks, but if you learn anything in the meantime, you'll let me know, right?"

"You have my word."

"Give Caroline a kiss for me when she wakes up, okay?"

Finley nodded as he turned to leave the cafeteria. She was pleased to see the women's heads turn to follow him on his way out. Only someone who knew him very well would recognize his stride was slower, his shoulders more slumped than usual.

"Could I have your autograph, Mr. Andrews?" One of the women asked. She was plump with greying hair, her eyes adoring as she tugged at his sleeve.

Chris flashed his famous smile and bent to sign the woman's napkin, all graciousness, all charm.

Finley, Emily and Meadow sat silently, each trapped in her own thoughts. They stirred cold coffee, ignoring the half-eaten sandwiches on the table.

"Lord, I wish it was still cool to smoke," Finley said.

"Over my dead body," Meadow replied, smacking her friend's hand. "I remember how you used to stink from those nasty things. I could barely stand to sit beside you in the movies."

"Really?" Finley asked, surprised.

"Really!"

"Why didn't you tell me?"

"I figured you had enough trouble with the divorce. Didn't want to add to it.

"When you gave up cigarettes at the same time you gave up David, I was impressed. Thought you were finally getting smart—about the cigarettes—not so much about the man."

Emily nodded. "He is sweet, Finn," she said, leaning in toward her boss. She lowered her voice to a whisper. "A major hunk, too."

"Hands off, twinkie," Meadow said to the younger woman with a grin. "If any friend of Finn's gets her mitts on David, it's gonna be me."

A surprising rush of jealousy jolted Finley. The thought of another woman with David troubled her more than the crisis brewing at the station. Why did she still care so much?

"You wouldn't really go out with David, would you?" she asked Meadow.

Meadow looked at her in disbelief. "Of course not. I have my scruples, corruptible as they are. Besides, I could never compete with you. The guy still loves you. That's clear every time he looks at you."

Meadow's comments both pleased and frustrated Finley. "Better get back to Caroline." She picked up David's sandwich. Emily had pre-paid the cashier for their food, and Finley put a ten-dollar bill on the table.

"No way, Finn. This feast belongs to me," Emily scooped up the bill and stuffed it in Finley's pocket. "Next time we're in New York, you can buy dinner...at Le Cirque."

"See you at the station tomorrow?" Meadow asked.

"Only if Caroline's better."

Finley hugged and waved goodbye to her friends before going to the elevator.

When she arrived back at the room, Caroline had wakened and was sitting up in bed with many of the bandages removed from her head. Her face was swollen and covered with bruises. An angry line of stitches circled under her chin. She looked as though she'd gone ten rounds with Muhammad Ali, but she was smiling. "The nurse removed some of the bandages," she said.

Finley embraced her daughter. "Your teeth aren't chipped."

"Good thing, Carrie," David added from the other side of the bed. "Those teeth cost us a fortune at the orthodontist."

David's eyes met Finley's, hers brimming with tears of relief, his glowing with affection. *Maybe it's not too late?*

~ * ~

Finley remembered when the problems with David turned serious. It was after he accompanied her to the Bahamas for a corporate meeting two years earlier. After a day at the beach soaking up sun and Mai Tais, they had returned to their hotel room to dress for the welcoming cocktail party.

Finley laid out her dress on the bed. She'd shopped for days to find the perfect look for this party. The dress was bright emerald green and strapless. When she had held the fabric against her face in the store, its softness and color brightened her skin. High-heeled sandals and gold earrings would complete her look. She wanted to look beautiful for this party. John Prescott and Austin Montgomery would be there, and it was past time she be noticed for more than Emmy and Peabody Awards. She wanted to move up in the company, and a woman needed all her tools to do that, including her looks.

As she walked toward the shower, David grabbed her by the wrist and whirled her around and into his arms. "Hey, gorgeous," he said, burying his mouth in her neck. She felt the rough scratch of his beard and pushed him away. She didn't want a whisker burn tonight.

"No time, darling," she said. "We have to be downstairs in forty-five minutes and I need to shower and take a little extra time with the makeup tonight."

He backed away, hands raised in surrender. "Sorry, Ms. Smith. Just thought a quickie would make you look even more beautiful than you already do with that tan. No problem." In spite of the complimentary words, Finley heard sarcasm in his voice.

Momentarily, she regretted her rejection of him, but she didn't want to be late for this party. "Catch you later, sailor?" she said.

"Who knows?" he answered. "Maybe I won't be in the mood later."

"Right," she chuckled. "That'll be the day."

Soon after they arrived at the party, she saw David cornered by Matt Marquand, the Vice President of Affiliate Relations, a man David detested. She started to walk over to rescue him but found herself surrounded by Austin Montgomery and other corporate officers. Their compliments and attentions engulfed her. She looked beautiful tonight and knew it. It was intoxicating to have these powerful men focus their concentration on her—men who were able to take her career to its zenith.

Back in the room after the party as she happily rubbed lotion on sunburned shoulders, David seemed distant and distracted.

"Hey, Finn, anything you should be telling me?"

She continued the circular motion of her hands down her arms. "What do you mean?"

"That Marquand creep in the bad toupee asked me how it felt to be married to the rising star of Prescott Broadcasting."

She put down the lotion. "He said that?"

"Yeah, that you're up for some job as V.P. of News for the Corporation. Did you know that?"

She shook her head, eyes widening.

"Said you'll be traveling so much I'll forget what you look like. That's what happened with him and his ex."

Her eyes blazed bright with excitement. "Tell me exactly what he said. Don't leave out a word."

"That you'd never be home...that you'd spend your life in airports and hotels." He looked startled by her rising enthusiasm.

She stood and started to pace the room, then went out onto the balcony overlooking the ocean. "That is amazing news. I sort of thought it was possible, but didn't know it was that far along. Did he say when this might happen?"

"Wait a minute, Finn. You'd take it?"

"Of course, I'd take it. Think of the money and prestige. I'd take it in a heartbeat."

When Finley climbed naked into the king-sized bed, she ran her tongue down his spine.

"No thanks, Ms. V.P." He moved to the far side of the bed.

~ * ~

After that night, Finley spent more and more hours at the station or at meetings where she could pitch her qualifications to decision makers. David tried to talk to her about the chasm growing between them, but she had been much too busy to worry about that. Until the divorce papers were served at work. And then, it was too late.

~ * ~

Sitting in this hospital room two years later, she regretted giving up her marriage so easily. The Vice President's job had not materialized. It was dangled before her by corporate, but never really offered. She knew that David, even if he still loved her, would not consider life with a woman caught in the wringer of her own ambition.

Fourteen

Thursday morning

Stephanie was laughing aloud into her mouthpiece.

"No, ma'am, we don't carry *Knots Landing*," she said, cocking one eyebrow at Finley. "That's on another network." Finley smiled as Stephanie continued to listen. "I don't know why we don't have it, honey," she said. "But we don't. You'll find it on Monday nights at eight. Just check your paper. Thank you for calling WABN, though."

Disconnecting the call, Stephanie lifted her eyes to heaven, "Lord, I'll be glad when that hokey show is off the air. I must get ten calls a day, most of them mad at me because Valene wore something the night before and I don't know the designer." She turned serious. "How is that beautiful little girl of yours this morning?"

"Really good, but this has been a tough time. She looks better every day. She might come home tomorrow."

"Hallelujah, praise Jesus." Stephanie jumped to her feet, raised her arms above her head and began to dance behind her desk. She stopped abruptly. "Oh, I almost forgot—been meaning to tell you. My sister Jenny is a private-duty R.N. She's really good with physical therapy and isn't on assignment right now. Would you like me to talk to her about staying with Caroline?"

"Oh, that would be fabulous. I was going to call the Nurses' Association. Caroline will need total care and lots of help with her therapy. As we both know, I can't stay home any longer."

"I'll check."

"Great. Let me know as soon as you reach her. I'll pay above her standard rate." She turned away, then back. "By the way, is Meadow in yet?"

"Yes, she's in a sales meeting."

"What about Ms. Reynolds?"

"Oh yes, she arrived before I did. Her line's been buzzing like a queen bee's hive all morning."

"Wish me luck, Stephanie."

"You know I do that, girlfriend. I'm afraid you might need a lot more than luck to deal with that one."

As she walked to the elevator, Finley scanned the glass-enclosed lobby. Six large television sets covered the walls, their volume muted. All were tuned to *Good Day Philadelphia*. The reception area had three elegant seating arrangements, each different, each blending perfectly into the others. The colors were rich ambers, chocolate browns, soft oranges. Some of the furniture was striped, some solid, some in delicate florals. Finley marveled that any decorator could have put the pieces and patterns together with such elegance.

When her secretary spotted Finley, she stood and ran to embrace her. "I didn't expect you back yet. God, I've missed you. So much weird stuff is going on here, and I need you to run interference."

Finley returned the hug. "I've missed you, too, Julie. Thanks for sending the cookies. Caroline loved them."

"How is she? I haven't been able to get over there. Jim's working nights and there's no one to stay with the kids."

Finley shook her head. "Don't worry about it. She's had too much company anyway, but she's doing really well—may even come home tomorrow." Finley crossed her fingers. "I'd better get some work done."

She went into her office and began checking the wire services for breaking news events. She was eager to see Meadow and share the good news about Caroline. She knew that would have to wait until after the sales meeting.

~ * ~

Meadow approached the conference room for the first sales meeting since Sylvia's arrival, and she heard her staff laughing. *Bet Marty Sax is telling one of his stories*. She paused outside the door. His tales were always worth a listen.

"I remember back in 1965 when a program called *Green Acres* came on this station," he said. "Everybody complained it was dumb, but I knew it would be a winner. How could it miss with that gorgeous Gabor gal? Back then, we sold sixty-second commercials for fifty bucks." The other salespeople shook their heads in disbelief. Today, a thirty-second commercial in prime time cost up to twenty thousand dollars.

"Those were the days," Marty continued. "There was no competition, no cable. And it was cool to sell TV ads back then. TV advertising was a brand new, exciting industry. Fun. I used to write the commercials, roll the camera and cut the tapes myself."

The younger members of the sales staff stared at him, envy widening their eyes. For them, television was not fun. It was full-on corporate pressure, the competition so intense many of them couldn't sleep nights. Meadow feared their nights would become a lot more sleepless now that Sylvia was in charge.

All eyes turned to her as Meadow closed the door behind her. "Better watch out, Marty. A new network called Fox starts up this October."

"Yeah, it's pretty trashy from what I hear," he responded.

Meadow scanned the people circling the table. Each man wore a well-tailored suit, except for Marty, whose grey glen plaid was rumpled and a bit worn. The two women had shiny chin-length bobs and the ten men forty-dollar haircuts, except for Marty, whose bald head's edges were trimmed by his wife, Barbara. All twelve of them sat stiffly, but not Marty, who relaxed in his leather chair. Marty's easygoing cheer was the result of a low-maintenance lifestyle, a long and trusting association with city power brokers and, most of all, his inherent niceness. Marty, the mensch, was a Philadelphia legend.

The other salespeople supported families in big houses. Each drove a late-model imported car. Beamers and Audis filled the parking lot. Marty lived in the same little house he and Barbara had bought when they married. He drove a six-year-old Buick. His son and daughter had gone through medical school and were practicing doctors in New York. Marty, sitting in the chair next to Meadow's, was surely the most secure person in this room.

Twelve pairs of eyes stared at her nervously as she sat down next to Marty. Meadow smiled and said, "So, heard any good jokes lately?"

They jumped with questions.

"What's gonna happen, Meadow?"

"Where'd she come from?"

"Any idea about her M.O.?"

Their raised voices became a clatter of nervous energy until Meadow held up her hands to silence them.

"Whoa," she said. "Let's settle down. I've hardly met the woman. Maybe all the rumors are baloney. Maybe she'll want to keep things on the same keel they are now. Give this some time."

She glanced at Marty. He smiled, looked down at some papers in front of him and shook his head from side to side.

"Let's not waste energy on speculation, okay? Catch me up on what's going on with your clients," Meadow said.

Marty started, as always. "No major problems with any of mine, though I still wish you'd let me drop my rates for Price Cutter Supermarkets. I'm worried about my share. It's a jungle out there and every station is hungry for a bigger chunk of the carcass."

"Set up a vendor-support program for them," Meadow said, knowing his answer before she finished her statement. "We have the best consultants in the country coming in to get vendor dollars for our clients."

Marty laughed, "Price Cutter taught those guys how to do vendor programs. They wrote the book on squeezing every nickel out of their suppliers in exchange for shelf space and signage. They'd howl if I suggested they meet with our consultants to teach them how to do their business."

Meadow rubbed her forehead. He was right.

"Oh, never mind, boss," he said, patting her hand. "I can handle Price Cutter. Been doing it for twenty years."

Meadow's youngest salesperson, Erin Sullivan, spoke next. Her eyes were troubled. "The media buyer for Pennsylvania Bank & Trust is making me nervous," she stammered. "Says he's having dreams about me.

He creeps me out the way he looks me up and down. I'm doing great on share, but I'm not sure it's because he likes my programming." Erin lowered her eyes and a pink blush worked its way from her neck up to her face.

"Things are creepy with him. He makes me super uncomfortable. I'm wondering, Meadow, if an account switch might be possible? Something with equal billing, or even a bit less. Maybe one of the guys would be better on this one."

Marty stared at Erin. His daughter was about Erin's age. "Hey Erin, how about I take over the bank and give you Abele Automotive? They bill about the same, and their media buyer is female."

"Oh, Marty, would you do that? I'd owe you big time."

"Consider it done," he said. "If it's okay with you, Meadow."

Meadow nodded. Thank God she had someone on her staff as smart and decent as Marty. It was rare in this business. "I'll arrange the switch with Accounting and Traffic. You two make appointments with the clients to introduce them to their new account reps."

One by one, the salespeople shared their concerns, their troubles and successes of the past week. The triumphs outweighed the problems, and Meadow was grateful for that. She didn't want to have any bad news for Ms. Sylvia Reynolds when she met with her tomorrow.

Fifteen

Friday, late morning

Finley's office phone rang. "Lunch?" Meadow asked.

"Absolutely," Finley answered, folding the newspaper. "One at Sam's."

Sam's was the lunch destination for many people at the station. Within walking distance, it had great burgers and salads. Its high-sided booths kept conversations private.

At ten till one, Finley left her office and found Meadow laughing with Stephanie at the receptionist's desk. "Want to come?" Finley asked Stephanie.

Stephanie held up a brown bag. "Not today...dieting."

"Heard back from your sister yet?" she asked.

"Nope, but I left word. Don't worry. She'll do it. Or find someone for you."

Finley smiled in relief as she and Meadow headed out into the first warm day of the season. "Man, this weather makes things seem a lot more manageable, doesn't it?" Finley said, adjusting her long stride to accommodate her shorter friend.

"Sure does," Meadow answered. "Makes my little heart sing and my boobs feel almost perky." She looked down. "Damn, I forgot—it's my new Wonder Bra—not the weather."

Strolling toward the restaurant, they watched as passersby turned faces up to the sky, luxuriating in the sunshine. Finley lifted her chin. She was happy. Both her phone calls to Caroline's doctor had elicited reports of continuing progress, and she could not wait to get back to the hospital room after work. David would be there, too, and hopefully they'd learn Caroline could come home soon. No matter how much some breaking news event might demand her attention, this would not be another late night at the station.

Sam's was crowded, as always. Luckily, Josie, their favorite waitress, whispered to them, "I'll have you a seat in a jiffy and that's a promise, even if I have to spill soup on that couple in the corner."

Five minutes later, they were seated in a corner booth with menus in their hands. Not that they needed them. They had memorized the familiar offerings and usually ordered the same things.

"Ladies?" Josie asked, pencil poised.

"Chinese chicken salad," Finley said. "Dressing on the side, extra mandarins."

"Ditto," Meadow said. "Oh, and iced tea."

"Make that two." Finley held up two fingers. "And water, please."

Meadow leaned in. "So, how's Caroline?"

"I hope she'll come home Monday."

Meadow squeezed her hand. "That's great, Finn. God, I'm happy for you."

"Thanks, love," Finley squeezed back. "Now, tell me something— why the trip to New York last Monday?"

"Holy crap!" Meadow exclaimed. "That seems a lifetime ago, but I guess I haven't talked to you about it. Randy showed up Friday night after you left."

Finley nodded. "I saw him at the elevator." She didn't mention her suspicion at the time.

"He wanted me to snoop at corporate about the Sylvia rumors first thing Monday morning. I met with Matt Marquand, the V.P. of Affiliate Relations, you know the stuffed shirt with the toupee?"

"Oh yeah."

"Marquand told me Sylvia might be replacing Randy. I argued my brains out that the station was in the best shape ever and it would wreck things if they replaced him. Obviously, Mr. Toupee was blowing smoke when he said they would take my comments under consideration."

Josie brought their salads and tea to the table. "Anything else?"

Meadow and Finley shook their heads.

Finley stirred one spoonful of sugar into her tea and tasted it. "By the way, have you heard the name Richard Stone?" she asked,

Meadow's eyes narrowed, trying to think. "Name's familiar. Is he from L.A.?"

"I believe so."

"I think he might be a right-wing anchor from the NBC affiliate out there. Why?"

"Sylvia gave me a Beta he produced. She wants me to sit in on their appointment next week."

"If memory serves, they call him the 'Rush' of television. He's lemon yellow. All righteousness and tabloid crap, if he's the guy I'm thinking of."

Finley dipped a walnut into her salad dressing. *Over my dead body he's joining my news.*

~ * ~

Finley spent the weekend catching up on paperwork and dashing back and forth between the hospital and her house where she cooked and froze some of Caroline's favorite dishes. When she arrived back at the hospital Sunday afternoon, Caroline was on her feet, her blue robe over her hospital gown, taking small, tentative steps in the hall. "Sweetheart," she said, taking her arm as they headed toward her room. "You're up. Want a wheelchair?"

"Nope, Mom. It feels good to be on my feet. The nurses helped me earlier, and I've been practicing ever since. Now, though, I'm ready for a rest."

Finley pulled back the covers and helped Caroline into the bed. "Where's your dad?"

"He left ten minutes ago."

Finley's heart sank. *Damn.* "Anything I can get you, honey?"

"Nope. I just want to sleep now."

"In that case, I'll head home. I'm bushed, and I want to make sure your room is sparkling for when you come home. Which might be tomorrow."

As she started out of the room, Caroline said, "Mom, I think I was being kind of a brat to you. I'm sorry."

Finley turned at the door. "I've been beating myself up about the way I've treated you lately. Guess we've both learned a lesson or two, right?"

Caroline yawned and snuggled down into her bed. "Right." In seconds, she was asleep.

She tiptoed out of the room to find the nurse. "I can't believe how well she's doing. Has the doctor said when she can come home?"

"He hasn't seen my report yet, Mrs. Smith, but once he finds out how she's ambulating, I'd bet it'll be tomorrow."

Finley drove home in a state of euphoria. Soon, she'd have her baby back. At the house, she changed into her robe and took out the package of hamburger she'd defrosted that morning. Once the meat was cooked and sizzling, she carried the burger and a cup of tea into the living room.

Then she remembered the Richard Stone tape that Sylvia had asked her to watch. Nibbling at her burger, she slipped it into the tape player and turned on the television.

The man was handsome, dark and intense. But so slick that she figured she'd need to wash her hands after she removed the disc—and not from the grease of her burger.

"Good evening, ladies and gentlemen." He nodded to the camera. "Not to be the bearer of bad news to you liberals out there, but one of your favorite Democratic Congressman was seen out in Washington last night accompanied by a well-known prostitute—a male prostitute." He drew out the last words of the sentence with a meaningful leer. "I won't name names, but you know who he is now, don't you?"

His rant continued for three minutes, slyly shifting negative innuendo to a well-known AIDS activist, a woman spearheading a global warming initiative, and a respected scientist involved in stem-cell research. Richard Stone finished his piece without ever mentioning a name but left no doubt about the identity of his subjects.

What garbage, Finley thought, swallowing the last of her tea. Freedom of speech is one thing, but this stuff is crap. Though these days, crap was exactly what some Americans relished.

She tucked the Beta back into. its sleeve and threw it in her briefcase. Before that meeting Sylvia had scheduled, she'd have her defenses in place. No way she wanted Richard Stone as part of her news team.

As she took her dishes to the kitchen, the phone rang. "Mrs. Smith, this is Dr. Epstein."

Oh lord, don't let anything have gone wrong, she thought.

As though he heard her gasp, he hurried on. "This is good news, Ms. Smith. We're going to release Caroline. You can pick her up tomorrow afternoon."

Finley was jubilant, though her joy was dampened by one thought. *How am I going to sneak out of the station before the evening news?*

Sixteen

Monday morning

Meadow ran to her car on the morning of her scheduled meeting with Sylvia. A grey drizzle turned to a downpour. "Perfect," she murmured. "My hair will be Brillo by the time I get to the station."

She dressed carefully, a well-tailored but not too expensive suit, a simple silk shirt and mid-sized heels. She wondered as she chose the outfit what image she was trying to project to a woman who was suddenly in control of her destiny. *No threat*, she admitted, feeling ashamed of herself.

Twenty minutes later, she knocked on Sylvia's office door.

"Come in."

Squaring her shoulders, Meadow turned the knob.

"Good morning, Ms. Reynolds."

Sylvia did not look up from her newspaper.

Meadow, always comfortable in this office when Randy occupied it, felt short of breath as she took the seat in front of the ebony desk. Sylvia closed the paper, folded it and tossed it in the wastebasket.

We recycle here. Meadow did not speak the thought.

"Good morning, Meadow. What can I do for you?" Sylvia arched an eyebrow.

Good God. You're the one who called the fucking command performance. "Uh, Ms. Reynolds, you asked for this meeting. Remember?"

Sylvia waved a dismissal into the air. "Ah yes, that's right. I'd forgotten. I want to talk about how we can increase your sales revenue s."

"Okay," Meadow responded. "I'll be happy to hear any ideas you may have. We do have a very successful vendor program operating with Martin & Associates and..."

Sylvia waved her hand again. "Those fossils? Vendor programs are pretty well tapped out now, wouldn't you agree?"

"To some extent," Meadow answered. "Although small companies still use us to help maximize their ad dollars from suppliers. Also, Dick Martin has branched out into some wonderful promotions for our clients. Some are charity based, like the Christmas campaign we do with the Make-A-Wish Foundation."

"How much do we get from Make-A-Wish?" Sylvia asked.

"Sixty-five thousand, all donated by their sponsors."

Sylvia sniffed. "That's all?"

"Yes, but it's good for the station to be associated with the Make-A-Wish mission. We work with local children and feature them in news stories during the Holiday season. Our anchors love the opportunity to work with hometown kids."

"All very sweet, I'm sure," Sylvia responded. "Nice, but certainly not a *must have,* wouldn't you agree?"

Meadow was stunned. "WABN has worked with Make-A-Wish for twelve years. It benefits children with life-threatening illnesses. Every department at the station supports it in one way or another. The good will in the market from the campaign is immeasurable."

"Oh well, let's not talk about that right now," Sylvia interrupted. "What we really need to address is your sales team." She lifted a nail file from her purse.

"What about them?" Meadow's throat tightened. She had never been very good at taking orders, particularly from a bottle-blonde stranger with little respect for anyone.

Sylvia pointed to a ledger on her desk with the nail file. "Some of your account executives are earning close to two hundred thousand a year. Don't you think that's exorbitant?"

"Not if they deserve it, Ms. Reynolds. They're on straight commission. If they don't sell commercials, they don't get paid. There's no dead weight on my sales team. They're the best in the city."

"Yes, but if we cut their commission by two percentage points, wouldn't that motivate them to work harder? Then we could hire some kids fresh out of college at a lower commission rate. In my experience, the more feet on the street, the better the revenues." She began to file her nails.

"Our revenues will fall—I guarantee it." Meadow's voice betrayed her frustration. "Every station in the market pays a five percent commission. If we cut ours to three, we'll lose our heavy hitters. They'll be scooped up by the competition the day they quit."

Sylvia poised the file in the air. "But that's your job, Meadow. To keep them motivated, now, isn't it?" Her smile was icy.

Meadow braced herself. "Ms. Reynolds, I must be honest with you. My staff is loyal. But they're all supporting families. Some have kids starting college. They have to think in terms of where they can make the best money. On a level playing field, WABN is the place they want to work, but if we cut commission two points below market standard, they'll walk."

Sylvia did not look pleased. "What about one point?"

"No," Meadow nearly shouted. "The equation remains the same. They're not in this for laughs. If they can't make the industry-standard commission, they'll be gone."

Sylvia pursed her lips and raised her eyes toward the ceiling. "All right, Meadow. We'll save this talk for another time. However, we need to discuss another matter."

Ah, thought Meadow. The commission talk was a smoke screen for what she really wants. "What's that?"

"Marty Sax. He's making an outrageous amount of money for such an old man."

Meadow took a deep breath. "But he's worth every penny. Again, it's commission. No one in the market can sell like Marty. His clients love him. Marty the mensch, they call him. He's been here since 1964 and is an inspiration to the entire team. When he retires, WABN will go into mourning."

"And when will that be?" Again, the cocked eyebrow.

"One or two years, I imagine."

"Hmmm, then he'll start liquidating his stock, right?"

"Maybe, but he could do that whenever he wants."

"How much stock does he own?" She returned the nail file to her purse.

"I've no idea, but a lot, I'm sure. Marty's been in this business for over twenty years and plunged every commission and bonus into stock. The station's changed ownership three times. Each time, Marty got premiums on his stock turnovers to the new companies. He's a major shareholder."

Sylvia paused and made a note to herself. "All right, Meadow. That will be all, for now, but I do think it's time for Mr. Sax to move on." She slammed her ledger shut. "It's embarrassing having someone his age doddering around the station."

Before Meadow could respond, Sylvia swiveled her chair and turned her back. Meadow felt as though she'd been gored by a battering ram, a ram with a soft Southern accent.

~ * ~

The migraine started when she left Sylvia's office. She had never had a migraine before in her life, but she knew she was experiencing her first. She just made it into the ladies' room before she vomited.

She splashed her face with cold water and tried to wash the sour taste out of her mouth. Popping a mint between her lips, she returned to her office and found Marty outside the door, talking to Heather. He took one look at her pale face and said, "Hey, boss, got a minute?"

"Sure, Marty, come on in."

As he settled himself on the sofa, she heard him chuckle.

"What's funny, Marty? I could use a laugh right now."

"Oh, it amuses me to see yet another hatchet man circling their wagons around this station...except this time it's a hatchet woman. Guess that's progress for *your* team, right?"

"That kind of progress I can live without," she answered, rubbing her temples.

"I've seen this happen three times already. You get used to it." He stared at her. "You look like crap, babe, and I don't like that. You've gotta learn to roll with these people until they burn themselves out. They always do."

She lifted her chin and studied his face intently. "Do they, Marty?"

"Absolutely. It's called karma or something. That's your generation's lingo for justice, I think. Don't worry so much. Turn it over to somebody else...God or me or whoever you trust. Don't do this number on yourself, Meadow. You don't deserve it."

She was surprised by the tears on her cheeks. "Oh, Marty, I hope you're right. But I don't know. Look what happened to Randy."

He smacked his head. "That's why I came to see you. I just hung up the phone with him. He already got himself a great job with the Long Island Cable system. He's not General Manager, but he'll be in charge of operations, and that market's an untapped gold mine. With his experience, Randy'll be a superstar."

The vise around Meadow's head began to loosen. Maybe Marty was right. Maybe things would work out for the best. Hearing the good news about Randy made that seem possible.

"Did Randy say how Phyllis is taking the move?" she asked him.

"Believe it or not, good," he laughed. "She found out there's a train from Great Neck right into Manhattan. She's chomping to hit Bloomingdale's. From what I hear, she's making an ass of herself telling all the folks at the club that she now realizes how provincial Wannamaker's is now that she'll be living near New York. She's happier than a pig in...oh, never mind, I don't want to corrupt your sweet young brain with curse words."

Meadow laughed in relief or hysteria and found she couldn't stop. *How long had it been since anyone had called her young?*

Seventeen

Monday afternoon

"Meet me for coffee," Meadow said. "Now."

Finley hit "save" on the news story about a middle-school shutdown and went to the elevator. The cafeteria would be empty at this time of day. She needed to finish up early because she and David were taking Caroline home tonight. But Meadow's tone was urgent.

When she entered the small, vending-machine-filled room, Meadow was seated at one of the five plastic tables. She waved Finley over.

The moment Finley sat, Meadow whispered, "She wants to get rid of Marty Sax."

"What? Why would she do such a thing?" Finley exclaimed. There was no need to ask whom Meadow was talking about.

"Not sure." Meadow looked around as if to make sure no one had come into the room. "She seems to think he's too old. Makes her look bad."

"She can't get away with that. Corporate would never allow it."

"Who knows what corporate would allow? Did you think they'd replace Randy with someone like Sylvia?"

Finley paused, then shook her head. "No, I suppose not."

"Well, I'll tell you right now," Meadow continued. "If she fires Marty, I'm gone. I won't put up with it."

"I think we'd better watch our threats," Finley answered. "And be sure we're prepared to carry them out. This bitch is hell bent on shaking things up and I, for one, don't want to abandon this station into her nasty little fingers too easily."

Meadow sighed. "I suppose you're right. If we don't fight this fight,

80

WABN might go the way of tabloid crap. Have you heard Rush Limbaugh? Total garbage. But it smells and it sells. Corporate wants those ratings."

"True," Finley nodded. "But as far as Marty is concerned, the big guys might be afraid of an age-discrimination suit." She stood. "Gotta get back to work. I'm leaving early."

~ * ~

Finley sang joyfully along with the oldies station on her car radio. "Just call me angel of the morning," she crooned, not caring that her voice was, as usual, off-key. It had been David's song for her when they first started dating.

Caroline was sitting impatiently with her suitcase, flowers and balloons beside her. David sat on the bed holding her hand.

"Finally, Mom," Caroline said. "I thought you'd never get here. I want to get out of here."

Finley knelt beside Caroline and wrapped her arms around her. "I can't wait to get you home, honey." Now that most of the bandages were removed, she could safely hug the girl she had nearly lost. Before, she'd been afraid of being rebuffed and then of hurting her daughter's injured body. Feeling her now brought back a memory of warm soft skin and the scent of baby powder as tiny arms hugged her neck and a baby voice said, "Mommy."

Startled, she realized that the word had not come from her memory. Caroline had said it now, in this hospital room. "Mommy...I love you." Finley lifted shimmering eyes to David.

God, is this a second chance? If so, please, please don't let me blow it.

David's voice cut into her reverie as a volunteer appeared, pushing a wheelchair. "Let's get all this stuff packed in our cars, Finn. I have her release papers and we're set to get out of this joint. By the way, as you asked, I interviewed Stephanie's sister, the nurse. She's great and will be at the house early tomorrow morning to meet you and Caroline."

~ * ~

Caroline chattered in the car about wanting to get back to her friends and about the cute young intern who had discharged her from the hospital. When they arrived home, Finley, fearing her daughter might tire herself, suggested a nap before dinner. She and David tucked Caroline into the white canopied bed they had bought for her when she was ten. When Finley handed her the ratty brown bear Caroline had loved since childhood, she took it into her arms and fell into a sound sleep. Before the accident, she would have called holding that teddy bear *juvie.*

Finley and David tiptoed out of the room, leaving the door ajar.

Downstairs, Finley said, "Why don't you stay for dinner?" She had bought three rib eyes on her way home. "Caroline would love it if you were here when she wakes up."

His eyebrows knit in thought. Hospital coffee breaks aside, they had not shared a meal since the divorce, except for one in a restaurant on Caroline's sixteenth birthday.

He seemed uncomfortable, but said, "Okay. Thanks. That'd be nice, I guess."

"Want a drink while she's sleeping?"

"Got a beer?"

"I think there's a six-pack in the basement. I could chill a couple in the freezer. Would you get it and I'll start the salad?"

~ * ~

David walked down the stairs into the basement of the home he'd shared with Finley and Caroline for fifteen years. Not much had changed. It was still cluttered, in spite of the shelves he'd built to hold the overflow of food cans and bottles that Finley insisted on keeping on hand, in case of some national catastrophe. He blamed her paranoia on the daily dose of disaster that assailed her over the wire services. His work bench was still in the corner, gathering dust. *God, I miss puttering around down here.* The basement had been his refuge when the torrent of estrogen in the house threatened to unhinge him.

Now, as he picked up the six-pack, he acknowledged that he missed that energy, that beauty, that rush of girly silliness more than he had known.

"Found it," he said, returning to the kitchen. Finley took the beer from his hands and put two bottles into the freezer.

"Should be cold enough in fifteen minutes." She set the timer.

Like I don't know how long it takes to chill beer in the refrigerator I bought three years ago. For a moment, he was angry at this woman, still living in this house he loved. Then he calmed himself, remembering that the final decision to separate had been his.

Finley had poured herself a glass of red wine and was tearing lettuce into a salad spinner. Avocado, basil and oranges sat on a wooden board, ready for chopping. She always prepared them early to keep them crisp but did not add the ingredients to the greens until the last minute.

A bottle of homemade vinaigrette stood next to the cutting board. Three thick steaks sat on another board waiting for dry rub. Watching her efficient movements, David remembered how much he had enjoyed the simple, delicious dinners Finley used to make, even after a long day at the station—before those long days had stretched into long nights which would become long trips when she finally got the promotion that jerk in the Bahamas had told him about.

As she prepared the food, humming some vaguely familiar tune, a rush of longing grabbed him. *Hold it. Nothing's changed. She's as ambitious as ever, and you don't want a life with a superstar, remember? Been there, done that, didn't work.*

"How's your practice going?" She looked up from her chopping.

"Good...really good. Full schedule of patients. I feel as though I'm making a difference for most of them."

"I'm sure you are. You're a wonderful counselor." She stared so deeply into his eyes he became edgy. The timer buzzed. "I'll check that beer."

She turned toward the refrigerator, graceful as a dancer, comfortable in her kitchen. He watched the slender, familiar body as it moved. He remembered how it had felt under his hands, how it had responded to his touch, opened with his kiss. Finley, economical in her movements, was nonetheless complete in everything she did.

As she bent over to retrieve the beer from the freezer, her hair fell over her face. That hair had shut out the world for him when it cascaded around his face, a silken veil against light and sound, leaving only the scent of her body and the low, rumbling sounds of her passion in his ears. *God, he had loved her.*

"Want a glass?" her voice jarred his reverie.

"No, the bottle's okay," he responded, grateful for the interruption. He couldn't afford such thoughts.

"Are you sure?" she asked. "Your beer mug is right here. Want it?" She moved to get the metal mug.

He took it from her outstretched hands. "Didn't I take that with me when I left?"

"Remember, we bought two so you'd have one for traveling."

Why did she keep that mug?

"Okay, I'm done," she said. "I can have dinner ready in ten minutes once Caroline wakes up. Let's relax with our drinks."

They walked to the two loveseats under the kitchen's bay window, left uncovered by curtains in order to let in light and the view of the large maple tree outside.

The kitchen had been awful when they first moved in, he remembered. They had spent hours steaming faded flowered wallpaper off its walls and painting them this creamy butter color that picked up the early morning sun in the summer and warmed their spirits against the snow during the long Pennsylvania winters. This corner of the kitchen was where they had spent Saturday mornings over coffee and evenings with cocktails. It had been the only place David could be certain that Finley wouldn't rush away from him to turn on a television set.

She slipped off her shoes and tucked her feet under her. "Lord, it's good to get away from that hospital and all the craziness that's happening at the station."

"Tell me about it."

"Oh heavens, where to begin...I'm worried about Chris. When his contract comes up at the end of the quarter, I'm certain that Sylvia Reynolds won't renew it. Oh, Meadow thinks she's even after Marty's scalp—which is insane"

"Is she right—about Chris, I mean?"

"Well, his Q scores aren't great, but I think with some coaching, they can improve. He's such a fixture on the News and even though things don't look good for him right now, my gut tells me this market isn't ready to lose him. People don't like change, even though they love to grouse about the status quo. Chris will be tough to replace, especially if Sylvia gets her way and brings in some right winger. She wants more sensationalism in the news."

"Yellow journalism," he said. "That's something you vowed you'd never be part of, remember, Finn?"

"Yes." She looked sad, as if she might be disappointed in herself. "I still believe that, but I won't let someone ruin our News without a fight...and I can't fight if I quit."

"Let's not worry about it tonight, okay?" he said. "This is a night for happiness. Our daughter has survived a terrible accident. She's home and healing and that's plenty to be grateful for, right?"

She clicked her glass against his mug. "Things do have a way of working out for the best sometimes, don't they?"

"Yep. This accident might be the reality check that sweet kid needs. Doubt she'll be out drinking and driving any time in the near future. Her senior year was scaring me, but I'm hoping this accident will make her think twice."

Finley smiled and relaxed into the soft cushion. Her question came out of the blue and startled him. "How're you doing alone, David?"

He sat silent, trying to think of a response that would be true, but not hurtful.

"Are you seeing anyone?" she continued.

He hesitated for a second. Could he tell her now, on the day of Caroline's homecoming? No, that would be cruel. He decided on a white lie. "No one in particular. Work keeps me busy."

He didn't intend to ask, but couldn't control the impulse. "How about you?"

"Nope," she laughed. "If it weren't for Meadow, I'd never have a date on a weekend. I don't know whether successful women intimidate men or I'm turning into an old hag, but my phone sure isn't ringing off the hook."

"Have you tried to meet anyone?"

"Went out with Meadow and Stephanie a couple of times, but the bar scene is awful."

He nodded, remembering.

"I came home more depressed than when I left. Emily says I should try a dating service, but when I think about that, something stops me at the moment they ask for my profile. Guess I'm not ready yet."

David was angry at himself for the relief he felt. God damn it, he thought, Megan's right. I'm not totally over her.

He stood and walked to the refrigerator to retrieve the second beer. "Want another glass of wine?"

She held up her glass to him, smiling. She patted the place beside her on the loveseat. "Sit here."

What the hell is she up to? And why did he so want to be close to her again, go down that path that had hurt so much when it ended?

He took the seat. As they clicked glasses once again, he was conscious of the heat of her thigh next to his, the familiar scent of this woman he had loved so deeply and for so long.

"I think it's better if I stay over here." He moved to the other loveseat.

Finley's smile faded, but that couldn't be his problem, not now, not ever again.

"Mom...Daddy. Could you help me downstairs? I'm hungry."

David stood, relieved to have a task, an excuse to escape the uncomfortable moment. "I'll get her. You start cooking those steaks."

Caroline's face glowed through the bruises, though she grimaced with pain as she tried to chew the steak.

"Oh, sweetie. I should've cooked pasta," Finley said, guilty.

"No, it's fine, Mom. It's so nice, all of us eating together again. Maybe we could do this once or twice a week?"

Finley looked at David.

He took Caroline's hand as he spoke, "Probably not, honey. You know how busy Mom is. It's hard for her to know when she'll be free in the evening. But I'll tell you what...when she has to work, I'll cook you dinner...deal?"

Caroline looked down at her plate. "Sure." She folded her napkin. "Think I've had enough. It was good, but I'm kind of tired. Daddy, could you help me back to bed?"

~ * ~

Caroline had scarcely touched her steak, so Finley wrapped and refrigerated it. She scraped leftovers into the compost pot, then took it to the larger container in the back yard. *Maybe Saturday, I'll plant some perennials. Nah—too soon. We're sure to have another freeze.*

She put the dishes in the dishwasher and set the steak griddle to soak, then crept up the steps. Standing undetected in the doorway of Caroline's room, she watched David stroke their daughter's hair.

"But Daddy, you and Mom should be together," Caroline said. "You still love each other. I can tell."

"Sometimes, love isn't enough, Carrie," he answered, wiping the tears from Caroline's cheeks with a handkerchief. "We just couldn't keep it together any longer."

Finley wanted to shout. *Yes, we can, David. I'll change.* She had almost voiced her thoughts when the ring of her phone jarred her. "Hello," she said.

David and Caroline looked up at her. When she heard the voice, her shoulders slumped and a feeling of absolute weariness washed over her. "Yes, Sylvia." She paused to listen. "You need me now?" She darted desperate looks at Caroline and David. "But I just brought my daughter home from the hospital. Are you sure this can't wait until tomorrow?"

The voice on the other end of the phone rose...enough so that David and Caroline could hear it ooze across the line—drawling, demanding syrup.

Finley closed her eyes, opened them, then cast them down in defeat. "All right. I'm on my way."

Eighteen

Monday night

Finley drove through the dark streets, her anger building with each block. *Damn it, couldn't she let me have this one night with David and Caroline? She knows we just got her home. Just because Sylvia has no life, does she have to mess up everyone else's? Can't she handle one fucking conference call without me there?*

She turned the key in the station's side door and headed for the elevator, taking slow, deep breaths in an effort to calm down. *Don't give that bitch the satisfaction of seeing how she riles me.*

When Finley entered the office, Sylvia was already on the phone. Sylvia looked up, relieved to see her. "Austin Montgomery," she whispered, her hand covering the mouthpiece.

She pointed to the phone on the table. Finley picked it up.

"Mr. Montgomery. Finley Smith here."

The deep voice was curt and efficient. "We've decided to make some changes, ladies.

Finley tensed at the condescension in his voice.

"What changes, sir?" Her heart quickened. Maybe this was her promotion. Even as the thought excited Finley, her mind grumbled. *Do I still want it?*

"Have you two heard of Rick Stone?" Austin asked.

Sylvia and Finley exchanged glances. "Yes, Austin," Sylvia responded. "He sent me a Beta of one of his news segments just today. Haven't had a chance to review it yet." She darted a warning look at Finley who raised her eyebrows at the lie.

She's had that tape for several days.

"Watch it as soon as possible. Both of you." Austin continued. "Mr. Stone has agreed to become our Vice President of News. He'll operate out of WABN and cut editorial segments for the other two stations. We'll syndicate them at stations across the country. He wants to be your anchor, too. You know, to keep his finger on the local pulse. He'll arrive Wednesday morning at nine to meet everyone and start on air that night. You'll love Rick. A good Christian family man. His wife Marjorie is a real doll, homeschools their daughters. I expect you girls to help her get settled in Philadelphia."

Finley mentally shook off the *you girls*. The impact of his words began to crystallize in her consciousness. V.P. of News was supposed to be her job—the job that had shattered her marriage—the job she wasn't sure she wanted now, but nonetheless, one she thought she owned.

Sylvia spoke, "Well, that's terrific, Austin. We both look forward to meeting him, right, Finley?"

Finley's voice sounded as though it came from a distressed animal. It was a voice she had never heard before. It was guttural, abrupt. "Certainly."

When they hung up, Sylvia stared at Finley for a long moment. Then, she whisked her hands as if to dismiss discussion. "Arrange the conference room for Wednesday. Make sure all the managers are there. And get that tape to my office in the morning. Did you watch it?"

"He's awful." Again, the voice sounded foreign to Finley. *Who is this stranger speaking through my lips?*

"You'd better start thinking he's terrific. He's your new anchor."

Sylvia's words jolted her again to reality. "What about Chris?" She gnawed on a ragged cuticle, dreading the answer.

"His contract expires in June and will not be renewed. We'll pay him for the remainder of it, but he should be out of here by close of business tomorrow. Jim Taylor will fill in until Mr. Stone is up and running." Sylvia turned away to rifle through her Rolodex, a clear dismissal to Finley. "Chris will get severance and a party. Tell him that it's goodbye time."

~ * ~

At seven o'clock the following morning, Stephanie's sister, Jenny, rang Finley's doorbell. In spite of a sleepless night churning with anger, Finley was impressed when she opened the door. "Wow, I thought Stephanie was a knockout. You're even prettier."

White teeth flashed against mahogany skin framed by straight ebony hair. "Don't let her hear you say that, Ms. Smith. She's competitive."

"Call me Finley, please."

Jenny nodded. "Okay. When do I get to meet my patient?"

"Caroline's still asleep, but she knows you're coming and will call for you when she wakes up. I wanted to let her rest as long as possible. She's been through a lot."

Jenny smiled again. "Just show me her meds, her physical therapy schedule and the instructions from her doctor. Don't worry about a thing. I'm a very good nurse, and I'll be with her every minute that you or your husband can't be here."

"Ex-husband," Finley said. Jenny's eyes flashed disappointment, and Finley turned to grab her jacket. "David plans to check in with you by phone before noon. Here's my number. Call me any time. See you tonight."

~ * ~

Chris clicked on his home answering machine after the Monday evening news and found a message from Finley requesting a four o'clock meeting on Tuesday. It was an unusual message but not unduly alarming. "That's the old news biz," he told his wife when he left earlier than usual on Tuesday. He patted her backside, gave her a kiss on the cheek and strolled out of their downtown condo. The air smelled of early spring and Chris put down the top of his yellow convertible. It pleased him to see heads in other cars snap in recognition when they saw him. *You've still got it, big guy.*

He navigated the same streets he'd driven for the past sixteen years, smiled and waved to the cops on the beat and made sure that the red-haired woman in the Chrysler next to him at the light got a good view of his profile.

When he pulled into the station lot, he was once again pleased with the parking sign that said *Chris Andrews, News Anchor*. He polished it with his coat sleeve.

Just before he entered the building, he paused to accommodate a young mother who asked for his autograph for her twelve-year-old son. "He wants to be an anchorman, just like you, Mr. Thompson."

Chris was annoyed. Willis Thompson was the anchor at the affiliate and Chris's arch rival. However, he recovered his smile quickly. "Well, bring him by the station sometime. I'd be happy to show him around."

Though gratified to see the stardust in her eyes, Chris remained disturbed that she could confuse him with that jerk at Fox.

He noted Stephanie's tight skirt as he walked into the lobby and said in a booming voice, "Looking good, gorgeous."

She dismissed him with a wave of her hand. "You say that to all the girls, Chris."

"Only if it's true," he shouted over his shoulder, heading toward the elevator.

Riding up to the News Department, he chided himself for worrying so much about his job. He was Chris Andrews, the most popular anchorman in Philadelphia. But, damn, how could that woman have thought he was a lamebrain like Willis Thompson?

~ * ~

Early Tuesday morning, Finley called Meadow and Marty Sax into her office.

"Hi Finn," Marty seated himself on her sofa and nodded as Meadow walked in.

"Close the door, Meadow, please," Finley said.

Meadow caught the urgency in Finley's voice. "What's up, Finn? You seem worried? Caroline okay?"

"Oh yes, great," Finley answered. "It's station stuff."

Marty and Meadow exchanged glances.

"Sylvia called me in last night for a conference call from corporate."

"Say what?" Meadow raised her eyebrows in disbelief. "Didn't she know you just got Caroline out of the hospital?"

"Yes, she knew, but Austin Montgomery had asked for the call and she felt it couldn't wait."

"What's going on?" Marty asked.

Finley closed her eyes and rubbed her right temple. "A guy named Rick Stone," she began.

Meadow interrupted, "Yeah, the right-wing wacko we talked about?"

Finley nodded, still rubbing her temple. "Seems he's going to be our new V.P. of News for the corporation and will use WABN as his base. We meet him at nine Wednesday morning. He starts that day, in time for the May sweeps. He wants to keep his finger in the local pie, so he'll become our new anchor and cut political segments here for the other stations."

Marty shook his head. "Are they nuts? This town'll never accept him."

"What are they thinking? Sales will drop into the dumper." Meadow exchanged a worried look with Marty. "Finn, I figured you'd get that job when it was created."

Finley's shoulders slumped for a moment. Quickly she recovered her erect posture. "Me too, but obviously things have changed, which is probably for the best. Don't know if I really wanted it anyway, especially now with Caroline being tutored at home so she can graduate on time."

Meadow's grin was instantaneous. "And maybe you're not ready to give up on Caroline's dad as well?"

"This isn't about me, Meadow. Right now, it's about Chris Andrews. I have to meet with him at four o'clock to tell him he's out at close of business."

Marty spoke first. "Shit...pardon my French, ladies, but shit. This is going to hurt him bad. He's close to my age but pretends he's thirty. This'll make him feel like a has-been, and I don't think he can take that. We need to find a fix."

"What kind of fix?" Finley asked.

Marty stood and began to pace, talking to himself, "Something with status...some kind of corporate spokesman job wearing a suit every day and looking good. Something that needs his charm and looks. Big companies love former anchormen."

He turned to Meadow, "Come on, boss. We'll go through our account list and find some lucky blue chip that will slobber over having Chris Andrews as their spokesman."

Finley tried to hide her skepticism. "By four o'clock?"

Meadow looked equally doubtful. "Yeah, Marty, I know you're a wonder worker, but this seems like a tall order."

"Let's just see." He grinned and ambled out of Finley's office with Meadow in close pursuit.

~ * ~

Marty and Joe Heaton went back a long way. Both had started their careers in the sixties. Joe was a media buyer for Blue Care when Marty was assigned to the account. Joe said there was no person in the world he trusted more than Marty Sax. Their friendship extended from business to social every chance they got. Marty had been there to cheer Joe on as he made his way up every step of the corporate ladder.

When Marty had been offered jobs in management, Joe was the first person he called to talk things over. "Joe, you know, they want me to become a sales manager, but I just don't think I'm cut out for it. I can make more money in sales and what I love is working with clients and making commercials. I don't want to manage people."

"Don't take the job, Marty." Joe had answered. "I couldn't stand to see you cry like a girl the first time you had to fire somebody. Do what you're good at. And there's no one better at that than you and no man in this town I trust more."

So, Joseph P. Heaton was Marty's first call.

"Mr. Heaton's office," the cool, professional voice answered.

"Sue, how've you been?"

The voice changed, became warm. "Hey Marty. I'm fine. How about you?"

"Great. Is the old man in?"

"Yes, give me a minute."

"Marty, you rascal. Haven't heard from you lately. What's up?"

Marty wasted no time. "Joe, remember how you were saying Blue Care could use a spokesman who was savvy in television—that your public relations were slipping?"

"Sure, I remember. Who're you thinking of?"

"Does the name Chris Andrews ring a bell?"

"Are you serious? Do you think he'd consider leaving the anchor desk? He'd be perfect."

By the time Marty hung up, Joe Heaton agreed Chris Andrews was roughly the equivalent of the second coming of Christ. He asked Marty to arrange a meeting with Chris for that evening.

~ * ~

At four o'clock, Chris sauntered into Finley's office. "Sit down, Chris," she gestured to the chair opposite her desk.

"Beautiful day, huh, boss?" He smiled at her. "What's up?"

"Something important. I got a call from Joseph Heaton, the President of Blue Care. Have you heard of him?"

"Are you kidding? Everyone's heard of Joseph Heaton. He's probably the biggest player in Pennsylvania."

"The call was about you."

"Me?" Chris looked worried. His face told Finley he could not imagine why Joseph Heaton would be calling her.

Finley smiled. "It's nothing bad, Chris. Blue Care needs a spokesman, someone with television and radio contacts, someone mature and credible. Mr. Heaton feels you'd be perfect for the job."

"He does?" The worry lines on Chris's forehead smoothed out. "He said me, in particular?" His eyes started to sparkle.

Finley nodded.

"He wanted to talk specifically about me?"

"Sure did. Can't blame him, Chris. I can't think of anyone who would bring more prestige to Blue Care."

Chris pulled himself to his feet and started to stroll around Finley's office, rubbing his hands together as he walked. "What do you think I should do, Finn?"

She hesitated, wishing she could cry on cue. "It breaks my heart to think of losing you, but you know how things are changing around here now that Sylvia's taken over."

"Yeah, and she doesn't like me. I'm not stupid, you know."

"Well, this job with Blue Care pays about the same as you earn here, and believe me, they *really* like you, so I think you should consider it. Mr. Heaton would like to meet with you this evening." She picked up a piece of paper from her desk. "Here's his number."

Nineteen

Tuesday afternoon

Sylvia's secretary rapped on her door softly.

"What is it?" she called out, annoyed at the intrusion.

The woman timidly walked into the office and closed the door behind her. "Ms. Reynolds, Finley Smith sent this to you. Said you were expecting it."

Sylvia looked up, then recognized the Beta. "Oh yes, good. I'll take it."

Sylvia tossed the tape into her briefcase. She would look at it later at her hotel. She wondered if Finley had broken the news of his departure to Chris Andrews. *Pompous ass, but harmless.* He wouldn't raise Cain over leaving. Couldn't afford to. Corporate had him tied in the knots of contracts, severance agreements and non-competes, just like they had all their on-air talent. He hadn't joined a union, felt it was beneath him, she'd been told. Fool. She imagined the reddening of his perfect complexion, the disbelief confusing his already addled brain and then, finally, the acceptance of the fact his life as an anchor was over.

With one problem dismissed, Sylvia pondered her next project. Getting rid of Meadow Marx. The clients and staff loved Meadow, but she was earning way too much, and Sylvia already knew she could hire Tom Turner from the Pittsburgh station for half of Meadow's salary. Tom wasn't as sharp as Meadow but was competent enough and would follow her orders without question. That's what counted.

As her mind coiled around the possibilities of restructuring the station, her phone rang. *Let it go. The girl will get it.* After a moment, though, the buzzer sounded and Sylvia picked up the secretary's line. "Yes?"

"Ms. Reynolds, your father is on the line."

Her breath caught. She hadn't spoken to him in months. She wrote him weeks ago about taking this job, but he hadn't responded. She snatched up the phone. "Father! How are you?"

"Okay. How's it going there?"

"Perfectly. According to plan."

"Crappy business you're in, you know," he said. "Not what it used to be. When I controlled the ad money for IBM and G.E., television was a great investment. Now, I think companies are throwing their money down the drain, what with shrinking audiences and your crazy prices."

Sylvia sank down into the chair, then straightened abruptly. Becoming the general manager of the top television station in Philadelphia was a coup, no matter how Michael Reynolds viewed the industry. "I think you're wrong, Father. It's still the best way to reach the masses."

His laugh was a hollow grunt. "Masses, that's right. Dolts who want to be spoon-fed pablum day and night." He paused. "Radio's the way to go."

"I disagree." Her voice sounded defensive, even to her, but she didn't care.

"Well, bully for you, girlie," he said. "Tell it to your clients. Maybe it'll impress them if they're naïve enough to believe your stats. I'm way too smart for that."

"Why did you call, Father?" she asked through clenched teeth. She brushed at her cheek, surprised to find tears.

"Oh, just checking up on you," he said. "You are my only progeny, you know." His laugh cut deep into her heart. "At least the only one who's legitimate." He snickered again. "Let me know when you get to the city. Maybe we can grab a drink."

She hung up feeling small, nearly insignificant in spite of the big office she inhabited. Sylvia was stung by her father's familiar dismissal. Nothing had ever been good enough...not the honor roll or the Magna at graduation.

"Should have been Summa," he had said as she approached him in excitement that hot afternoon in Boston, diploma extended from her hand toward him.

"Screw him," she said aloud.

~ * ~

After an exhausting weekend search for an apartment, Sylvia finally signed a lease for a place in King of Prussia. When she arrived at her hotel room at nine-thirty Sunday evening, her body ached with fatigue. She called room service and ordered a bottle of wine and a steak. Then she climbed into the tub, kneading her body to ease the tension from her shoulders and neck. The water had nearly lulled her to sleep when the room bell rang. "Damn," she said, "Wouldn't you know that for once they'd make it fast." She grabbed the thick terry robe off the hook, stepped into slippers beside the bed and pulled her hair back into an elastic band.

"Anything else, miss?" the man asked as he placed the tray on the small table in her room.

"No, that's fine," Sylvia dismissed him with a five-dollar tip. She wanted to drink her wine, fill her empty stomach and fall into bed to prepare for yet another long tomorrow.

After she had swallowed a half glass, she remembered the tape in her briefcase and her nine A.M. meeting with Richard Stone. "Shit," she said, retrieving the tape and hoped it was brief.

She slipped it into the tape player and turned on the television. As the opening credits played with music rising under them, she cut into the first bite of meat. It was satisfyingly rare. She started to chew just as he appeared on the screen.

The steak caught in her throat. "Oh, my God."

Twenty

As Finley prepared to meet with Richard Stone, Chris Andrews walked into her office. He looked sheepish but slightly giddy. "I met with Joseph Heaton last night," he said.

"And?"

"Finn, honey, I can't tell you how tough it is to tell you this, but I took the job." He handed her his letter of resignation.

Her heart unclenched in her chest as she took it from his hand. "I'm not surprised, Chris. It sounded perfect for you."

"Yes, and the best part is, he really likes me. I can tell. Told me to call him Joe. After the way that bitch Sylvia has been acting, it'll be such a relief to work for someone who treats me with respect."

Finley stood, circled her desk and put her arms around his shoulders. "I could not be happier for you, Chris. When do you start?"

"Well, this is the tough part, Finn. He wants me right away. I'd like to tell the audience tonight on the news that I'll be starting on a new adventure." He looked so pleased with himself that Finley's heart nearly broke with joy. "Is that okay?"

"Absolutely. I'm taking your notice to leave by close of business today. Congratulations, my dear friend."

~ * ~

"How about that Marty?" Meadow said thirty minutes later when she met Finley in the ladies' room. "Saved Chris's ass when he didn't even know it was about to be chopped off."

"Man, the word sure circulated quickly, didn't it?" Finley put her lipstick back in her purse. "Yes, it's great for Chris. But I still have an anchor coming into this news department I can't stand. This headache just won't quit," she said, popping two aspirins into her mouth and cupping water from the faucet into her mouth.

Meadow walked behind Finley and rubbed her neck. Her friend's slender shoulders relaxed under her fingers. "How's Caroline?"

"Great." Finley wiped the water from her lips. "This Jenny is a treasure. She even manages to give Caroline hair and makeup tips while pushing her through the physical therapy. She had dinner with us last night."

"Was David there?"

Again, Finley's shoulders tightened. "I invited him, but he had other plans."

Meadow changed the subject. "Has Sylvia gotten the word about Chris yet?"

"I told her ten minutes ago. She actually seemed disappointed that he's landing on his feet. Asked a lot of questions about the *fortuitous* timing of his getting such a plum job. I played dumb, let her think it was a coincidence it happened on the very day she wanted me to fire him."

Meadow chuckled, "Poor Sylvia...disappointed. Breaks my heart." At the door, she said, "Gotta get ready for the nine o'clock meeting to introduce us to Mr. Richard Stone." As she said the name, she faked a gag.

At precisely nine o'clock, all the WABN managers were gathered in the conference room. They knew what was coming. Phone calls had been circulating the entire weekend. Tension was high.

Sylvia's secretary entered with a dark-haired man and a petite blonde woman. Finley's first impression of the man was the overpowering scent of a very expensive cologne. He must have bathed in it, she thought.

"Ladies and gentlemen," the secretary said. "Meet Mr. and Mrs. Richard Stone."

Everyone stood and applauded politely as the couple took their seats at the head of the long table. "Rick will be taking over for Chris Andrews who will be the new corporate spokesperson for Blue Care."

Finley thought she saw Richard Stone's wide smile falter when he shook hands with Sylvia, but dismissed the impression. *Perhaps he's nervous about coming to a new station. Strange, though he doesn't look the type to be nervous about anything.*

"Welcome, Mr. and Mrs. Stone." Sylvia shook the woman's hand "Pleased to have you as part of the WABN family. Mrs. Stone, if there's anything I can do to help you settle in, please let me know. I'm in the midst of doing so myself, so I have contacts you might find useful. Please call me Sylvia. May I call you Marjorie?"

"Oh yes, Sylvia—make it Marge."

Sylvia frowned. Finley's grin was internal. *Bet she's afraid that good old Marge will want to be her girlfriend. What a freaky pair those two would make.*

"And call me Rick," her husband added.

Marge burbled on. "I'll take you up on your offer. We need to find a house and activities to keep our two girls out of mischief. *And* we need to find a good church. Where do you attend?"

Sylvia looked startled by the question then quickly recovered her composure, "I haven't really looked into churches yet, but perhaps someone else has recommendations?" She looked around the faces in the conference room.

Mark Scott, the chief engineer, raised his hand and said, "I'll introduce you to my secretary right now if you like, Mrs. Stone. She knows all about churches."

Marjorie Stone clapped her hands together in pleasure, rose from her chair and kissed her husband on the cheek, adoration glowing in her eyes. A quick glance of recognition flashed between Finley and Meadow. *Stepford.*

As his wife left the room, dutifully trailing behind Mark Scott, Rick stood. "I'm very happy to be here," he said. "I have some ideas I'm sure you'll find innovative and look forward to sharing them with your news director." He scanned the room until Finley waved to indicate herself. "Thank you, Ms. Smith, I'll catch you as soon as we adjourn here. In the meantime, do any of you have any questions for me?"

Tim Schneider, the production director, raised his hand. "How many cameras are you used to on set, Rick?"

Finley knew that Tim was itching to get another camera on set.

"Usually, I like three cameras for optimal vitality and movement. I don't want to be positioned at the anchor desk constantly. Let's work out some alternative places on the set. I like close-ups and to be shot standing more than seated."

"We can get together this afternoon," Tim said. "I'll show you the set and our camera layout and see what we can do."

Rick nodded. "Thanks. I'll stop by your office later."

Emily raised her hand. "Mr. Stone, I'm Emily Sanders, your co-host on the eleven and weekend anchor. I'd like to talk to you later about my reports on the newscast and how to make this transition seamless."

"Great, Emily," he responded. "I like having a female partner. You can do the softer pieces and leave the hard stuff to me."

Emily jumped in her seat. Finley read her mind. *Softer pieces, my ass.* Finley shot her a look assuring Emily that she would not be relegated to the status of twinkie.

Meadow had invited Marty Sax to the meeting as a nod to his seniority and status. "Mr. Stone," Marty said. "How would you describe your news philosophy? Do you lean to the right or to the left? I come from the days when news was objective."

Rick Stone's spine stiffened visibly. "Well, sir, whoever you are..."

Marty stood and extended his hand. "I'm Marty Sax, senior account executive, and member of the WABN family since 1964."

Rick ignored the offered handshake. "Well, Marty, my feelings are that most network news programs are leaning toward liberal. That is not part of my belief system. Philadelphia is the rock upon which this nation was founded. It deserves a news reflective of those conservative settlers."

Marty smiled. "Conservative? Philadelphia is the cradle of liberty, though my friends from Boston argue that point. Its people are descended from rebels. Our greatest pride is our Liberty Bell. I mean no disrespect, sir, by my comments, but I would hardly call the citizens of this city conservative."

"No disrespect taken, Marty," Rick Stone answered smoothly. "I realize Philadelphia leans somewhat to the left. I simply bring a broader perspective, a new look at things." He paused. "And that's what corporate wants."

Ouch, Finley thought. That's clear enough.

The room immediately silenced. His remark confirmed the rumors that had rumbled all weekend.

"While here, I will be taping segments to be aired by all the other Prescott stations and other stations across the country who want a right-wing presence on their newscasts. They will be generic, political statements that reflect what our owners believe. Corporate chose WABN for my headquarters because your production facilities are tops in the chain."

He surveyed the faces around the table, his smile never wavering. "Well, if that's all the questions you have, I'd like to get together with Ms. Smith to discuss specifics."

As Finley led Rick into her office, he put his hand on her shoulder. Surprised at herself, she recoiled. She didn't usually shy away from touches, but his fingers felt intrusive. She remembered the tape and its effect on her. More than anything, Finley wanted this man gone from her space, but politeness dictated she ask him to sit down.

"Well, Finn, I guess we'll be seeing a lot of each other."

How dare he call me by a nickname? Her arms prickled into goose bumps. "Yes, indeed," she said. "But I need to be clear. My feelings about news may be at some variance to yours."

"How so?" He crossed a slim ankle over his well-groomed knee and positioned his legs at a wide angle. Finley told herself his body language was not as insinuating as she perceived it to be.

She thought hard about her next words. She didn't want any misunderstandings between them. The issue was too important. "I don't like slants," she finally said. "Either to the right or the left. I expect straight reporting and investigations when warranted. Frankly, some of your comments in the meeting and on your videotape disturbed me. WABN did not become the top news station in Pennsylvania by delivering a product even slightly yellow. Philadelphia doesn't want that, and neither do I."

"Whoa." He reared back in his chair as though she'd struck him. He laughed the cocky chuckle she'd heard on his tape and continued. "I do hope we will be able to come to terms, Finn. I'm doing the job that corporate wants me to do. We needn't be adversaries." His grin was dazzling. "I'd rather we become good friends." The way he said "good" sounded dirty. Finley felt as though ants were crawling under her skin.

She shook off the feeling. "We'll be fine, Rick, if you remember that at WABN, you report to me."

"Well, *Boss*," the word was sarcastic. "I have a few calls to make." He sauntered to her door, turned with a wave and a wink and slammed it as he left.

Twenty-one

Wednesday afternoon

Rick Stone opened the door to Sylvia's office without knocking. She leaned back into her chair and stared directly into his eyes. "Yes, Austin," she said into the phone. "Rick met the staff this morning. As did his wife." She flipped on speaker.

"Isn't she nice?" Austin asked.

"Yes, very nice. Sweet. Asked about churches. She's having coffee with our chief engineer's secretary to get information on which ones she might like." She paused, clicked off the speaker and held the phone to her ear. Rick seated himself on the red sofa.

"I'm sure everyone will come on board, Austin. Give me time. Finley's stubborn. But I'll take care of her. Don't worry." Her eyes never left Rick's.

Finally, she spoke again. "Good. I'll get back to you next week with the format for producing his syndicated pieces...yes, yes, I know the message corporate wants to convey...loud and clear." She laughed and put the phone down.

She pushed her chair back from her desk and crossed her arms, never breaking her stare. "Well, well, Mr. Stone—or should I call you Daniel? As I recall, that was your name when last we met—Daniel Brower, attorney at law."

"And you were Avery something or other that night." He rolled his eyes up as if trying to recall the last name.

"Ah yes," she laughed merrily. "You do remember." She lifted her glasses to the top of her head. "Did you try to call the name on my card?"

Her voice was casual.

He hesitated.

"I thought not. Neither did I," she lied. "Ships that passed in the night, right? And that's how I want to keep it. Agreed?"

Rick leaned toward her. "Of course, Syl...Avery. It's best for all concerned if both of us forget that snowy night at O'Hare, although..."

"Although what?"

"Well, we'll probably be traveling together often to New York. It would be comforting, wouldn't it, after a hard day to have a soft place to fall? Nobody'd ever have to know. Discretion is my middle name, and I'm sure that you're equally careful about such things."

She laughed again. "You have an amazing capacity for forgetting that you're married—to little miss church mouse."

"Don't dis Marjorie. She's a wonderful mother and my best friend."

"Just a little dull, right? Wonderful mothers don't always make exciting, soft places to fall, I hear." She balanced her chin on her hands, smiling at him. "But how would I know? I've never been a mother, but I have been complimented on other talents. You might remember them."

He rose from the sofa, walked to her door and closed it. "Oh yes, I remember them well." He sat back down on the couch, his smile a leer.

Suddenly, Sylvia was tired of the game. She stood. "Well, that's enough of that. You need to meet the people in the news department."

He looked confused at her abrupt dismissal, and that pleased her.

A sharp knock came on Sylvia's door surprised them both.

"Come in," she said.

Mark Scott's secretary, Mary Brennan, led Marjorie Stone into the office. "Mary has been so helpful," Marjorie said, hugging the secretary. "She marked all the appropriate churches in Philadelphia and the good neighborhoods." She laughed. "So, when we start house hunting, we'll know just where to look." She turned to Sylvia, "I can't thank you enough, Sylvia, for letting Mary help me. Saved me hours of interviewing pastors."

"I'm delighted she could lend a hand." Sylvia said, patting Mary Brennan on the shoulder as she ushered her out of the office.

Marjorie never lost her excited smile.

Like a puppy dog. Wagging her tail in gratitude, Sylvia thought.

Without warning, an image popped into Sylvia's mind—of her devastated mother on the day she learned of Michael Reynold's infidelity. A touch of remorse softened her heart, but she slammed the feeling away.

~ * ~

As he drove to the real estate office, Marjorie still babbling from the seat beside him, Rick pondered the conversation in Sylvia's office.

This could be perfect. She'd never tell anyone, couldn't afford to. Neither would I. That night in Chicago was good—not great—but good. Sylvia's attractive and probably in need of physical attention. That Finley Smith is really something, though. That one could really ring my chimes. Beautiful. That hair, those legs. He imagined them wrapped around his back and felt himself harden.

Marjorie pointed to the map in her lap. "I think we should focus on Rosemont. The Covenant Community Church there has a dynamic minister. Mary says he really knows his Bible. State Senator Cummings goes there, too."

He listened quietly. *Good place to network.*

"Ridgewood, right next to Rosemont, is nice, too. Beautiful homes and parks. But I noticed there's a synagogue there."

He glanced over and saw her raised eyebrows.

"Be careful at the station, Marge. Lots of Jews there."

"Oh, I'd never talk like this except with you, sweetie. I know you feel the same way." She rubbed the back of his neck. "That's why our marriage is perfect, Rick. We feel the same about the important things in life, don't we?"

She's right, he thought. He'd never associated with Jews. That Marty Sax and Meadow Marx turned him off. No matter how they cleaned up, they were different, pure and simple. As to blacks, though that receptionist was a stunner, he couldn't imagine laying a finger on her.

"Once you go black, you'll never go back," his fraternity brothers said. Rick never sought out that opportunity. Enough sexy white women in the world, women like Finley Smith. He needn't dip into dark meat for satisfaction.

Yes, Finley had it all—elegance, breeding, class. Compared to a thoroughbred like her, Sylvia Reynolds was little better than a lead pony.

Twenty-two

As Chris Andrews said goodbye to his viewers, Finley stood in the control room between Meadow and Marty. They had their arms around each other's waists, and when she glanced in either direction, she saw tears on their faces.

"I'm gonna miss that old coot," Marty said, coughing and pulling out a handkerchief.

Meadow shook her head. "This feels historic, like the end of something."

Finley didn't speak. She couldn't trust herself. Her thoughts jumbled between sadness and distress over the changes ahead. How could Rick Stone, a cold right-wing automaton, possibly replace an anchor Philadelphia had trusted for the past sixteen years? How could she stay at a station who would hire such a man?

She shook away the thoughts. This was a night for happiness, for celebration. Chris's departure deserved that much.

A large crowd from WABN was taking Chris and his wife to dinner, but the three huddled in the control room would not be among them. Finley needed to get home to Caroline, and Meadow had dinner already scheduled with her parents and Marty and Barbara Sax.

"You get on home to that little girl," Chris said to Finley. "You, Meadow and I'll have dinner in a few weeks and catch up about my new job at Blue Care." His eyes shined with anticipation. "I can't wait for you to meet Joe Heaton, Finley. He's gonna love you."

As she drove home, Finley's sadness over losing Chris began to dissipate. She felt blessed that Caroline was healing quickly and keeping up with her class, thanks to Jenny's teaching skills. How lucky she was to have Jenny around to handle the therapy, tutoring and doctor's appointments.

Her feeling of gratitude expanded when she saw David's car in her driveway. He must have come over to be with Caroline, but Finley admitted to herself how thrilled she felt over the chance to see him again.

At her front door, her senses were assailed with heavenly scents of andouille sausage, peppers and thyme. Hurrying to the kitchen, she found Caroline and David sitting together while Jenny stood at the stove.

"Mom, Jenny's making an authentic creole dinner."

"I can tell. The smell is making my mouth water. Jenny, is there anything you can't do? Where'd you learn to cook?"

"Our mama was a great cook," Jenny said as she added more oregano to the simmering pot. "She catered for some of the richest families in Philadelphia when we were kids. She made us learn, too. Stephanie's boyfriend says I cook better than her, and Lord knows that man can eat! Don't tell Stephanie I told you."

"Promise," Finley said, crossing her heart.

"Glass of wine, Finn?" David rose to his feet and picked up the uncorked bottle.

"Absolutely. I'd love a glass. It's been a bear of a day."

"You go on in the living room and enjoy your drinks." Jenny shooed them out of the kitchen. "I'll call you when dinner's ready."

Caroline excused herself to make a phone call.

As they settled on the couch with their drinks, Finley noted the lighted candles. Musky incense exuded an exotic fragrance. She smiled. Caroline wouldn't give up on her parents, and she'd found a perfect co-conspirator in Jenny. A pang of guilt hit Finley. She knew Jenny spent more time with Caroline than she did.

David clicked his beer can against her wine glass. "So, tough day, huh? What's happening?"

"The new anchor, Rick Stone, arrived this morning with his perfectly proper spouse." She put her glass on the table. "He's a Nazi, David. And I'm not kidding. He's so far to the right he tilts. This is not going to be okay. If corporate continues to back him—and they will, of course. He's their golden boy. I'm afraid I'll have to leave."

"Would you do that—after all your hard work?"

His words made Finley question her resolve. "I think so. I could go back to reporting. It might be fun to get out on the street again. Bottom line, at this stage of my life, I will not manage a yellow newscast.

"Enough about me and the station. Frankly, I'm sick of thinking about it." She leaned in his direction. "How's life?" she asked. "Still mending the broken minds and hearts of Philadelphia?"

"Trying," he answered with a self-deprecating chuckle. "Though I wonder sometimes what makes me the great god of mental health. My patients seem to buy it." He shook his head.

She leaned closer. "You are a healer, David," she said. "So centered—you always have been. You saved my sanity after Caroline's accident. Sure held *me* together."

He grinned. "I'm a good actor, I guess. I was as scared as you. I just can't shake that old garbage that guys shouldn't show it. I know better here," he tapped his head. "It's just here that gives me trouble." He touched his chest.

She took the hand resting over his heart and gently touched the finger that once wore her gold band. She brought the hand to her face, nestled her cheek against it and turned her mouth to kiss it. He pulled back. Their eyes met for a moment. He began to move toward her. Time and space hung silent, each of them unsure of the next move.

At that moment, Jenny's voice trilled from the kitchen. "Dinner's ready."

~ * ~

Meadow hurried into Klancy's Kosher Kitchen at seven o'clock. Her parents sat in a corner booth with Marty and Barbara Sax. They waved her over. The familiar smells of latkes, knishes and simmering brisket wafted from the kitchen. Red-painted walls glowed warmly under dim lighting and cast a rose blush on the tables covered in white linen. *This'd be a great place for a wedding reception*, Meadow thought, surprised at the speculation. *Silly girl, like you'll ever have one of those again.*

"Bubella," Stan rose to hug his daughter. "Marty was just now telling us about the *swell* new fella at the station."

"Oh, he's swell all right," Meadow said. "If you think Hitler was a good guy with a bad haircut."

"Chris Andrews got himself a good job with Blue Care, we hear," Arlene said, kissing Meadow's cheek as she nestled in beside her.

"A great job, actually, thanks to this angel." She put her arm around Marty's shoulder and smiled at his wife. "Barbara, your husband pulled off his greatest feat on this one."

"Don't be telling him that." Barbara dismissed Meadow's words with a brush of her hand. "Already his head's too big for his yarmulke."

"So, what're you gonna do about the news jerk?" her father said.

"Not much I can do, and I certainly don't envy Finn right now. She's worked so hard to make our news top in the state. Now, corporate wants to screw with it."

"You're surprised?" Marty asked.

"Guess I am. Ratings equal dollars after all. Isn't that the equation?"

"Usually," Marty answered. "This time it seems Austin Montgomery has another agenda. I'm not sure what it is. The rumors are flying how he plays ball with the governor and his corporate supporters. There's even talk of an FCC investigation."

"I hope you're wrong, Marty," Meadow responded. "That would make me sick."

"Don't get sick yet, darling." He patted her shoulder. "It ain't over 'til the fat lady sings, and she hasn't even opened her trap yet. Now, let's order before I starve to death."

They studied their menus and made suggestions to each other about what sounded good. They agreed to order different dishes and share.

"I'm not very hungry," Arlene said quietly. "Just some kugel for me."

"Not hungry?" Meadow turned to her mother. "Mom, you usually eat us all under the table."

"She hasn't had any appetite lately," Stan said, his eyes anxious. "She's tired all the time and her back seems to be hurting more than usual."

"Have you seen a doctor?" Meadow turned toward her mother.

Arlene took a sip of her wine. "Oh yes, honey. Two of them.

They're doing lots of tests. I'm just a little anemic. Don't worry. It'll pass."

Meadow couldn't help but worry. This was the first time in memory she had ever heard her mother complain about not feeling well. "Promise me you'll see a third doctor."

Arlene dismissed her daughter with a wave of her hand, "It's nothing."

"Like I said, promise."

"All right, all right, I promise. Now order already."

~ * ~

Sylvia, wrapped in the hotel's thick terry robe, lay in bed sipping her martini. A game show flickered on the muted TV. The excited contestants did not distract her from the thought that had deviled her the entire day. Should she take a chance on a dalliance with Rick Stone? The one night had been spectacular, and this period of celibacy had gone on much too long. Sometimes, she thought, life really is stranger than fiction. She reminded herself that she mustn't let her physical need cloud her objectives. There was no reason to make any decisions about Rick tonight. Other matters were more pressing.

First, she must consider the best way to get rid of Meadow and Marty. With their salaries and commissions eliminated, her bottom line would soar. She stared into the propane fireplace and sipped the drink. Bet they both have a nest egg stashed away. Their kind usually does.

She didn't need just cause to fire either of them, but neither did she want to deal with an age discrimination suit. Marty only had another year until retirement. Best to suck it up and leave him alone. Of course, if he decided to keep working after sixty-five, she'd have to reconsider—but not tonight.

Meadow Marx was another story altogether. If Sylvia's plan worked, Meadow would be gone after July sweeps.

Twenty-three

Thursday morning

"This is absolute trash!" Finley shouted as she previewed the first of Rick Stone's syndicated programs. The fabricated story indicted Stephen Aldquist, a respected New Jersey senator. It implied bribery, infidelity, and the possibility of a gay tryst during the *anonymous* senator's college years. No name was mentioned and images were blurred, but enough hints peppered the commentary to ensure that any viewer could draw a conclusion. Because the audience so trusted the WABN news, Aldquist's reputation would be damaged, especially after Rush checked the wire service and picked up on the rumors.

She jerked her phone to her ear and punched in a number. "Rick, please come to my office immediately."

Five minutes later, he sauntered in. "Hi, Boss lady. What's up?" He plopped down on the sofa and cocked his foot onto his knee—his usual posture, open and suggestive.

She grabbed the tape from her desk. "This is what's up. What sources did you use for this piece?"

He smiled. "Now you know a good reporter never reveals his sources."

"You will if you want it aired on my newscast."

"*Your* newscast? Hmmm, I thought it was Prescott Broadcasting's newscast. At least, that's what they think...besides, Austin Montgomery read and approved the script yesterday."

Finley's breath caught in her chest. She could barely speak. "You submitted it to corporate before you brought it to your News Director?"

"'Fraid so, Finn. See, I'm getting the feeling you're not a team player. I mentioned that to Austin when we talked. He said he'll support an end run around you whenever I need one."

Her mind shifted into overdrive then screeched to a halt. What could she do if the company chairman backed Rick, however he distorted the truth? Her heart hurt with the frustration of her situation.

Feeling defeated, she murmured, "That'll be all."

He grinned, took the Beta from her hand and sauntered out of her office.

Finley began to analyze the situation in earnest. What are my options? Resignation? A telephone confrontation with Austin Montgomery? Murder? No, not that.

Finally, realizing she had no answers to the problems assaulting her mind, she called Meadow. "Lunch, half an hour?"

~ * ~

"I ordered your usual," Finley said.

Meadow nodded. "What's up, Finn? You look like you walked through a chalk storm." An alarm rang in her head. "It's not Caroline, is it? Nothing's gone wrong, has it?"

Finley smiled. "No, Caroline's doing great. I think she'll graduate with her class, thanks to Jenny." She covered Meadow's hand with her own. "Thanks, pal, for putting things in perspective. That would be real trouble."

"So, what's the not-real trouble?"

Finley put down her fork and stared into Meadow's eyes. "Rick Stone."

"Oh, so the Rick shit is beginning to hit the fan, huh?"

"Yes. He and I just had it out about his first syndicated segment. It'll be on our six and run on all the others in the chain tomorrow." Frustration knitted her forehead into lines. "And there's not a thing I can do about it. Meadow, it's pure libel against Stephen Aldquist."

"What? That guy's as pure as a politician can get. What could he possibly have on Steve?"

"Absolutely nothing. Aldquist's never identified. It's all rumors and hearsay, but it's clearly Steve he's talking about. Nothing is substantiated, but you know as well as I do how the average viewer hears this kind of crap."

"What if the Senator sues Prescott?"

"He won't. A lawsuit would just bring more attention to the story and Aldquist is too sharp not to know that. Believe me, Rick Stone is a master on how to smear someone without getting his hands dirty."

"Have you called corporate?"

"No." Finley shook her head. "Rick cleared the story with Austin Montgomery yesterday—before he showed it to me. He has Austin's full support."

Meadow sat silent as Josie brought their lunch to the table.

Finley picked up her fork and stabbed at her salad. Finally, she put the fork down on her plate and rested her chin in her hand. "I seem to have lost my appetite."

"You and my mother."

"Arlene?"

"Yes." Meadow's eyes clouded with fear. "Something's wrong with her. She's not okay. She promised to see another doctor next week. I've never seen her sick before, and it scares me."

Picking up her fork, Finley looked ready to cry.

Meadow feared Finley was ready to resign, and that mustn't happen. From a personal standpoint, she adored Finley as her best friend. Beyond that, though, Finley was the best news director in the business, and if the ratings dropped, sales revenues would plummet like a rock tossed off the Prudential Tower.

"Eat, Finn," Meadow ordered firmly. "We're going to need all our strength to win this war with corporate...and war it is."

~ * ~

Meadow called Marty into her office and closed the door. She needed someone with his kind of experience and wisdom as a sounding board. She told him about Rick's nearly libelous story. Surprised by the slight smile playing around his lips, she said, "What's funny, Marty? Share the joke. Believe me, I could use a laugh right about now."

"I've seen corporate pull shit before, but this time they're getting nastier than ever. Let me think about this."

Meadow didn't know why his words made her feel better, but they did. Marty the mensch could make anything okay.

~ * ~

Marty held the receiver to his ear. "Hi, Dolly. How's the prettiest gatekeeper in Philly?"

"Oh Marty, you old smoothie. If I didn't know better, I'd swear you had some Irish blarney in you. Want Joe?"

"Yes, please."

Within seconds, the familiar voice came across the line. "You looking to get your clock cleaned on the golf course again, Marty?"

"Not today, Joe. I do need to talk to you though. Drinks after work tomorrow?"

"Sure. The Pendleton?"

"See you at seven thirty, and thanks. By the way, try to catch our six o'clock news before you meet me, okay?"

Twenty-four

Friday night

David had Caroline for the night. "You need a break, Finn," he'd said. A night with your wacky buddy may be just the tonic you need. Call Meadow."

What a sweetheart, Finley thought. *The only better tonic would be lying in your arms*, but the words remained unspoken.

Finley and Meadow made a pact to keep talk about work to a minimum. Both of them were sick about the new atmosphere at WABN. From janitors to anchors, people walked on eggshells as they waited for the next firing, fearing it would be their own.

As they sat in Meadow's cozy living room, the two women yielded to one of their deepest cravings—a pizza from Mozzarella's. When it arrived, Meadow moaned in ecstasy as melting cheese ran down her chin. She lapped it up like a cat enjoying its cream. "God, if there is a heaven, I bet they serve this every night. How can anything this good be unhealthy? Carbs, schmarbs...it's worth it. I'll starve tomorrow."

Finley grinned, then picked up a piece of pepperoni and laid it on her tongue like a communion wafer. "There is a heaven, Meadow, and we'll be there together unless I screw up, murder Sylvia and make God mad at me. We'll eat this pizza every day and never gain an ounce. That's what heaven is for."

"Absolutely, and gorgeous male angels will fly around us ready for stud service at any time. By the way, they'll be hung like stallions, oh, and circumcised, too. Gotta keep my mother happy, you know. I try to drive her nuts here on earth, but in heaven I'll be more charitable."

"How's she doing?" Finley asked. "Did she see another doctor?"

"She has an appointment next week." Her face darkened. "I'm scared, Finn. She's always been so healthy." Meadow picked up another slice. "Which reminds me," she said, taking a bite. "If you could pick a man for me who would make my mother berserk with joy, what would he be like?"

"What a weird question," Finley said. She began to ponder. "Well, Jewish, for sure."

Meadow nodded.

"Of course, he'd be a liberal. Oh, and employed. Gainfully. In some kind of, umm, caring job that would suit your mom's hippie sentiments. And he'd love you like mad, Meadow. That would matter most to her."

Meadow smiled. "Wanna show you something." She stood up and wiped her hands down her yoga pants.

"What?"

She picked up a glossy magazine from the table.

"Hey, we agreed to leave work out of this night."

"This has nothing to do with WABN."

Finley set her wine glass on the coaster and sat down next to Meadow. "Have you heard of Classmatch?" Meadow asked.

"Classmatch? No." Finley leaned closer. "What is it?"

"It's for professionals. They advertise in Airline magazines. Keep a much lower profile than the other dating sites. I heard about it from a buyer in New York." Meadow opened the magazine.

"Oh, Meadow, matchmaker dating? Didn't you try that once? Isn't that how you met Harry, the hairy hun, who considered burping the perfect complement to a great dinner?" Finley laughed out loud, recalling the hysterical double date when she and David were still married.

Meadow smiled and thumbed through the pages.

"Oh, and that Fred guy?" Finley continued "He wore more makeup than I do."

"He had eyeliner and lip liner tattooed on. He was in a band. It was my toy-boy phase."

Finley started to recount other lemons that Meadow had tried to turn into lemonade when, suddenly, a dark-haired man appeared on a page.

Horn-rimmed glasses shielded warm eyes. His grin was open.

"Mmm," Finley said. "He's different...looks nice. Who is he?"

"That, my friend, is what we're going to find out."

"What?"

"We're going to meet him at Gallagher's at eight. I told him I didn't want to come alone, so he's expecting you, too. When David called and asked me to be home for you this evening, I knew this was the night."

"David. Called...?"

"Sure, didn't you know?"

He does care. He must. "I can't go out dressed in sweats," Finley said.

"At Gallagher's, you'd look weird dressed in anything else. It's a hangout for gym rats. You look great. Come on...it's seven fifteen. We gotta hurry."

Finley groaned, but stood up, wolfed down a last piece of pizza, and carried her empty plate to the dishwasher. "You owe me, big time."

Meadow nodded. "I know, I know. I'd do it for you and you know it."

Twenty minutes later, after a quick touch up of their makeup, Finley and Meadow began a fast clip to Gallagher's. "What do you know about this man?" Finley asked.

"You're gonna die when I tell you this. He's a doctor. A Jewish doctor. Don't know what specialty, but he's involved in Doctors Without Borders, so he fits all of Arlene's specs. Don't know if he's circumcised, though. Yet."

Finley laughed. "A Jewish doctor? Oh my God, Meadow. Do your folks know?"

"Nope, haven't even laid eyes on him yet, so I think a gathering of the clan is a tad premature. I sure like his picture though."

~ * ~

Finley spotted him first. He was sitting at the bar with a Miller Lite in front of him. Miller Lite? She stuffed her snobbishness, nudged Meadow and pointed. As their eyes connected, he stood and smiled. Finley could almost feel the electricity that passed between this stranger and her friend.

"Ohhh," Meadow said. "He's tall, not too tall, just right tall."

"Hello." He walked toward them, never breaking his stare into Meadow's eyes as he took her hand. "Ben Freedman. I know you from your picture." He tore his eyes reluctantly away from Meadow and turned to Finley. "And you must be Finley."

She extended her hand and he grasped it firmly. "Good to meet you. Meadow says you two are like sisters."

His hand felt strong and slightly calloused. This is a man unafraid of hard work, Finley thought. David's hands felt like this, she remembered with a jolt that nearly brought tears to her eyes.

Ben turned back to Meadow. "You, by the way, are an absolute doll, even better than your picture."

"Doll?" Meadow exclaimed. "You called me a doll, and it didn't piss me off. That's a first."

Ben laughed. "That's how you look to me, pretty as porcelain."

Finley felt Meadow melt against her side. She nudged hard with her elbow. "Okay, doll, let's get a table."

Ben pulled out two chairs, and Finley said to the waiter who materialized next to her, "Just a seltzer, please. I'm driving." She leaned back to observe Meadow and Ben.

He put his elbows on the table and tore his glance away from Meadow to include Finley in the conversation. "So, you both work at WABN? Great station. Best news in town."

"Thanks to Finn," Meadow said, patting her on the back.

Finley decided to conduct her own mini focus group with this stranger. "Have you seen our news lately?"

"Been in Somalia," he answered. "Caught it last night for the first time in weeks." He hesitated for a moment, looking uncertain. "Not sure I like your new anchorman. Hope that doesn't offend you."

"Offend me?" Finley laughed. "On the contrary, Ben. I don't like him much either, but I'm stuck with him." She sipped her seltzer. "Thank you for being honest with me." She shook her head. "However, Meadow and I made a pact to not talk business tonight, so I'm going to change the subject if you don't mind. Where is your office?"

He described a street that bordered an African-American and Hispanic neighborhood. "Lots of Medicaid cases and way underserved medically."

As time passed, Finley found herself becoming more and more comfortable with Dr. Ben Freedman. A kind intelligence radiated from his dark eyes and his wit was nearly as sharp as Meadow's. Finley could see him becoming a very good friend.

That was a relief because Meadow obviously was falling for him quick and hard. *Nothing worse than having your best friend fall for a loser you can't stand, she mused. No problem here.*

Meadow filled him in on Caroline's accident, and he asked Finley questions about her physical progress. Finley watched as Meadow appeared more smitten by the moment. She and Ben laughed at the same things and interrupted each other's sentences with easy candor. Their spark was obvious.

It had been like this from the beginning with David and me, too. The memory was sweet and painful. On their first date, they sat up until dawn in an all-night diner talking and laughing together.

At nine thirty, Finley stretched and yawned. "I need to get home. I want to call David and see how Caroline's doing. It's my first night away from her since the accident. You two stay. I'll walk back to my car. It's parked near Meadow's apartment. Not far."

"No way." Ben jumped to his feet and put his credit card on the table. "Just let me settle this and we'll walk you back."

"Can I help with the check?" Finley asked.

"Nah, let me be a gentleman."

She glanced at Meadow's glowing face. Finley understood exactly what she was feeling. It was a good thing—women's lib be damned—to have a man take care of you, escort you to your car, pick up the check.

The three of them strolled the bustling streets back toward Meadow's apartment, and Finley saw Ben take Meadow's hand. He walked nearest the curb...old-fashioned, maybe archaic, but lovely. David always did that, too.

When they arrived at her car, Ben asked for Finley's keys and opened the driver's door before handing them back to her. "Night, Finley.

Been a pleasure."

"Me, too, Ben," she said sincerely. "Now you two kids behave yourselves, okay?"

When she looked back, she couldn't believe her eyes. The two of them stood under a street light staring into each other's eyes. Hard-boiled Meadow Marx was blushing like a teenager.

As she pulled away, Finley rolled down her window and asked, "By the way, Ben. What's your specialty?"

"Gynecology," he answered.

She drove off fast, before Meadow could catch her eye. Finley laughed all the way home.

~ * ~

The phone rang the next morning just after ten. "What'd you think of him?" It was Meadow.

"I think he's great. But more important. More important, what did you think?"

"Even greater. He came up and we talked forever. When he kissed me good night, swear to God, Finn, I saw stars."

"Did you...um, you know?"

"No." Meadow's voice drifted dreamily. "I would have, but he says he wants to get to know me better. He doesn't believe in sex unless the couple is in love. Wouldn't you just know it? The first guy who's turned me on in three years, and the son-of-a-bitch has scruples."

Twenty-five

Friday night

Marty glanced around the Pendleton bar. It was jammed with men in suits and women wearing high heels and dressy casual. Marty knew most of the crowd. He recognized the ones schmoozing clients over drinks and others discussing strategies that could change the landscape of their businesses. This was the favorite watering hole in Philadelphia for bo th the "up and coming" and the "already arrived" crowds. The place was packed as usual on this Friday night.

Soft classical music muted the buzz of conversation. The lights were low, and curving earth-toned walls showcased the longest mahogany bar in the East. The wooden masterpiece had been transported in pieces from New York's Tammany Hall in the early part of the twentieth century. The historic bar heightened the sense of affluence which made the Pendleton "the place to meet" for Philadelphia power brokers.

As his eyes adjusted to the dim lighting, Marty spotted Joe Heaton waving to him from the bar. Joe's briefcase sat on the stool next to him.

"Hi pal," Joe said as Marty placed the briefcase on the floor between them and slid onto the stool. "Been too long."

"Sure has, Joe. How's Diane?"

"Good. Nagging at me to retire. What else is new? Barbara okay?"

"Great. Busy with grandkids and volunteering. She hounds me to quit, too. Says she wants to learn golf and play with me. She should know the only reason I play is to get some guy time. Hate the game, love the conversations."

Joe laughed. "Me, too. Love Diane to death, but after forty years..."

He left the comment unfinished, obviously knowing Marty would understand.

"Still keeping our nation's hospitals afloat?" Marty asked.

"Trying, but it gets tougher every day."

"Think things'll change with the election?"

Joe shook his head. "Hope so, but those schmucks in Congress are mighty comfortable. Donations from big pharm and insurance keep them fat, happy and employed."

"What can I get you, sir?" the bartender asked Marty.

"Same as him." He gestured toward Joe's Scotch.

"Coming right up."

"You know, Marty, most hospitals in this country are operating in the red. I'm getting mighty tired of fighting those deep-pocket bastards who buy Congress. Tim Clancy, my priest at St. Matt's, is on my ass all the time to help the folks in our parish who can't afford health insurance. He keeps throwing that Bible stuff at me about taking care of the sick."

Marty shook his head and remembered their last meeting. "By the way, how's Chris Andrews working out?"

"Great!" Joe answered, patting Marty on the back. "Best tip you gave me since you told me to start buying television stock back in the sixties. I owe you. Never seen a better spokesman on TV. Not the sharpest tack in the pack, but he reads whatever's on the Teleprompter like Moses from the mountain. People believe him. Nobody has a clue he doesn't know what the fuck he's talking about."

Marty laughed. "Glad to hear it. We miss him at the station. He was like a big puppy dog that everybody liked to stroke." He took a long swig of scotch. "Did you watch the news tonight like I asked you?"

"Yeah, why?"

"What'd you think of our new anchor guy...Richard Stone?"

"Slick as spit," he answered. "Don't think I like him. How can he get away with that piece of shit about Steve Aldquist?" He shook his head in disbelief. "Why'd they get rid of Chris anyway? He was a hell of a lot more credible than Richard Stone."

"Well," Marty said, grinning, "better order another drink. This may take a little time."

Twenty-six

Monday, 6:00 p.m.

Jenny put on her coat to leave for the night. "Caroline's almost ready to go back to school," she said. "Guess you won't need me much longer."

Finley's heart sank. In the short time she'd been there, Jenny had become a part of her little family. Caroline loved her, and Finley found Jenny's solid presence a rock she could depend on. "I suppose you're right, but I hate to see you go. You're like a favorite sister and aunt to me and Caroline. I can never thank you enough for helping me keep her up to snuff with her classes."

Jenny's smile beamed from the lovely mahogany face. "I feel the same way about you two. But I need to help other people heal. I'm a nurse. That's my mission."

Finley lowered her head. "I know, but we'll miss you so much."

"I'm not falling off the planet, girl, and I sure don't plan to give up your great kitchen. The one in my apartment is a closet. I'll be under your feet whenever I feel like cooking something special. Deal?"

"Deal," Finley answered. "Any time, you know that."

"Well, I suggest we start with a real fine dinner this Saturday night. I'll cook and we'll invite Meadow along with Stephanie and Anthony...Lord, I'd better get a lot of meat...that Anthony can eat...and, of course, I'll invite Mr. David." As she said his name, she paused. Finley knew she was checking for a reaction but gave none.

"Great idea, Jenny. Better count on one extra guest. Meadow's new friend, Ben Freedman. I have a feeling they'll be together Saturday night."

126

"Really? Meadow has a boyfriend?"

"And how. They just met, but I think they're already falling in l...o...v...e."

"Any special dietary considerations you know about?"

"Mmmm, maybe not pork."

~ * ~

Saturday evening

Meadow and Ben arrived first. Meadow was gaping at Ben like a love-struck school girl and her chin showed definite signs of whisker burn.

Finley took Meadow into the kitchen while Stephanie got Ben a Miller Lite. "So?" she asked.

"Omigod, Finn, he's amazing. I definitely recommend sex with a gynecologist. Oh, and he is circumcised. Fits all my mother's specs."

The doorbell interrupted. When Finley went to answer it, she found Caroline already there, embracing David. He came in and hugged Finley. *Like a brother*. She was saddened by that.

Finley took drink orders and as they settled down to talk, the doorbell rang again. "I'll get it," she said.

"Hi, girlfriend," Stephanie fluttered in. "Nice place," she said looking around with an approving nod. "This is Anthony. Tell him to mind his manners tonight."

The man filled Finley's entire doorway. His gentle handshake surprised her and his dark eyes gazing at Stephanie were adoring. "Pleased to meet you, ma'am."

"Call me Finn, please."

She led them into the living room, asking what they'd like to drink. Ben stared at Anthony, star struck. "Aren't you Anthony Jones?"

"Yessir."

"Meadow, this guy is the best halfback ever to play for the Eagles."

"The rock group?" Meadow's eyes twinkled, but Ben looked startled, not sure that she was kidding.

Finley groaned. Meadow was certainly sports challenged, but this kind of ignorance for anyone living in Philadelphia went way beyond possible, even for her.

David and Ben positioned themselves next to Anthony on the sofa and peppered him with questions about the Eagles.

"Oh Lord, this happens every time I introduce him to new men," Stephanie said. "Hey Jenny," she called out. "Need some help in there?"

The women headed for the kitchen to put the finishing touches on the meal. Jenny carved the rare filet of beef wrapped in pate and thin pastry. Juices simmered on the stove. Butter-drenched mashed potatoes warmed on another burner. Finley carried a high, browned broccoli soufflé to the candlelit table. Stephanie tossed a green salad loaded with feta cheese, walnuts, cranberries and Jenny's special vinaigrette. Meadow pulled biscuits from the oven and gingerly tossed them into a bread basket.

"Soup's on." Jenny called out. David escorted Caroline to the dining room.

As they gathered around the table, Finley asked them to join hands, "I don't know how religious all of you are, but I'd sure like to thank God and Jenny for getting Caroline better." Every person bowed their head.

"Now, let's eat," Jenny said, passing the meat platter.

Twenty-seven

May 1, at night

A light snow fell as Sylvia left the station. God, she thought. It's May. I was certain we were through with winter. She stepped carefully to the parking lot and lifted her face to the cold mist. Snow always reminded her of a December evening years before when she had visited her father in New York.

Eight-year-old Sylvia boarded the plane that cold afternoon in Raleigh as her mother cried piteously. Sylvia ignored the tears. Her mother cried every night once she'd finished the half bottle of bourbon that was her custom. Each Thursday after dark, Sylvia hid the empty Jim Beam bottles in neighbors' trash cans so gossip wouldn't spread on Friday, the day the garbage trucks came.

That frigid day in Raleigh, Sylvia ran up the steps of the plane happy to escape the nosey nuns at her school and, most of all, the embarrassment of being the daughter of the town drunk in Beaufort, North Carolina, a small town on the coast. She was thrilled to be escaping to New York City for Christmas with her father.

That night, she walked with him from his Park Avenue apartment to Radio City Music Hall. Snow was falling in huge, wet flakes and quickly covered all the cars and sidewalks. The Fifth Avenue storefronts were alive with dancing dolls and toys. Each window excited Sylvia's imagination. When her father took her hand to cross the street, she pressed herself against his side, loving his nearness. Stepping up onto the opposite sidewalk, he dropped her hand instantly. Sylvia grabbed his hand back but again, he dropped it.

Sitting in the sixth row in her red velvet dress, she felt like a princess whose daddy was the handsomest king in the world. As he scanned the program, she could not stop herself from gazing at him. His strong profile. His dark hair styled to perfection.

He never returned her glance.

"Oh, Daddy, look at the people sitting up there in those boxes. How do they get up there?"

"There are stairs, Sylvia." His voice was sharp and made her feel stupid. She should have known, of course. And she did know but just wanted him to talk to her.

"Michael," a voice trilled across the rows of seats. Sylvia watched as a tall, blonde lady floated down the aisle. Sylvia's father stood and opened his arms.

"Natalie," he said, holding her close and kissing her on the cheek. "Wonderful to see you."

"And who is this young lady?" she asked.

"My daughter, Sylvia. She's visiting from North Carolina."

The woman took Sylvia's hand into her own, and her skin felt soft as a peach. "Hello, Sylvia. Are you having fun with your daddy?"

As Sylvia started to respond, her father said, "I certainly hope so. Though it's not my idea of nirvana, carting a child all over the city. Especially one who looks like my ex." He put his hand over his mouth, but Sylvia heard what he said next. "She was homely, too."

"God, Michael," the blonde lady said. "You really are a prick." She turned to Sylvia, "Don't pay any attention to him, honey. I don't think he likes girls."

Homely. Sylvia had never heard the term before. What did it mean?

The great organ started the overture for *Babes in Toyland* and when the heavy maroon curtain parted, the Rockettes stood there, poised like dolls in Santa's workshop. One by one, they came to life, first stiff, then looser, their costumes casting a rainbow of pastels across the vast stage. Sylvia willed the image to burn into her brain so she could remember this moment forever. They were the most beautiful girls Sylvia had ever seen.

When they got back to his apartment after the show, Sylvia crept into his office and, on tip toes, pulled the big dictionary down from the top shelf. It was heavy and nearly toppled her over as it fell into her arms. She turned the pages until she found the H section.

Homely—not attractive or good looking, lacking elegance or refinement. Sylvia carefully replaced the book, climbed down from the chair and sat on the floor. As the meaning sunk in, she started to cry. Each time she gained control, she remembered—her father called her homely. That was why he wouldn't hold her hand after crossing the street or talk to her in the grand theater.

The lady named Natalie was beautiful. The Rockettes were beautiful. But Sylvia was homely, and so was her mother. Yes, her mother was homely, with puffy eyes and red veins popping out all over her nose. Sylvia decided not to visit her father again. She didn't want him to be ashamed of her.

From then on, she fought each time she had to board the plane in Raleigh. Her father said it was part of some agreement, but she knew he didn't want her. He just wanted to keep the agreement, whatever it was.

That Christmas was the last time they were ever alone, without an ever-present nanny or one of his business associates joining them at meals.

Snow always reminded Sylvia that underneath the makeup and hair dye, she was—homely.

~ * ~

As she unlocked her car, Rick Stone came up behind her. "Hi there, Sylvia. Time for a drink?"

She questioned the wisdom of being seen with him in Philadelphia. But then, as she knew she would, as he surely knew she would, she said, "Sure, Rick. Your car or mine?"

Her attraction to him was now tinged with anger. She saw him staring at Finley during staff meetings. Obviously, he didn't find Finley *homely*.

Rick drove to Malone's, a dark pub, miles from the station, far from where he had settled with Marjorie and the children.

"Hungry?" he asked after the martinis had arrived.

"Not really. I had a late lunch."

His smile across the table was insinuating.

She nibbled the olive and decided to test the waters. "Finley Smith giving you any trouble?"

He laughed. "She tries, but with my pipeline to Austin, we both know she'll lose. She's out of touch with corporate's objectives. And I don't see her changing any time soon. If I were you, I'd prepare for a resignation from little Ms. Smith."

His callous words cheered her. "Worse things could happen. She's good, but there are other good News Directors around who are more agreeable and less expensive."

"Anything else going on?" he asked.

She thought for a moment. "I'm planning to give Meadow Marx notice after the May book comes in. Her revenues are down." She took a sip of her drink. "She blames you."

Rick's lips tightened. She could see her words peeved him. He read overnight ratings. The station's news shares were trending down. She had expected a dip. That always happened when a long-time anchor was replaced. Only not one this deep. It felt good to dent Rick's cockiness, to keep him bound by a small thread of fear.

"Just a glitch," he said. "By the November book, they'll be back up."

"Actually, I'm happy for that glitch." She sipped her drink. "Gives me one more excuse to unload Meadow. Sales dollars have been trending down since Chris Randall left. It's perfect."

"Happy to help." He put his hand on her arm. "Anything I can do, just say the word. Any service you need."

She smiled.

After a second drink, fatigue hit Sylvia, hard. "Take me back to my car. Have to get home."

Pulling into the station's lot, he braked hard, and his tires slid on the new snow. "Whoa, easy," he said. "Don't need a fender bender at this hour, especially with *you* in the car. I'd have a devil of a time explaining that to..."

Sylvia's fatigue flared into anger. "Bye, Rick," she drawled. "Have a nice night with Marge." She slammed the door and walked away.

Later, as she soaked in her tub, she struggled to soothe her irritation with logic. *I am a very successful woman in charge of the top television station in Pennsylvania,* she told herself. She thought she had convinced herself to relax when unexpected tears invaded her eyes—bitter and icy against the jackhammer of her throbbing head. Hurt beyond consolation, she began to moan, exactly like the discounted, homely girl whose hand had been dropped that snowy night in New York.

Twenty-eight

June 1, early morning

Finley ruffled through the stack of press releases piled in her inbox. The Nielsen ratings were expected tomorrow, and she wasn't sure what she was hoping for. If numbers were as far down as overnights indicated, would Austin recognize this golden boy might have been a mistake? Or did he have a different agenda than just advertising dollars? And, if corporate kept Rick, kept the station in this purgatory of yellow journalism, what would her next move be?

The ring of the telephone interrupted her thoughts.

Meadow's voice was tight. "Finn, the bitch wants to meet next week."

Finley swiveled her chair around to face the window. "Maybe she just wants to go over ratings. Discuss how to market a lower-rated news."

"Doubtful. She knows my team will sell the sizzle…rationalize the dip as a hiccup. I think there's more."

Probably, Finley thought. *Time to change the subject.* "So, since we can't read her mind, let's talk about something pleasant. How are things going with the good Dr. Freedman?"

Meadow's voice softened. "Great. Yesterday was his afternoon off, and when I got home, he'd cooked me a brisket. A brisket! I haven't had one of those since my mom made them for Passover. And don't tell Arlene, but his was better. How'd I luck out like this? Sex with Ben leaves me famished, and he feeds me brisket."

Finley looked at her watch. "Which reminds me, I'm hungry. Lunch?"

"Can't. I'm helping Erin put together a summer schedule for the Toyota dealers. WRQA has come up with a dynamite promotion, and we need to top it to keep our share from last summer. Maybe tomorrow."

"Okay. Give my love to Ben and tell him I want his brisket recipe." She put her computer to sleep.

As she pulled on her jacket, the phone rang again. She nearly let it go, then changed her mind. What if it was Caroline?

"Hello, Finley Smith," She answered.

His voice was soft. "Hi, Finn. Could we have lunch? I need to talk to you."

Her heart leapt. "Sure, David. I was going to eat alone."

"I'll pick you up in fifteen minutes."

What could he want? She hadn't seen him since Jenny's dinner. Maybe he missed her? In the ladies' room mirror, she dabbed some lipstick on her mouth and blush on her cheeks. *I'm so glad I wore a skirt today. A short one.*

She ran back to her office and retrieved the high-heeled sandals she kept in her bottom drawer. They were there in case a special occasion cropped up at the end of the day, and this definitely qualified as special, no matter that it was afternoon.

The trees along the sidewalk looked ready to burst awake after their dreary winter's nap. She rummaged sunglasses from her purse. Just as she put them on, David's car pulled up.

As she eased into the front seat beside him, she hiked up her skirt and crossed her legs toward him. "Hi stranger."

He nodded and put the car into drive. She snuck a glance in his direction and caught an unusual set to his jaw. "Everything okay in your practice?"

"Oh yeah, fine. No problems *there.*"

There? What did that mean? Where were his problems? She didn't speak until they stopped in front of the small Italian restaurant that had been their favorite.

"Carlucci's." she said, delighted. "I haven't been here in ages. I can already taste the eggplant. Do you still come here?"

"Not really, but I know you like it, so..."

They walked into the small dark space and she inhaled the familiar scent of tomatoes and garlic. "Yum. I miss this place."

"Dr. and Mrs. Smith," a voice boomed from behind the bar. "Where have you been?" Tony Carlucci, the owner, rushed around and hugged Finley.

Finley decided not to mention the divorce. "Tony, it's good to see you again," she said. "Hope you're serving the eggplant parm today."

"Always, Mrs. Smith. If I weren't, I'd make it special for you, you know that."

He ushered them to the back. There were only twelve tables in the restaurant and the others were filled. "Do you mind being near the kitchen?"

"Not at all," she answered as he held her chair. "The better to smell the garlic."

David seemed distracted which made Finley nervous. She began to peel the wax from the side of the Chianti bottle in the center of the red-checked tablecloth.

"You always do that," he said.

"I like the way the wax feels under my fingernails, but I'll stop. Don't want to make a mess on Tony's tablecloth."

David ordered two glasses of wine. Finley nearly stopped him. She never drank at lunch, but surely one glass wouldn't fuzz her up too much. Maybe this is to be a celebration, she thought. Tony brought a basket of hot, crusty bread and a plate of olive oil mixed with cheese and basil for dipping.

Finley couldn't resist a piece of the bread and when the wine arrived, she raised her glass. "To us, David. For getting Caroline back to school in one piece. In a way, I think that accident was a blessing. She seems a lot more grown up now."

"Yes, she does." He sipped quietly.

She needed to break this silence. "So, why the invitation?"

He hesitated. "There's something I need to tell you."

"Okay, what?" His tone sounded ominous, but she figured her imagination had kicked into overdrive.

He put down his glass. "I've been seeing someone, nothing serious at this point, but I'd like to introduce her to Caroline and I don't want to do that without telling you first."

"Oh." Finley struggled to swallow. "Who is she?"

"Megan Stritch. Another counselor. I met her during a consult about a patient, and..."

The sentence hung between them.

"And, you care about her?"

"I like her. She's sweet and we have lots in common. I didn't start seeing her again until I was sure Caroline was out of the woods."

"Of course not. You wouldn't."

"How do you think Caroline will take to meeting my *friend*?" The word sounded fake even as he said it.

Finley struggled for the right response. "She'll be disappointed. You know she wants us back together, but if it's important that they meet, they should." *Say it's not important, her mind implored.*

He seemed relieved. "Thanks, Finn. This may not go anywhere, but I'm not good at keeping secrets."

No, he wasn't. Mr. Honorable, that was David, the man who had never kept a secret from her in his life.

"Here you go, eggplant for the lady and Puttanesca for the good doctor." Tony served the plates with a flourish. "Now be careful. That plate's a little hot. Don't want you to burn your fingers, Mrs. Smith."

"It's Finley, Tony. Please call me Finley."

"Okay, pretty Finley. Just watch that plate." He refilled their wine glasses and tossed the napkin over his shoulder. *"Buon appetito."*

Bile rose into Finley's throat. She would not be able to swallow the food. She poked at the eggplant with her fork and stirred it around under its cheese, her head bowed over the plate. She put a morsel in her mouth and washed it down quickly with wine.

"So, how's the eggplant?" David asked. "Good as you remembered it?"

"Yes, some things never change." When she looked up at him, he was staring at her as if trying to read her mood. "I'm not as hungry as I thought, though. Oh, and darn it, I just remembered a meeting I scheduled at one-thirty. So silly I didn't think of it before. Why don't you ask Tony to box this up and take it to Nancy? I've scarcely touched it."

She stood.

"You're leaving?"

"Yes, I'll grab a cab. Tell Tony it was wonderful, that I just forgot a previous appointment. Tell him I'll come back to see him soon. Tell him...tell him I've missed him."

She raced through the restaurant and out the door. Her eyes stung as they adjusted to the sunny day. She walked aimlessly down the street in the opposite direction from the station, trying to absorb David's words. *Sweet, lots in common, my friend*. This woman was more than a friend. He would never introduce anyone to Caroline who didn't have an important place in his heart. Perhaps the place Finley once occupied.

Suddenly aware she was walking away from the station, she turned back in the direction of WABN. It was two miles away. She was so numb as she walked back she was unaware of the straps of the linen sandals tearing into her feet. When she limped into the lobby, Stephanie's words surprised her.

"Finley, what happened to your feet?"

She looked down. Blood stained her shoes. "Oh, didn't notice. I'll change them."

Stephanie's eyes followed her. "How could you not have felt that?"

Finley didn't answer.

Twenty-nine

June 2, afternoon

Meadow lay back in her bed drenched with perspiration.

Ben's voice jangled her afterglow. "What would you think if I moved in here? It's getting to be a pain, carting my clothes over every day. You could move into my place, but yours is bigger."

They had taken a noon lunch break because neither could wait until evening to be together. Lying in his arms, the heat of their lovemaking still warming her body, Meadow's muddled mind careened around his words. She hated spending one night without him. But they'd been together such a short time, and her practical brain urged her to hit the brakes. *Too hot not to cool down.* Was it?

She pulled herself up to her elbow, covered her breasts with the sheet and stared into his eyes. "I love you, Ben Freedman. I really do. But shouldn't we wait? Maybe let this passion part simmer down a bit before we live together?"

He laughed. "Look, you've been married and I've been in at least a half-dozen relationships in my time. I've never felt like this before, and neither have you. Admit it."

Her laugh was giddy.

"We're hardly teenagers," he continued, "and it's not just the sex. We like the same movies, TV shows, people. I even forgive you for being an idiot about sports. That's big, trust me." He grinned at her. "Let's take a leap, baby."

God, she loved him. Had she loved her husband like this? No. That relationship happened because it was time to settle down, be a wife, have babies. This was different. She was flat out mad about Ben.

She lay back on the pillow, trying to think. "Well, suppose, just suppose, you're right. Suppose this is the big enchilada, that we're 'soul mates' or something. God, I hate that term. But suppose, just suppose, we are." She grinned up at him and could not believe her next words even as she heard them. "Don't you think a girl should get a ring on her finger before she makes this kind of leap? Maybe an old class ring with lots of twine around the bottom?"

He laughed and kissed her. "You bet you'll get a ring, baby. I'm gonna buy you the biggest rock in Philadelphia tomorrow morning."

"No, Ben, nothing big. I don't want you becoming an expensive uptown doctor in order to pay the bills. I like you too much as the kindly Dr. Freedman, sort of Marcus Welby, gently treating all the underprivileged vaginas in Philadelphia. As long as I'm the only one you really treat." Her eyes danced with merriment.

He had pulled her over on top of him when the phone rang.

"Hello," she said, tugging up the sheet again.

"Meadow, honey." It was her father. "I called you at the office, and they said maybe I could reach you at home. Mom and I would like to talk to you. Could you come over here?"

"Now?"

"Yes, honey."

"What's wrong, Daddy?"

"We'll talk when you get here."

"Ben's here with me."

"Bring him."

The ride to her parents' house in the suburbs seemed interminable. Ben drove silently, one hand on the wheel, one caressing her neck.

When her father opened the front door, his face looked old.

"Daddy?"

"Come, sit. Your mother's in the living room."

Meadow tossed her jacket on a chair in the hall and didn't notice it fall to the floor. Ben picked it up and hung it on the coat rack. She hurried to the living room and sat close beside her mother. As usual, even in daylight, candles burned and incense drifted through the air. Pictures of

140

Meadow and her son as a little boy covered the mantle above the fireplace and the old dream catcher macramé still hung on the wall over them.

"I'm going to make us some tea," her father said, going to the kitchen. Meadow noticed a new stoop to his back and turned back to her mother, unspoken questions in her eyes.

"I saw the third doctor, just like you said." Arlene stared into the fire.

"What did he say?" Meadow leaned forward, holding her breath.

"She, actually. Someone Ben recommended." She patted his arm. "When I showed her the results of my blood tests, she thought a bone-marrow biopsy would be in order."

"Biopsy? What does she think this is?"

"Won't know till after the biopsy, which is scheduled for Thursday."

Meadow's heart tightened as if in a vise. She could not catch her breath for a moment. Ben's arm encircled her shoulders, squeezing. "Easy, honey. Don't panic."

He spoke to Arlene. "Not to get too personal, Arlene, but how old are you?"

"I'm sixty-three."

"So, no Medicare yet. You do have health care insurance, right?"

"Of course, we do. Didn't have it when we were young hippies, but let's face it, at this age..."

"Who's your insurer?" Ben asked.

"Sheldon Compassion Network."

Meadow felt Ben's reaction without looking at him. A slight tension in his body. But his tone was steady. "Okay, we'll deal with that later." He sounded professional, soothing. Meadow didn't recognize this Ben. He made it seem as if a bone-marrow biopsy was of no more concern than a runny nose.

"So, the biopsy's Thursday, right?"

Arlene nodded.

"Is it okay with you if I call your doctor tomorrow and see if she'd like me to assist? We often collaborate."

"Thank you, Ben. I'd like that." Arlene took his hand, tears glistening in her eyes. "You'll be such a comfort to Meadow, in case..."

"Now don't you turn doomsday on me, Arlene," he said, laughing. "It may be nothing, but if it is, you're gonna lick it. And I'll be much more than a comfort to Meadow. I promise."

Is he going to tell her about our moving in together? Meadow squirmed.

"We're engaged," he said.

Meadow jumped in surprise "Huh? It's official?"

"What'd you think? I'd live in sin?" Ben's grin was devilish.

When Stan carried the tea tray in, Ben stood. "Stan, I love your daughter with all my heart. I would like to ask her to marry me. Do I have your permission?

Cups clattered on her father's tray, tea spilling. Meadow watched as he steadied himself, his mouth agape. Arlene looked up at her husband, then raised her hands toward heaven. "So, answer the man already."

"Well sure, Ben. You're a great guy, if Meadow's willing."

Doubt melted from Meadow's mind like sour cream on a warm blintz. He was doing this to take her mother's mind off the biopsy, and she loved him for it.

He knelt before her. "Will you marry me, Meadow Marx?"

With tears in her eyes, she answered, "I would love to marry you."

"Okay then," he said, taking her into his arms and kissing her. "You're gonna have to learn something about sports."

"Stan," Arlene said, her voice strong. "Forget the tea. Remember that champagne we bought for our anniversary? Break it out. Oh, and call your grandson. His mother must tell him the good news."

"Yes, dear," he said. Arlene followed him, taking the tea back to the kitchen.

When her parents left the room to get the champagne and glasses, Meadow turned to Ben. "Why the reaction about her HMO? Something wrong with them?"

"In the medical field, we call them Sheldon non-compassion network. They'll make her jump through hoops for reimbursement on every step of her illness, if there is an illness. They're bastards, but don't tell your folks now."

Meadow nodded and went to take glasses from her mother's hands. Stan made a great ceremony of popping the cork. Smiles beamed as they raised their glasses. As Meadow took her first sip, she thought, *perhaps my love might cure her. It will at least make her forget for a while. No, it will cure her. She will dance at my wedding.*

As though he read her mind, Ben said, "Arlene, I'm planning on watching you and Stan dance the hora at our wedding. Is that a deal?"

Arlene tapped her toes joyfully. "You bet it is, Ben."

~ * ~

The following morning, Finley was surprised at Arlene's phone call inviting her to dinner that night.

"What's the occasion, Arlene?" she asked. Meadow had already told her about her mother's impending biopsy and Finley had planned to call, but Arlene beat her to the phone. She sounded joyous, upbeat, anything but what Finley expected from a woman facing such a procedure.

"Oh, just a little celebration of life, Finley," Arlene answered. "Nothing fancy, just us and Meadow and Ben and the Saxs and you. Can you make it?"

"Wouldn't miss it for the world," Finley replied, still confused by Arlene's bubbly attitude. You'd never guess this woman is facing a biopsy.

~ * ~

So it was that Finley was present in the Marx living room when Ben put the diamond on Meadow's finger. Finley shot Arlene a look that said, *You are one cagey lady, now aren't you?* The look was rewarded by a wink.

The ring was beautiful, a simple diamond solitaire set high on platinum prongs. Finley lifted Meadow's left hand for a closer look. "Wow, you didn't tell me things had progressed this far with you two. But I'm happy for you. You're perfect for each other."

"Where will you be married?" Barbara Sax asked.

"Temple Emmanuel," Ben said. "Arlene called them today and booked December sixteen."

Meadow looked at him, dumbstruck. "Hold your horses, folks. Don't you two think I should have been part of the planning?"

"You get to pick the reception hall, darling." Arlene answered.

Finley chuckled to herself. Arlene's banking on the fact that because she's sick, Meadow will allow her to take charge, just this once.

Meadow's steam of indignation huffed once more, then quieted.

"I called Mikey again last night, Mom," she said. "Right after we left here. He's anxious to meet Ben. I know they'll like each other."

"Did you tell him about my little problem?" Arlene's eyes lost their luster.

"Yes, and he's coming home this weekend to see you. He is concerned, of course, but Ben told him to expect the best."

"He's such a good boy. I don't want him worrying. He needs to keep his grades up."

Barbara Sax moved to sit next to Arlene and rested her hand lightly on her friend's shoulder. "Mazel tov," she said, kissing Arlene on the cheek.

Finley marveled at Arlene's courage and Barbara's ability to hide her worry. *I'll learn a lesson here*, she thought. *As we celebrate here in this warm place, David is probably introducing Caroline to Megan Stritch tonight. I must not allow that to interfere with the happiness I feel for Meadow and Ben. It's best to rejoice when we can. The problems will take care of themselves.*

When she left the celebration later that evening, Finley pulled Arlene into her arms for a long, tight hug, willing some of her own strength and health into the older woman's body. "I love you, Arlene."

Driving away, she thought to herself that the prospect of this wedding will be just the tonic Arlene needs to get through what's ahead.

As she pulled into the garage, Finley was surprised to see lights burning in the living room. Once inside, she found Caroline sitting on the loveseat, her legs pulled up under her.

She tossed the *People* magazine onto the coffee table. "Mom, did you know Dad is seeing someone?"

"Yes, honey," Finley replied, taking off her shoes and sitting beside Caroline. "He told me he wanted to introduce you to someone named

144

Megan, and I figured it might be tonight. Was it?"

"Yes. Don't you think you should have warned me?"

"Probably, but with the news about Meadow's mom, I just didn't have the energy. I'm really sorry if you got blindsided." Finley was silent until she could hold her tongue no longer.

"What did you think of her?"

Caroline stared at her, obviously still miffed, then spoke in a soft voice. "She's nice. I think she really likes Daddy, and that bothers me."

Me, too, Finley thought. "I'm sure it does, honey, but he has a perfect right to be happy, don't you think?"

"Yeah, sure, but I was hoping it would be with you."

Finley began arranging magazines on the coffee table. Finally, her curiosity overwhelmed her. "So, what's she look like?"

"Pretty. About your size, I guess, but younger."

Finley's heart sank.

"Not real young or anything," Caroline hurried on. "Probably about thirty." As if able to read Finley's mind, she added, "But Mom, she's not nearly as pretty as you—and I mean that. Her hair's frosted like something out of the seventies, probably at Budget Cuts."

In spite of her jealousy, Finley laughed out loud. Caroline knew her mother well. "Thanks, honey, true or not, that makes me feel better. How about some ice cream? There's Chunky Monkey in the freezer."

"I'm there," Caroline jumped to her feet, then pulled her mother up to follow her to the kitchen.

~ * ~

The day of Arlene's biopsy dawned with a crystal blue sky and the scent of cherry blossoms. Strange, Finley mused, driving toward the hospital, how creation never seems to reflect the worry of its people.

The waiting room was hushed except for the ringing of the receptionist's phone. Stan, Meadow, Barbara and Marty were already there and motioned Finley over when they saw her come in.

"What time did they take her in?" she asked, walking over to Meadow.

"Just a few minutes ago." Meadow answered. "They're going to do a bone marrow aspiration followed by a trephine biopsy from her hip." She walked over to pick up a newspaper off a corner rack. "She was in good spirits, and Ben is in there, so that makes me feel better."

"Do you know when she'll get the results?" Finley asked.

"Ben put a rush on it to the pathologist. We hope we'll know something by the end of the day."

Each of them dug in for the long wait, using whatever was available to distract them from their worry.

"Anybody know a four-letter word for *without repairs?*" Marty asked.

Stan shook his head. Finley's mind stalled and Meadow seemed too distracted to respond.

"As is," Barbara said to her husband, a smug look on her face.

"That's five letters," Marty said, sounding exasperated.

"No, it's not. You don't count the spaces in crosswords, dummy."

"Damn," he said as he figured out the words around the space. "She's right."

Barbara nodded, smiling.

Time slipped away, and Finley's thoughts drifted to the last time she had been here. In her mind's eye, she saw Caroline lying in the hospital bed, unconscious and scarcely breathing. Who would have believed then that she would be preparing for graduation now? Miracles do happen.

Two hours later, Ben walked into the waiting room, an older woman at his side. Both wore scrubs. Masks hung from their necks. Everyone got to their feet.

"The procedure went very well," the woman said. She had a badge on her left shoulder that read Patricia Warren, M.D. "She'll likely be in some pain today, but this prescription will manage that." She handed a piece of paper to Stan.

"She's in recovery now and will be going to a room as soon as she's fully conscious. I expect she'll go home tomorrow."

"Will there be chemotherapy?" Meadow asked, nestling herself against her father.

"Until we get the biopsy results, we won't know what modality will be most effective. If chemotherapy is necessary," the woman's voice was kind, "new treatments are much less invasive than those you've heard of in the past."

Ben moved to Meadow and wrapped his arm around her waist. "We really don't want to project beyond the biopsy results, honey." She put her head on his shoulder. He turned to Stan. "Why don't I take you to recovery so you can see your wife. She's a little groggy from the sedative, but wants you with her."

Stan turned to follow Ben out of the room. "Call me Dad," Stan said. "Call me Dad."

~ * ~

At four thirty that afternoon, Ben and Dr. Warren found them as they sipped coffee in the hospital cafeteria. "Mr. Marx, we got the preliminary biopsy results," Dr. Warren said.

Stan stood and stared at Ben.

He looks so old and frightened, Finley thought. Meadow gripped her hand, hard.

"Our initial diagnosis is multiple myeloma, a blood cancer. I suspected it before the biopsy because we saw some signs of bone damage in her X-rays. That's the reason for her bone aches and the fatigue. We did an MRI after the biopsy and found two plasma cell bone tumors. That makes it likely that she's at stage two."

Stan's knees buckled, and Ben caught him under the elbow. "Easy, Stan. It's treatable."

Marty and Barbara put their arms around each other's waists.

"Treatment?" Meadow murmured, her voice hollow.

"We'll begin with radiation therapy coupled with some drugs now in clinical trials," Dr. Warren answered. Our best course of action is aggressive. That means twenty weeks of high-dose chemotherapy after the radiation." She walked to Stan. "You look pale, Mr. Marx. Let's all sit down."

All of them sat down at the cafeteria table and pulled up two more chairs for Ben and Dr. Warren, who continued. "High-dose chemotherapy has proven twice as effective as conventional chemo in long-term clinical trials, Mr. Marx. After we've shrunk the tumors with the chemo, we may do an autologous stem-cell transplant. Your wife's kidney function is still good, which means such treatment could be highly beneficial to getting her into remission."

"Autologous?" Stan said, looking confused "What's that mean?"

Ben spoke, "That means we'll use Arlene's own stem cells, Stan. We'll harvest them first, before any treatment is started."

Stan put his head into his hands, shaking it from side to side.

"Mr. Marx," Dr. Warren continued. "Please know that though this condition is not curable, it is eminently treatable and that we will take every possible measure to make sure your wife lives many more years."

Stan looked up, tears in his eyes. Then, he squared his shoulders and said, "Do everything you can, doctor. I must not lose Arlene."

Thirty

The day after her mother's biopsy, Meadow approached Sylvia's office for their meeting. She was filled with an eerie sense of calm. Arlene's illness had numbed her to a state approaching tranquility. *Guess this what you call a reality check.*

She knocked, opened the door, walked in and sat down. She studied the familiar office which felt unfamiliar now. So cold. Nothing had been hung to replace Randy's pictures except a black and white drawing of Sylvia. *Looks like a starving artist flattery job.* Meadow studied it closely. *Wonder how much she paid the poor sap to soften her jaw like that.* The thought made her smile. It was the first smile she had been aware of since she got the diagnosis.

No touch of color brightened the black and white surfaces of the office. The red pillows and coffee mugs were gone. It appeared that all the soul had been blanched from this space. Nothing warm remained. Nothing human. Most especially the woman sitting across the desk from her.

Sylvia wasted no time. "Meadow, as you know, sales revenues are trending down." She picked up a spreadsheet and indicated the red line jagging downward.

"Yes, they are." *What'd you expect with an asshole like Rick Stone in the anchor chair?* The calm remained.

"I'm afraid this station can no longer afford the salary you are earning, given the economic climate we're operating in."

"So?" *So, you finally have the excuse to get rid of me, you bitch.* In spite of herself, Meadow grinned.

"So," Did Meadow detect a slight hesitation, a look of something almost fearful on Sylvia's face? "I'm going to have to let you go." Sylvia's exhale was audible. "I realize you've been here a long time and have done a very good job, but I can't afford you now. I'd like you to clear your desk by close of business today."

Sylvia's shoulders slumped. She looked exhausted. Clearly, she had practiced her little speech but now seemed weakened by it. When she lowered her head, Meadow noticed a line of muddy brown at the part in the yellow hair and a slight sag to the powdered jowl.

Silently, Sylvia put on her glasses and returned to the papers on her desk.

Meadow sat quietly. What did she feel? Was it shock or relief? All she knew absolutely was that she didn't want to be here, in this ugly office, with this frozen yellow-haired creature. She wanted to be with Arlene. She wanted to make her laugh. Her mother would ooh and ahh at her daughter's language, but she'd smile. Nothing could ever again scare Meadow as much as the day she heard the word cancer. Nothing. Sylvia Reynolds was an annoyance, no more, no less.

"I've arranged severance." Sylvia continued, extending a sheet of paper to Meadow. "Six months. You shouldn't have any trouble finding something else." She refused to make eye contact and continued to sort through her papers.

How sad she is, Meadow thought. Strange that I almost pity her. *Almost.* Finally, Meadow spoke. "Okay, Ms. Reynolds. Oh, fuck it…Sylvia. I'll be out of here by five. The severance will be fine."

Sylvia's eyebrows lifted in surprise. She had obviously expected a fight. "All right then." She paused, seeming confused about what to say next. Her hands began to clench on her desk. Meadow watched, feeling calm as a windless sea, then rose from her chair and started to leave.

"Do you need a letter of recommendation or anything?" When Meadow turned toward her at the question, Sylvia glanced away again.

In that instant, Meadow's calm dissipated. Her temper flared and she stormed back, furious. Bracing her hands on the desk, she leaned into Sylvia's face. "Are you kidding me? When I choose to go back to work, and I will, I'll get a job with your competition in a day." She anticipated her next words hungrily. "Then, Sylvia, I'll clean your clock." She smacked her palm on the black desk, scattering papers across it and onto the floor. "I don't need any recommendation from you. No offense, sweetie, but my reputation in this town is a hell of a lot better than yours."

She lifted her left hand in a grand gesture of goodbye.

Sylvia saw the diamond. "Are you engaged?"

"Yes," Meadow waved her left hand directly under Sylvia's nose until the other woman flinched as if she feared being hit.

"Who is he?" Sylvia asked, ducking back into her chair.

"Nobody you'd know. Just a gorgeous, sexy doctor who makes the best brisket on earth. The wedding's in December."

All pity was gone now. She savored the pain coursing over Sylvia's face. She swept to the door, grinning, then pivoted and faced the sharp-faced woman behind the desk. "Oh, and by the way, don't expect an invitation." She laughed as she left. *Now that was an exit,* she exalted.

Meadow stuck her head into Finley's office, still laughing. "Finn, ta da." She threw up her hands and twirled in a dance of joy. "It's happened. I'm officially fired."

"Oh, Meadow, no," Finley said, coming around her desk to embrace her friend. "I was afraid she'd do it, but I thought maybe the news of your mother might stall her. Should have known better. The woman has no soul." She looked as if her own heart might break.

Meadow pulled away from the caress and took Finley's shoulders into her hands. "Chill, Finn," she said, looking hard into her friend's eyes. "Actually, the timing is good. I have money put aside."

Meadow plopped down onto Finley's sofa and kicked off her shoes. "Ever since Austin took over, I've been worrying about this. With my savings plus six months' severance, I'll be able to help Mom through her treatments and organize the wedding, too. I'll find a job next year. I need a break. This station is arsenic. Don't cry for me, Argentina. I couldn't be happier."

Finley stared at her friend's face, as if trying to gauge whether Meadow's joy was genuine. Finally, she spoke. "I know you'll land at another station when you're ready. But, God, what will we do without you? The station will just keep going downhill." She looked ready to weep. "I can't bear the thought of losing you."

"You're not going to lose me, ever, Finn. You're my soul sister, remember? Now don't forget our date on Saturday to shop for a wedding dress."

"Are you sure you're up to that?" Finley said.

"Absolutely! The Rabbi says he'll tolerate a shiksa at his altar, so we'll need a dress for you, too. You're the maid of honor." She kissed Finley and sailed out the door.

As she walked lightly back to her office, she passed Marty's desk. Tapping him on the shoulder, she said, "Come with me, please." When she closed her office door behind him, she picked up her phone. "Hi Matt," she said. Matt was the head of security. "Could you have about ten big packing boxes brought up immediately?"

Marty figured it out without being told. "Do you want me to fix this?" he said.

Meadow looked at him, puzzled. "Oh Marty, I know you mean well, but no. I want time off anyway. A lot going on in my life."

He nodded. "Yeah, but if you change your mind, say the word."

Meadow picked up her sons' pictures and wrapped them in the newspaper on her desk. What did he mean? How could he *fix* this? Was he getting senile or something?

Thirty-one

June 4

WABN ground to a shocked silence when news of Meadow's dismissal spread. As soon as word spread, the buzzing began. People spoke behind covered mouths and congregated behind closed doors.

Finley tried to maintain a composed demeanor in front of her staff, but her heart ached. That afternoon, as she headed to the A.P. press release box to check breaking stories for the evening news, she noticed Rick Stone and Marilyn Whitmore huddled in a corner talking, their heads nearly touching. When they saw her, Marilyn stopped whispering and scurried back to her desk. Rick sidled to the other side of the desk. Finley nodded but did not speak to him. She expected him to comment about Meadow, but he never mentioned her.

Instead, he said, "Hey boss lady, been hearing some weird stuff from my contacts in Harrisburg."

Finley continued to scan the papers in her hands.

"Seems that Emily has been asking a lot of questions around the Capitol."

"So?" Finley turned to look at him.

"Just wondering who assigned her to spend so much time on stuff away from Philadelphia. I'm told she's taking trips to hospitals and companies all over the state. What's she working on?"

How did he know what Emily was doing? Finley smacked her hand down on the desk. "Rick. I'm fully aware of Emily's assignment, and it's confidential."

"Even from the Vice President of Prescott News?"

"Even from you," she said. *Especially from you.*

"Well, I guess I'll have a little chat with Austin." Rick said.

Finley felt her face go crimson, started to respond angrily but composed herself. "Have your chat, Rick," she said, her voice calm. "I'm the news director of WABN, and it's time for a decision about who's in charge of this newsroom. My position is that you're the anchor. You report to me."

Rick flinched slightly before he regained his erect posture and strode back to his desk, then yanked the phone to his ear.

Finley knew that Marilyn Whitmore had been observing the conversation. When she looked at the girl, she began stuffing papers into files on her desk. Marilyn was employed at Rick's request shortly after he came to the station. Finley had argued the hire. Marilyn's writing and performance were below average, but Rick had pushed for Marilyn to become an editorial assistant.

"Over my dead body," Finley had told him. "She scarcely knows her way to Independence Hall."

Rick had continued to press his point, but Finley held her ground, "I'll hire her as a secretary, but I will not put her in a position that requires constant attention to detail. I don't have time to babysit."

So, part of Marilyn's secretarial job involved booking hotels and rental cars for staff. Was little Ms. Whitmore his spy?

As soon as Finley returned to her office, she closed the door and called Emily. When the beep signaled, she left a message. "Emily, from this point forward, make your own reservations on the road. Hotels, rental cars, restaurants. We have a mole in the office."

When she hung up, the phone rang instantly. Caller I.D. gave her all the information she needed. "Austin," she said in the cheeriest tone she could muster. "Long time, no talk. How are you?"

He sounded surprised at her good spirits. "Fine, Finley. Just checking in. Wondering how things are going with Rick."

"Great," she lied. "Couldn't be better. Are you happy with his tapes?"

"Yeah, they look good. Little concerned about the ratings dip, though."

Remember, Finley, this is Austin's boy we're talking about. Be smart. "Oh, that's to be expected. Chris was a fixture in this market. It'll take time for Rick to find his audience. Don't worry about it."

Obviously surprised, Austin stammered, "Oh, very well then. Anything else I should know?"

"Nope. All is copasetic. See you at the shareholders' meeting in November, if not before."

Hanging up, she noticed Rick standing just outside her door, his back to her. She laughed. "Guess what, Rick? That was Austin Montgomery. Wanted to know how things are going with you. I covered for you about the ratings drop. You can thank me later."

Thirty-two

Saturday morning

Caroline threw jeans, tops, bras, socks and panties into a suitcase in no particular order.

"You know, honey, if you roll those things, it'll be easier to fit more stuff in and they won't get as wrinkled," Finley said.

Caroline gave her the familiar butt-out look and tossed in a hairdryer, shampoo and conditioner, then shut the bag and zipped it resolutely. "There," she said with satisfaction. "I'm ready to go." David was picking Caroline up in twenty minutes to drop her off for freshman orientation at Penn State.

Finley glanced at her watch. She would have time for a quick shower before she met Meadow at the bridal salon at ten thirty. Another bridesmaid's dress, she thought ruefully. Maybe she'll let me wear black.

Finley helped her daughter down the stairs with her suitcases and, as she kissed her goodbye, Caroline surprised her with an unexpected question.

"Mom, are you sad that Dad is involved with Megan?"

Finley was blindsided by the query and stared, open mouthed, at Caroline until it was repeated.

"Well, are you?"

What's the right answer, she wondered? She opted for honesty. "I suppose so, a little." she answered. "I'd hoped that maybe we could put things back together, but you know what? It's the right thing for him to do. My job pushed him out of my life. It always came first. Your dad deserves better."

Caroline responded with the sage wisdom of the young and untested. "That's ridiculous. I see no reason why a woman can't be a wife and mother plus have a career in this day and age. That's what I intend to do."

Good luck, my darling, Finley thought. You sound exactly like me at seventeen. "I hope you can pull it off, sweetheart. Maybe you'll be better at it than I was."

~ * ~

Finley zipped the navy silk gown and knew without looking that it was a perfect fit. Her body was cradled and caressed as though the bias-cut dress was a nightgown. "Ohhh, I like the way this one feels, Meadow."

Meadow appraised Finley as she swayed and posed in front of the three-way mirror. "No kidding. It couldn't be sexier unless it was body paint. How much?"

Finley pulled the tag out of the strapless top. "Three twenty-five."

"Not too bad," Meadow nodded. "Go for it."

"Are you sure it's appropriate for a temple?"

"Absolutely, though you'll probably give the Rabbi a boner." Meadow held glittering earrings to Finley's ears, then put them back on the accessories table the clerk had arranged. "Too much. No need to shine perfection." She sat down on the tufted dressing room chair and crossed her legs. "By the way, do you want me to invite David?" she asked, *too c*asually.

Finley stopped her movements. Her shoulders slumped and the reflection in the mirror changed in her mind's eye. Less seductive, more mother of the bride. "To tell the truth, I don't think I can handle seeing him with a date, so no, if that's okay with you."

"Of course, it's okay. He's still seeing the counselor, huh?"

"Guess so. I haven't really talked to him since he told me about her."

"Well, don't you worry, love. Ben'll have some doctor friends at the wedding. And you'll be swarmed once they get a look at you in that dress."

That's the last thing I'm interested in, Finley thought. *I don't want to meet another man for a long time. Ever.*

She stepped down from the platform in front of the mirror. "I want to see your dress, Meadow. Put it on, veil and all. I'll look for shoes."

Outside, Finley picked up a pair of silver sling sandals and dangled simple silver earrings beside her face. Yes, perfect, she decided. She took them back to the dressing room to show Meadow.

When she entered it, Meadow was standing on the platform in a long white silk sheath, her face glowing under a tiny veil. Finley gasped. "You look beautiful. You really do. It's a dream dress. Simple and elegant. Ben'll love it. I love it."

"Are you sure, Finn? It has to be perfect. This is the last wedding dress I ever intend to wear, by God, so if it isn't positively right, you've gotta tell me."

"I would tell you, Meadow, but it's perfect. You look about twenty-five."

Meadow turned and examined the sides and back of the dress. "Twenty-five, huh? I was kind of going for nineteen, but I guess twenty-five will have to do. Now, unzip me. I'm hungry and we have an hour 'til I have to pick up Arlene and Stan at the oncologist's office."

After a hurried lunch, the women gave each other a quick hug and Finley drove home, looking forward to an evening alone. She hung the navy gown in her closet and put the shoe box on her top shelf with the earrings tucked in it. She was as tired as she had ever been in her life, depleted by the problems at the station and worry about Arlene. She spent the afternoon reading a novel she'd picked up at the book store and then ran a tub for a hot bath. She would soak away the aches of the week and climb into bed early. She had just finished shaving her legs when the phone jangled. She jumped out of the tub and grabbed the receiver. "Hello."

"Finn," the voice was deep, warm. "It's David."

"David, is everything okay? Did you get Caroline settled in?"

"Yes, she couldn't wait to get rid of me. I was only there about fifteen minutes before she made it clear I was no longer needed." He laughed. "I make a good chauffer and porter, but she was much too busy looking at those hunky freshman boys to want me around."

Finley smiled. "Guess our little bird is leaving the nest, right?"

"Absolutely. And that's as it should be." He paused and his voice changed, turned husky with what sounded like nerves. "Just wondered if you have plans this evening," he continued. "I'd like to talk to you. Can I come over?"

Her fatigue lifted in an instant. "Sure, David. I'm not doing anything tonight. Come ahead."

"Good—be there in twenty minutes."

She raced into her bedroom and yanked new cashmere sweats from the Wannamaker's bag. She pulled them over her naked body, loving the soft caress of the fabric and knowing that the periwinkle color flattered her. *What does he want, she wondered?*

As she dried her hair, her heart plummeted in her chest like a stone. She could hardly breathe. *Maybe he wants to tell me he's moving in with Megan, perhaps marrying her.* The doorbell startled her, and she braced herself for any possibility.

When she opened the front door, his eyes ran over her body appreciatively. "That's pretty."

"Thanks. Just bought it today. I was shopping with Meadow and needed a splurge. This is it." She swayed before him, preening and posing.

"Good choice."

"Help yourself to a beer. Have you eaten?"

"I'm not hungry, Finn. Just want to talk."

"Fine," she said, leading him to the kitchen and gesturing to the refrigerator as she poured herself a glass of wine, then nestled down on the loveseat.

He pulled out a bottle of beer, opened it and sat next to her. She vowed to remain quiet, even as her curiosity urged her to ask the questions. *Why are you here? What do you want?*

His voice was a whisper. "It's about Megan."

Oh no, here it comes. She cleared her throat. "What about her?"

"She dumped me."

She startled, nearly spilling her wine into her lap. "Why?"

"Says she doesn't want to be with a man who's still in love with his wife." His laugh was hollow. "Guess she's a better shrink than I am.

Figured it out much faster than I did."

"Still in love—with me?" *He still loves me.* The warmth of the thought was replaced in an instant by an apprehension that nothing had really changed in her life.

Her fear didn't stop her from touching his face.

His kiss was long, yearning. There was no need for words. He lifted her from the couch and carried her up the stairs. Her ear, nestled against his chest, could hear his heart pounding furiously.

In the bedroom, when he set her on her feet, the blue cashmere drifted to the floor before she even knew he'd unzipped it. He looked at her naked body like a starving man. He kissed her again as they edged toward the bed, moving as one.

As he began to caress her, she opened herself to the familiar feel of his hands. *He knows my body so well. He knows just how and where to touch me. His fingers feel like fire on my skin. No man could ever make me feel this way. No man but this one.*

At last, she stopped thinking and turned her body over to feeling the expert caress of the man who used to be her husband.

Thirty-three

Monday morning

Stephanie's mouth opened when she saw her. "Hey Finley," she said. "You look incredible. Good weekend?"

Finley smiled. *Great weekend*, she thought. *Now I need to figure out how what to do about it.*

When she got to her office, her secretary looked dour. This was strange. Sandy was the most unflappable person at the station. Cheerful to a fault.

"Something wrong, Sandy?"

"Mr. Montgomery called at eight fifteen." She answered, raising her eyebrows. "Wants to talk to you right away. He sounded pissed."

Finley dialed Austin's private line. Listening to the buzz of the connection, she pondered over reasons he might sound *pissed.*

Were the projected revenue losses over Rick's poor ratings beginning to sink in? Doubtful. Rick was Austin's boy, and he'd give him time to bring them back up. Or perhaps this had nothing to do with the station. Maybe Regina was asking him for more money. That always put Austin in a vile mood. Don't borrow trouble, she told herself. Just wait and see.

"Austin Montgomery." His voice sounded as though it had been squeezed through a lemon.

"Hello, Austin. Finley Smith."

He inhaled raggedly. "Over the weekend, I heard some disturbing information over the grapevine."

Grapevine? Then, she remembered...Rick. "What information is that?" she said, measuring her tone.

"That your Ms. Sanders is nosing around all over the state digging up dirt on a company called Cavaleri Construction. Is that true?"

Finley's mind churned, trying to formulate the correct response. Her job was to protect her reporters. This unexpected question from the company chairman threw her. And that made her angry because she should have anticipated it. Stupidity was the one thing she could not forgive in herself or others. And it was stupid she didn't suspect Rick would run to Austin like the sneaky rodent he was.

She answered, finally. "Emily Sanders is doing her job, not digging dirt. And she's working with my full support. It is this station's job to get the truth to our viewers. Right Austin?"

"Your job, Finley, is to obey my orders. I didn't authorize any investigation on companies associated with Governor Morgan."

Finley's face flushed. "I have never had to clear a story with corporate before. Mr. Prescott gave me the authority to run this news department as I see fit. No one has changed that order."

She knew the remark would anger him. He hated to be reminded of how his former father-in-law had run the company. His already cold voice turned icy. "Mr. Prescott," he said, "is no longer chairman of this company, in case you've forgotten. I am telling you, Finley, to call off your dogs on Morgan."

"Mr. Montgomery," she said formally. "Are you ordering me to squelch the truth? Because if you are, I will discuss it with John Prescott. Though you are the chairman, he is still president of Prescott Broadcasting."

The slam of the phone reverberated in her ear. *I don't care*, she thought furiously. *I will not turn the news yellow for Austin Montgomery or anyone else.* Shaking, she returned to her work.

That afternoon, Finley, buried in press releases and stories for the evening news, let her ringing phone go to Sandy. "Finley," Sandy buzzed in. "The old man is on the phone." When Finley didn't respond, Sandy continued, "John Prescott."

Surprised, Finley picked up her phone. "Mr. Prescott," she said. "Haven't heard from you in a long time."

His voice sounded tired and very old. "I know. I've been remiss. But Finley, Austin tells me that one of your reporters is probing into Governor Morgan's business dealings. Is that true?"

"Yes, Mr. Prescott. There are rumors of improprieties that could endanger the citizens of Pittsburgh. If our investigation reveals that the story is true, we will report it."

He sighed deeply. "There's a lot you don't understand about how television runs now, Finley. Things have changed. I'm afraid I have to ask you to lower the heat on this one. I'm sorry."

Her heart sank, souring the pit of her stomach. *John, too*? "I'm not sure I can do that, sir. I'll think about it." When she hung up, she felt bruised by the sadness in the old man's voice. If John Prescott could be bought, she no longer wanted to be part of this business.

She was putting the finishing touches on her letter of resignation when Marty Sax stuck his head into her office. "Hey, Finley, got a minute?"

"Sure, Marty. Come on in. I can use a shoulder."

He studied her red-rimmed eyes as he sat down. "I just wanted to ask you for ideas of what to buy for Meadow and Ben for the showers and stuff."

"She's registered at Macy's."

"Okay, I'll tell Barbara." He gestured toward his left shoulder, "So, why do you need the shoulder?"

"It seems John Prescott is standing behind Austin's order that I call off an investigation. I can't tell you what it's about, but it's not one I can quit."

"Anything to do with Governor Morgan?"

Her mouth dropped open. "How did you know that?"

"Finley, everybody knows. Joe Heaton talks all the time about how rotten Morgan is. I've heard about the Governor's mob connections from Tom Armstrong at the bank and Jim Fieldstone at Pennsylvania Builders, too."

In one sentence, Marty had mentioned the three biggest power brokers in Philadelphia.

"Mob connections?" she asked.

"Sure. How do you think he got elected? He's a schmuck—an equal opportunity payola whore. The Mafia is his biggest contributor, followed by HMOs and big pharma."

Emily had once questioned whether there was a mob connection to the governor. The awful thought made her ask the question. "Do you think John Prescott has been bought?" She held her breath, scared of what she might hear.

Marty shook his head. "I don't think so. He's just old and tired. It's easier to give Austin his way than to fight the fight. The other two stations in the chain are in the ratings dumper, and our revenues are still pretty good. You figure it out. He's sent Sylvia here to make sure WABN stays in lockstep. If everybody plays nice, we get the lion's share of the political revenues, plus the biggest bucks from the HMOs and pill pushers. That's why the dragon lady handles the buys from the national agencies. Haven't you noticed that we have a medication in every break, day and night?"

Finley recalled all the pink capsules and green pills that paraded constantly across her television screen promising to fix everything from insomnia to high blood pressure. She had discounted their frequency as unimportant. Bad mistake.

"One slimy hand washes the other," Marty continued. "The politicians take care of the insurance and pill rascals, and then they put their ad dollars on stations that play ball. Classic yellow crap. It smells but it sells."

Finley said. "I don't want to be part of that kind of journalism."

"So, you'll quit," he said, shaking his head. "And Sylvia will hire some robot to follow orders and kiss Morgan's ass like Austin does. And so it goes, and goes, and goes."

"What can I do?" As Finley said the words, she thought about the unsuspecting citizens in Pittsburgh who would cross that bridge.

As if he had read her mind, Marty said, "The bridge project won't start until next year. We have time. Let me talk to some people."

As Finley considered his words, her phone rang. She looked up at Marty and answered it. "Finley Smith."

"Finley," the voice was soothing. "John Prescott here again. I've talked to Austin about our conversation and we both feel troubled about how things were left with you. Would it be possible for you to come to New

York tomorrow so that we can sit down and discuss the matter in person?"

She silently mouthed the words "John Prescott" to Marty. He smiled.

"Yes, Mr. Prescott. I could do that. I'll catch the eight thirty train and get to your office around noon. Does that work for you?"

"That's perfect, Finley. Thank you. I'm asking Sylvia and Rick to come along, too. It'll be good to have the WABN family all together again for a friendly luncheon."

When she hung up, she looked at Marty. "They want to see me tomorrow. Sylvia and Rick, too. What do you think they want?"

He laughed. "To figure out your price."

Thirty-four

Tuesday morning

Finley was lulled into dozing by the repetitive rhythm of the train's wheels. Sylvia and Rick sat across from her, sipping Bloody Marys and chattering cheerfully about the upcoming day. Austin had booked rooms at the Waldorf for all three of them so they would be staying over tonight. Caroline had planned to spend the night at Jenny's apartment, so Finley was free from obligations at home.

David had called the night before. Her face had flushed with sensual memory when she heard his voice. First, he asked about Arlene's condition, but Finley knew his call had a different purpose. Finally, it came. "Saturday night was terrific," he said trying to sound casual. "Care to repeat, tomorrow, my place?"

When she told him about this appointment in New York, he'd sounded disappointed, then angry. She tried to explain the importance of the trip, but he'd grown distant and finally answered, "Okay. Guess some things never change."

Damn it, he's right, she admitted.

"Drink, Finn?" Rick said, interrupting her half-asleep reverie.

She straightened up and shook her head.

He and Sylvia stood and walked toward the dining car. Finley's eyes followed them as they laughingly collided with seats along the swaying corridor. Rick put his hand on Sylvia's waist to steady her when the train lurched sharply to the right. They looked like old friends. *Why not?* she thought. *They're cut from identical cloth.*

When the taxi dropped the three of them in front of the skyscraper that housed Prescott Broadcasting, Finley checked her watch. It was exactly noon. She craned her neck to look up to the top of the imposing brick and glass building. This would be a long day and night. She *must* keep her wits about her.

The ride up to the thirty-seventh floor was so rapid that Finley's ears plugged. She swallowed to clear them. The elevator glided to a smooth stop and when the door opened, she saw the familiar receptionist's desk with the big gold Prescott Broadcasting sign over it. They greeted the woman sitting there and, within minutes, she escorted them to the conference room.

John Prescott stood, smiled and embraced Finley as she entered the room and then turned to Rick and Sylvia. "Good to see you again," he said, pumping Rick's hand and putting an arm around Sylvia's shoulders. "We thought we'd order in today."

Finley was struck, as always, by the stature of the "old man." He was tall, erect, though over eighty, and his full head of grey hair was cut short. His blue suit was soft, loose fitting, and draped his shoulders as comfortably as a flannel shirt. *This is probably the way my father would look had he lived to this age*, she thought.

Austin Montgomery, as always, was perfectly groomed. To Finley's taste, over groomed. His hair was styled and sprayed and had clearly been low lighted by an expert stylist. His suit was tailored to showcase his spare physique.

As the others exchanged pleasantries, Finley looked around the conference room. The floor was a shiny mahogany as was the long conference table sitting over an ancient oriental rug. Camel-colored curtains covered the vast windows, but they were so sheer that the Manhattan skyline appeared like spires through them. It was so quiet she could scarcely recall the cacophony of voices and horns that had assaulted their ears on the street below. It feels otherworldly up here, she thought.

A small dining table, to the side of the conference room, was topped in creamy damask. Five chairs sat around it. Simple white china was set and heavy sterling flatwear and linen napkins completed each place setting. Fresh red roses floated in a low bowl in the center of the table.

Sylvia and Rick accepted wine. "Water for me, please," Finley said to the server. *I must be sharp.* Salads were served and. dressings offered. "Vinaigrette," she said.

The server in the white shirt placed a piece of perfectly poached sea bass into the center of each luncheon plate. Bowls with tiny roasted potatoes and broccoli swimming in hollandaise were offered. As they began to eat, Finley realized she was famished. In her haste to catch the train, she had skipped breakfast, and she ate the delicious meal eagerly.

Conversation at the table shifted from the latest Broadway musicals to what new promotions competitors were instituting and then on to gossip about what was happening at the other stations in the chain. Finley smiled and nodded but did not join in the banter. She helped herself to more vegetables.

"My, you have a marvelous appetite for such a slender woman," Austin said.

She stopped chewing, mid bite. She didn't want to appear to be wolfing down her food. She began to stammer a response, but John Prescott interrupted her. "Eat up, Finley. You can afford it. You never seem to gain an ounce."

Sylvia sniffed and put down her fork.

After the meal was cleared, coffee was served. A plate of cupcakes was placed in the center of the table. "Mmmmm," Finley said. "My weakness." The little white cake was piled heavy with chocolate frosting, and Finley peeled the paper from it as she nodded to the server, accepting coffee. Brandy was offered and served to Sylvia and Randy. Again, Finley declined. Her hosts both put their hands over their glasses as well.

As she finished the little cake, she carefully wiped her mouth with the napkin, making sure that her lipstick didn't stain it. "That was wonderful, John. Thank you, and you, too, Austin."

"You're more than welcome," John said.

Austin led the group into his office which connected to the conference room through carved wooden doors. "Sit down, please, everyone. Make yourselves comfortable."

He wasted no time. "Finley, as you may know, we are concerned about your reporter's investigation of Governor Morgan."

Ah, now we're getting to the point of this meeting.

"The governor's been a friend to Prescott Broadcasting for many years," he continued. "We need to make this unsavory matter with Emily Sanders go away."

Marty had coached her the evening before, and Finley was prepared. While pretending to read her book on the train, she had formulated her plan of action. Her tone was measured, calm and quiet when she answered. "Austin, we have reason to believe the governor has contracted with a disreputable construction company for repairs to a bridge in Pittsburgh." She stared into his eyes. "It's a highly-traveled bridge. Shabby work on such a project could result in a tragedy for the citizens who cross it."

"The port authority people have to approve any work that is done, Finley," Austin said. "Your concern is unwarranted," He raised his hand in a dismissive gesture and turned to Rick. "So, is Marjorie adjusting well to life in Philadelphia?"

"Oh yes, she loves..." Rick began to answer.

Finley interrupted. "Excuse me, Rick, but I'm not finished." Sylvia looked as startled as if she had thrown a rock through the gleaming window. "Austin, the governor contracted with Cavaleri without taking bids." Shaking her head from side to side, she continued, "That is odd."

Sylvia sniggered nervously. "Oh Finley, grow up. This happens in every state, except maybe Vermont. Those greenies like to think they're holier than God."

Rick laughed and nodded in agreement.

Finley glanced at John Prescott. He looked somewhat saddened at Sylvia's comment. She decided to test her instinct and directed her words to him. "Mr. Prescott, do you think Governor Morgan's behavior sounds ethical?"

He took a white handkerchief from his pocket and wiped it across his face. "Oh, Finley, I'm afraid I gave up on what I thought was ethical a while back. This business will do that to you."

His defeated tone hurt. But it cemented Finley's plan. She turned back to Austin. "I can't promise anything, Austin, except that I will consider your request." Marty had told her she might have to play dirty if the stakes were important enough. "Certainly, I will expect to be compensated *if* I decide to cooperate.

Sylvia and Rick darted furtive glances toward John and Austin.

"What do you want?" Austin said.

She squared her shoulders. "To be named Executive Vice President of WABN News." She heard Rick inhale sharply across the table. "You can manage the other two stations, Rick."

Sylvia's jaw dropped open. The sight amused Finley so much that she nearly laughed out loud.

Rick attempted to stammer out an argument, but Austin interrupted him. "We want Rick's taped segments to continue."

I'll bet you do, Finley thought. *Have to grab those ad dollars from the corporations who control the elections, don't you? Just a friendly game. One filthy hand washing the other.*

"The segments will continue," Finley answered. "But I will have control of their content." She felt sick to her stomach, but at the same time, proud of her newfound ability to bluff.

"Now, wait just a minute, here," Rick sputtered

Austin shook his head, obviously prepared to argue.

Finley interrupted before he could speak and spoke with eyes narrowed. "Oh, by the way, you should be aware that I've been contacted by the *Philadelphia Inquirer*." This was not a bluff. It had happened frequently over the years. "I'm quite certain that they would be interested in hearing about Morgan and that bridge if you're not able to meet my requirements."

An eerie quiet settled over the room. Finley did not move. Austin and Rick exchanged quick glances. Austin's subtle nod told her all she needed to know.

Austin spoke, "Very well, Finley. You and Rick will collaborate on the tapings."

Rick's jaw clenched.

"Thank you, Austin."

"Are you looking for a salary increase?" Sylvia asked, obviously thinking of her bottom line.

"Actually, I'd prefer to be compensated in company stock," Finley said, crossing her knee toward Sylvia. "If I make more, the feds will take it in taxes anyway. Stock will ensure my future." *Which is a very good thing when you work with vipers*, she thought.

"How much stock are you talking about?" Austin said.

"Forty-thousand shares," she said, crossing her arms over her chest in a gesture that showed no room for negotiation.

The atmosphere of the room turned hollow. Then, Austin jerked in agitation and Sylvia and Rick laughed nervously. Finley noticed that John Prescott's mouth twitched in a slight smile.

Austin finally spoke. "That's two million dollars' worth of stock."

"Yes, I know," Finley answered calmly.

"That will have to be cleared through the Board of Directors."

"Of course." Finley pretended this was a simple matter. "But I really don't want to work at a newspaper, if I don't have to."

"I'll contact the board this afternoon and, if they agree, put the stock purchase into motion," Austin said. "If it's approved," *And it will be*, Finley thought, "I'll post the news of your promotion in the trades tomorrow."

She rose to her feet and extended her hand. "Good. I look forward to reading them."

"Very well, I guess we're finished here." Austin stood and shook her hand. "Why don't you three get settled in at the hotel. You're on your own until dinner. We have reservations at eight at Ducasse's in the Essex House. It's excellent."

Finley had heard of Ducasse's. It was one of the most elegant and expensive restaurants in the city. *My, they're not holding the horses on this one*, she thought. I must have really scared them. This power trip feels good.

Their cab ride to the Waldorf was silent, broken only by the cabbie's indistinguishable Middle-Eastern cursing.

When Finley walked into her room, she threw her overnight bag on the king-sized bed and picked up the phone. "Marty," she said, falling back onto the cushioned brocade of the coverlet. "It worked."

Thirty-five

Tuesday afternoon

Finley left the message for Austin at four o'clock. "So sorry, Austin, I'm not up to dinner tonight. Please extend my regrets to the others. I have some reading to do." She offered no further explanation and settled back into the soft hotel bed.

She could not stand to play the game again tonight. She felt slightly sick to her stomach from the phoniness of the afternoon. They think they bought me with their stock, she thought, shaking her head. *Let them think what they wish.*

"I need to talk to somebody I trust," she said to the walls and picked up the phone in the room. She dialed David's number first and got his answering machine. She didn't leave a message because she didn't know exactly what she wanted to say to him. He would not be pleased if she told him about what had happened that afternoon.

Next, she called Caroline at Jenny's apartment. Her daughter's cheery description of the phone conversation she'd just had with her future college roommate lifted Finley's spirits.

"We talked for nearly an hour, Mom," Caroline said in an excited voice. "She sounds really cool. She's from Cleveland and wants to major in insects. I told her that's weird, but she says she's always been a little bit buggy." Caroline laughed into the phone. "She's really funny and likes Justin as much as I do. I can't wait to meet her next month."

Her daughter's excitement eased somewhat the tension of the day. Her mood lifted. "Great, sweetheart. I can't wait to hear more when I get home tomorrow. I'll pick up something really good for dinner. Dessert, too."

"I love you, Mom."

The memory of those words warmed Finley's memory after the conversation ended.

Nested now in her pajamas, remote clicking away in her hand, Finley enjoyed a chicken sandwich and glass of red wine from room service. Lunch had been filling, and she was grateful that she didn't have to dress up and eat another rich meal in the company of people who turned her stomach.

She fell asleep with the remote still in her hand and was in the middle of a wonderful dream about David when she was startled awake by noise outside her door. She looked at the clock—two fifteen a.m. She muted the television and crept toward the hotel room door. Through the peep hole, she saw Rick.

"Finn," he whispered drunkenly. "Can I come in for a nightcap? We should talk about our collaboration."

He was grinning drunkenly, and the meaning of this late-night visit made Finley's skin crawl. *Thank God I chained the door before I settled in*, she thought.

Again, he whispered, this time louder, "Finley, how 'bout it? I think we should get to know each other better. Let me in."

She held her breath on the other side of the door, afraid he could hear any sound she might make.

Finally, he shook his head, turned and staggered down the hall toward Sylvia's room. Finley quietly turned the lock so she could crack the still-chained door and watched.

When he got to Sylvia's door, he knocked softly. "Hey, Sylvia. It's Rick. How about a nightcap—or something?"

Moments later, Finley heard the door open. Rick smiled and entered the room.

Finley closed her door and checked the lock. She walked back to bed. *He's a creep and she's a fool*, she thought, falling instantly into a deep and dreamless sleep.

~ * ~

The taxi ride to Grand Central on Wednesday morning was quieter than the one they'd taken the day before. Sylvia had decided to stay an extra day. She said she wanted to have dinner with her father. Rick sat beside Finley in the back seat of the cab looking angry. The pungent smell of stale alcohol filled the cab.

"Good night?" Finley asked him, deliberately cheerful.

At Grand Central, as Rick scavenged through his pockets searching for his train ticket. Finley perused the newspaper kiosk until she found *Variety*.

As the train sped back to Philadelphia, Rick looked sicker each time it lurched. Finley said, "Perhaps a Bloody Mary would help."

He opened red-streaked eyes and answered. "Maybe you're right." He stood up, lurched to the aisle and headed toward the bar car.

Finley thumbed through *Variety* until she found it. She nearly laughed aloud as she read the article on page six. Austin didn't waste any time, now did he, she thought? How could he have gotten the article placed so quickly? She considered showing it to Rick when he sat down with his drink but decided that he looked miserable enough already. He finished his drink in two gulps, shut his eyes and fell asleep.

How attractive you look, Rick, Finley thought. *With your jaw hanging slack and a bit of pink drool sliding down your chin. Wish I had a camera.*

When the two of them arrived at WABN, Stephanie spied them, stood up and started to clap. "Way to go, Finn," she said, holding up *Variety*.

"What's she mean?" Rick said.

Yes, Finley thought, *sometimes patience is rewarded. This feels much better than if I'd told him.*

"Thanks, Stephanie. It just happened yesterday."

"Well, girl, nobody deserves it more than you. You still gonna have lunch with me once in a while?"

Finley started to answer when Stephanie said, "Oh Lord, nearly forgot. Meadow called you first thing this morning. Wants you to call her ASAP."

"Did she sound okay?" Finley asked.

"I think so. Probably just heard the news and wants to congratulate you."

Rick strode toward Stephanie and grabbed the newspaper from her hands. "Let me see that." He read the article as the elevator door closed. "Well, this is very good. Congratulations, Finley." His voice was tight, unnatural. Finley grinned at its hypocrisy.

As soon as Finley closed her office door, she dialed. "Meadow, oh good, I caught you. What's up?"

"What's up with me? What's up with you? Why didn't you tell me you were getting this promotion?"

"Didn't know it myself until yesterday. What do you think?"

"I guess it's great. This is what you've wanted all along, right?"

"I suppose. Not sure I like what I had to do to get it, though."

"Meet me at Joe's at one thirty. This sounds serious and I want to see your face when you explain."

"How's your mom, Meadow?"

"Well, some good news, some not so good. I'll tell you everything when I see you."

~ * ~

When Finley walked into Joe's, Meadow stood up from the booth and ran to embrace her. Meadow's arms felt strong, warm and so comforting and Finley didn't want her to let go.

When Meadow stepped back, she said, "What's with the teary eyes, Finn?"

Finley didn't realize her eyes had filled, and she snatched up a paper napkin and dabbed under her lashes. "Just really glad to see you again. I need a friend."

"Okay, spill."

"I will in a minute. First, tell me about your mother."

Meadow spoke nervously as she sat down. "The PET Scan showed some involvement around her bladder. The docs are huddling again to try and determine what's next."

"Oh, Meadow, that's scary."

"Ben says, 'not necessarily.' I'm hanging onto that until they figure out what protocol is appropriate. He keeps me centered."

After Josie delivered their lunches, they sat there for a long moment studying each other's faces. Meadow was the first to speak, "Finn, what's up? You look troubled."

"I am. To get the job, I had to agree to let Rick Stone continue with his garbage. I have some control over the segments, but it's going to be a struggle."

Meadow tried to interject a comment, but Finley rushed on. "Plus, I had to play dirty and threaten them with spilling the beans about Cavaleri to the Inquirer. That's how I got what I was after."

"You mean the job?"

"Not just the job. My main objective was to get forty thousand shares of company stock out of them."

"Forty thousand?" Meadow looked astonished.

"Yes, it's part of a plan Marty and I discussed, but I'm not totally comfortable with this kind of hard ball. If it works, I think it'll be good for the company, but is so nasty."

"I don't like to see you like this, Finn. You're acting like you've compromised something important. Is it David?"

"That's part of it. David and I had a wonderful night together."

"You did?" Meadow said, leaning forward. "Tell."

"He broke up with Megan and came over Saturday night. It was incredible. He wanted to continue it on Monday, but I took the trip to New York instead. He's angry." She put her head into her hands.

"You don't look like someone who just got everything she's worked her ass off to get all these years. Maybe it's time to reevaluate."

"Not today, Meadow. Not today, please. I need to sort things out." She raised her head from her hands and extended them across the table to Meadow.

Meadow grasped them. "It's gonna be okay, Finn. We'll get through it together, just like always."

Thirty-six

Tuesday evening

Sylvia was excited. She had called her father the afternoon before on the outside chance that he could see her during her visit to New York. She was thrilled when he invited her to meet him for dinner at Jean Georges, the elegant restaurant near Trump Tower.

She hadn't spoken to him since their nasty conversation right after she had started her job at WABN and she was eager to tell him about the changes she'd made at the station.

The night spent with Rick had left her a bit hung over but flushed with sexual satisfaction. Her skin always looked better after an encounter with a man like Rick. She had let him come into her room, even though she knew he'd tried Finley's door first, because she wanted to look good for her father. It was that important.

Sylvia pulled the phone book out of her desk drawer and started flipping through the yellow pages for Beauty Salons.

She ran her finger down the list of names and stopped at Angelo David. She remembered an article in the *Inquirer* that said this was one of the top new salons in New York.

A heavily-accented female voice answered her call. "Angelo David Salon. How may I help you?"

"Yes, my name is Sylvia Reynolds, and I'm hoping you might have a stylist available today." Sylvia held her breath expectantly.

"What would you like done, Ms. Reynolds?" the woman asked."

"Wash, cut, highlights—wait a minute, maybe extensions—do you do extensions?"

"*Mais oui*, Ms. Reynolds. We are considered the finest in the city for hair additions."

"Good," Sylvia answered. "And I'd also like a full makeup done. Is that possible?"

"Of course—if a stylist is available on such short notice. Let me check my book."

Sylvia drummed her fingers on the open telephone book, hoping against hope that she could be seen.

The woman came back on the phone. "Ah, Ms. Reynolds. You are a lucky girl. We have had a cancellation today at two p.m. It would be with Claude, one of our best stylists. Does that work for you?"

"Yes, put me down."

"See you at two o'clock then." Click.

Excited, Sylvia looked at the clock on the bedside table. It was just past ten. That would give her plenty of time to shower, eat brunch and head to Saks to find something extraordinary to wear.

At two o'clock, Sylvia, Saks bag in hand, strode into the tony East Side beauty shop. The receptionist greeted her and offered her a libation. Sylvia asked for white wine.

A slender young man appeared. "Bonjour, Ms. Reynolds. I am Claude. I will be doing your hair today." He circled around, studying her closely. "Please stand," he said. She did as told, and he looked her over some more before running his hands through her hair. "Ah, nice texture. So, what are we looking for today—professional, tousled and easy or all-out glamour?"

Sylvia thought for only a second before answering resolutely. "As glamorous as you can make it, Claude. Pull out the stops."

Ninety minutes later, after Claude had worked his magic with scissors, highlights and extensions, Sylvia looked in the mirror and saw a new and transformed creature. "I'm gorgeous," she said, her eyes brimming.

"But of course," Claude said. "I am the best."

Next, Sylvia met with Lucianno who polished her face with makeup. By the time she walked out of the Angelo David Salon she was a new woman, a beautiful woman, and a woman no man would call *homely*.

~ * ~

Just before leaving for dinner, she took the stationery from the desk in her room and listed some of her accomplishments since coming to WABN: lowering the station's bottom line by three quarters of a million dollars, hiring Rick Stone and generating revenues of over a millio n dollars from his syndicated reports and cutting all charity campaigns to free up inventory for the big spenders. Michael Reynolds would be impressed. He'd have to be impressed.

As she rode up to the restaurant, her excitement rose as quickly as the elevator. She looked around the elegant space and spoke to the Maitre d'. "Has Michael Reynolds arrived yet? I am to meet him."

The man checked his roster of guests and nodded. "Yes, Madam. He's sitting at table number thirty-two. I'll take you there."

She followed the black-coated man to the table. Her father stood, embraced her briefly and pulled out the chair opposite him. "Sit down, Sylvia. Long time. How're tricks?"

"Good, Daddy. Great, actually.

She had dressed very carefully in the black cocktail dress from Saks. It was sleek, elegant and sophisticated. Just the look she knew her father liked best. The dress and beauty makeover had set her back nearly three thousand dollars, but all of it was worth the look of admiration he gave her. "You look good, Sylvia. Lost some weight?"

She smiled. "Maybe a couple of pounds. I'm working very hard at the station."

He ordered drinks, then sat back against the cushioned booth. "You're not the only one, apparent ly."

Sylvia was confused but began to tell him about her accomplishments. She mentally scanned the list she had compiled just before coming here. "I've cut the bottom line enormously and increased revenues by over a million. And..."

"Yeah, yeah, yeah. I'm sure." He took a large gulp of Scotch. "But what about this Finley Smith broad?"

Sylvia felt as though he'd slammed her against a wall. What was he talking about? Why would he bring up Finley during their dinner together?

Finally, she regained her composure. "What do you mean, Father?" she asked.

He pulled a copy of *Variety* from beside where he was sitting. "This!"

She shook her head. "I don't know what you're talking about." She hadn't seen *Variety* that day.

He reached across the table and shoved the page into her face. There, swimming before her eyes, she saw the picture of Finley and the headline about her promotion. She took the paper from his hands and read the article.

"She's quite a dish, isn't she?" he said. "Tell me about her. Is she married?"

The rest of the evening—a night of too much alcohol, rich food and talk of Finley—was one Sylvia would never forget. In spite of the expensive black dress and the afternoon spent in the best salon in the city, Sylvia felt again like the homely girl he had called her years earlier.

As his interest in Finley increased, Sylvia's anger deepened. Deepened into a pit of total hatred.

When he put her in the taxi and paid the driver to take her back to her hotel, his parting words were, "Maybe you could set me up with Finley sometime? What do you think?"

Sylvia knew at that moment that only one thing could ever satisfy her hatred for Finley. Revenge. Revenge because Finley was beautiful, revenge because she was clever, revenge because her father would have rather spent this evening with her than with his own daughter. Only one thing could take the pain away for Sylvia—Finley's absolute destruction.

That was when Sylvia Reynolds began to plot her next steps.

Thirty-seven

Wednesday afternoon

Marty Sax arrived at Joe Heaton's office precisely on time. Punctuality had always been one of Marty's tenets, and he believed it had much to do with his success in selling.

"Marty Sax, you rascal," Mildred, Joe's private secretary of thirty years, exclaimed when she saw him.

"Milly, you doll. You never age a day. What're you taking, some secret youth serum or something?"

"I wish," she laughed, fluffing her short brown hair, even as she shook her head at the credibility of Marty's compliment. "Joe told me you were coming in this afternoon. Let me buzz him."

Joe Heaton emerged seconds after Marty was announced. He clapped his hand on Marty's back. "Come on in, you old bandit. Good to see you."

The two men entered the large office and Joe gestured Marty toward a chair as he settled himself down on the opposite sofa. Marty picked up the picture of Joe's wife and family from the coffee table. "How many grandkids now?"

"Seven," Joe answered, "and counting. Thank God most of them live in New York or Joanie and I'd never get any time to ourselves. The two that live in Philadelphia keep us plenty busy babysitting. What's fun is that we don't have to keep them."

Marty laughed. "I know what you mean. We have four. It's great when they visit and greater when they leave."

Joe crossed his legs and Marty unbuttoned his jacket and put his arms up on the arms of his chair.

Joe broke the silence. "So, my friend, what's up?"

Marty leaned forward. The time for small talk was over. Now he needed to get down to business. "Remember when I told you to start buying stock in WABN back in the sixties?"

"Yep, and I've never stopped. Every time the station changed ownership, I rolled it over and bought more. Once Prescott took over, they tried to stop me, but I threatened to take them to the SEC and they shut up fast."

Marty smiled. "Yes, they tried to take it private, but that didn't hold up in court. Too many of us at the station had invested our life savings." Marty opened his briefcase and took out a sheaf of papers. "Me, for instance." He laid the papers on the coffee table. "Every time they offered me a raise or a bonus, I just plopped it into stock. Barbara and I live a simple life. This," he smacked his hands down onto the pile of papers. "is our retirement, our legacy to our kids, everything we have."

Joe Heaton raised his eyebrows. "That's quite a pile.

"Yep, if my estimates are correct, I own about eighteen percent of the total shares of Prescott Broadcasting. Any idea how much you have?"

"Not off the top of my head, but I could check with my financial guy and get back to you. By the way, did you know Austin Montgomery tried to buy me out a year ago?"

"He did?"

"Yep. I told him to put his offer where the sun don't shine."

Marty laughed. "So, you'll find out how many shares you have and get back to me?"

"Sure I will. Anything for Marty the mensch."

"I'm going to contact Tom Armstrong and Jim Fieldstone, too. They took my advice back in the sixties and should have a pile of stock, too. I need to get my ducks in a row before the shareholders' meeting in October."

Marty rose to leave, buttoned his jacket and extended his hand to Joe. They shook and, as Marty turned, Joe put his hand on Marty's shoulder to usher him out.

"So long, Milly," Marty said. "Keep this old man honest, you hear?"

"I try, Marty, but he's a wily critter."

~ * ~

Finley called David at four o'clock that afternoon. "Hi, David. Hear the news?"

His voice was chilly. "Sure did, Ms. V.P. So, you finally got your promotion."

"Yes, but it's only for WABN. Rick will oversee the operations for the other two stations' news departments, so—"

"So what?"

"So, I won't have to travel as much as if I were managing all of them. I'll be in Philadelphia most of the time."

She heard the deep sigh on the other end of the telephone line. "Finn, I've been thinking about the other night. It was great, but sweetheart," Her heart leapt at the word. "Sweetheart," he repeated. "I know you well and I know you love me. But, let's face it. You love the rush of television news more." Finley's heart sank. He continued, "doesn't make you a bad person. Just the wrong person for me."

Finley's head ached, but she continued on. "David," she said, trying to hurry her words before he could hang up on her. "There's something else. I need to make you conservator of the stock for Caroline. She can't have it until she's of age."

"Why, Finn? You going somewhere?"

"No, but I want it protected for her. I've already talked to my attorney, and it's in process. Just wanted you to know."

"Okay. But I really can't talk now. Patient waiting. Must go."

She started to protest, but the dial tone stopped her. Leaning back in her chair, she looked around her office. A huge congratulations sign hung in its center. Her staff had put it up as soon as the story broke in *Variety*. She closed her eyes and remembered David's words. *Was he right? Was she such a work junkie that no man could compete with the excitement of a breaking story? And if so, what was she supposed to do about it?* She picked up the press releases on her desk but then dropped them back, unable to concentrate.

At that moment, her phone rang. It was Emily Sanders. "Finn, I have enough on Cavaleri to do a series that'll knock your socks off. I have statements from across Pennsylvania about the fiascos he's been constructing. Hospitals, orphanages, shopping centers. That bridge is a disaster waiting to happen."

Finley's heart quickened. "Will your witnesses appear on air?"

"Every one of them. They're furious about the money they've had to spend to fix Cavaleri's mistakes. I have five stories written. All I need is a cameraman to travel with me so we can interview his clients, or I should say, former clients. Morgan will never be able to justify signing a contract with this sleaze for the bridge."

Finley's temples started to pound. Her thoughts of David dissolved into the excitement of bringing down a corrupt state administration through her news. "Be in my office at two o'clock, Emily. Let me see what you've got. If it's as solid as you say, you'll get your cameraman."

~ * ~

When Meadow called Finley at home that night, her voice was angry. Finley recognized the tone from other times when frustration had coiled her friend's voice into a bitter knot.

"What's the matter, Meadow?"

"Well, you know that Mom's surgery was to be followed by chemotherapy and radiation?"

"Yes," Finley answered.

"Remember when Ben explained to us about the autologous stem cell implantation?"

"Yes, I remember. The stem cells are to be harvested from your mother before she begins chemo, right?"

"Right, and that's the problem. Sheldon Compassion Network is denying coverage for that procedure. They say it's still experimental, but that's bull. It's been approved by the A.M.A. and is her best chance for remission."

Finley took a deep breath to calm her anger. "Remember how Ben looked when your mom told him about her HMO?" she asked.

"Sure do. Now I understand why. Sheldon's one of the biggest advertisers on the station. All that warm and fuzzy *Sheldon Cares* horseshit had me convinced they meant it. Ben knew better."

"How can I help? I'll do anything." Finley said.

"For starters, join our picket line on Saturday at Sheldon's home office. We're having protest signs printed. Ben's getting his doctor friends to join us and Stephanie's spreading the word all over WABN. I think we'll have a good crowd. Marty's contacting Joseph Heaton at the hospital union and he's going to have representatives there with Chris Andrews broadcasting on a loudspeaker. Will you come?"

"Of course, I'll come. Better than that, I'll have a news crew there to film it for the six o'clock news and call all the other stations in the state. This story should not be an exclusive."

Meadow's voice broke. "Thanks, Finn." Finley heard her sobbing on the other end of the line, and couldn't bear the sound. Meadow never cried.

"Meadow, love, don't worry. Sheldon will cave on this. They can't afford the bad publicity they're going to get."

~ * ~

Saturday

The afternoon was warm and sunny. "A perfect day for a protest," Finley said, hugging Meadow.

The glass and stone skyscraper with the sign "Sheldon Compassion Network" in ten-foot blue signage was set back from the street by at least thirty feet. Not a square inch of that frontage was empty. Protestors screamed their anger and the crowd crawled with reporters.

Chris Andrews ran to embrace Finley as soon as he saw her. "Hi, Finn. Good to see you again." He pulled a balding man up to meet her. "Meet Joe Heaton, my boss. Joe, this is Finley Smith, my former news director."

"Now the Vice President of News, I understand." Joe Heaton took her hand into his.

She smiled and shook his hand. "I hear you're a friend of Marty Sax, Mr. Heaton."

"Call me Joe, please. And yes, I've known Marty since we were pups. He's the best."

Finley smiled, squeezed his hand and turned to Vince Simms, the WABN cameraman who stood at the front of the mob. "Good God, Finley," Vince said. "I haven't seen such a big protest since Vietnam," he said.

The crowd was packed with cameras and radio station microphones from across Pennsylvania. Her phone calls had worked.

Anderson Trenner, the chairman of Sheldon, appeared at the front door. His P.R. Department had been informed of the protest or he would never have been there on a Saturday. He was obviously startled at the screams of protest that greeted him and resonated to the top of the building. He was assaulted by cameras and reporters clamoring for an explanation of why his company would refuse a treatment recommended by a patient's physicians and approved by the A.M.A.

Mr. Trenner stood calmly in his impeccable navy suit. *He's trying to retrieve the placid smile he's so famous for*, Finley thought—the same smile that appeared in all Sheldon's television commercials and newspaper ads. He removed his glasses and spoke, playing to the cameras surrounding him. "Studies on autologous stem cell transplants are inconclusive in treatment of multiple myeloma and—"

Before he could complete his statement, he was silenced by the shouts of physicians raising papers showing research from across the world. The cameras immediately panned the screaming doctors. They were dressed in surgical greens with logos of every major hospital in Pennsylvania blazoned across their chests. Many had stethoscopes hanging from their necks. There was no mistaking who and what they represented.

Ben had been designated as their spokesman. He approached the ring of microphones, pushing Mr. Trenner to the side. "Mrs. Marx's oncologist, Dr. Jonathon Horner, verifies that autologous stem cell transplantation will offer Mrs. Marx the very best chance for remission. Dr. Horner is one of the most respected cancer physicians in this nation. Sheldon Compassion Network has a record of denying treatment routinely approved by other insurers. Sheldon seeks out obscure, poorly conducted studies and ignores the vast wealth of research which supports appropriate treatment—if such treatment is expensive." The last sentence was addressed directly to Anderson Trenner.

A cheer went up from the crowd. Anderson Trenner attempted to stammer a reply, gave up, and retreated back into his building. *Like a rat seeking his lair*, Finley thought.

At four o'clock, Arlene's doctor received a call from the Sheldon Compassion Network informing him that their decision to reject autologous stem cell treatment had been reversed and that Mrs. Marx could have her stem cells harvested for later transplantation.

~ * ~

Sylvia, her head covered with aluminum foil in Salon de Jolie, was trying to replicate the look she'd gotten in New York. At five thirty, she was called to the salon phone. She grabbed it from the receptionist and was assaulted by Austin's angry voice. "How could you allow the WABN news to cover that rabble-rousing monstrosity at Sheldon? It's breaking news on every station in Pennsylvania and on ABC here in the city."

Before she spoke, she covered the mouthpiece for fear Austin would hear the scratch of the foil against it. She pulled the foil behind her ear and spoke. "I know nothing of any demonstration, Austin." It was the truth. She had no idea what he was talking about. "I haven't seen the news. Finley must have ordered coverage without consulting me."

"Sheldon's a big donor to the governor. Morgan called me twenty minutes ago furious about the demonstration. We're making enemies, Sylvia. Enemies we can't afford. Something must be done."

Sylvia was quiet for a long moment, again covering the receiver to mask the sound of two gossiping women behind her. "I will do whatever you wish."

"What I wish is for you to control Finley Smith. That's what I hired you for."

~ * ~

Monday morning

Sylvia entered Finley's office looking ragged and angry. Her eyes were puffy, and her suit rumpled. *She looks like a drunk*, Finley thought. Sylvia sat down, daggers darting from her eyes across Finley's desk.

"Morning, Sylvia."

"Good morning," Sylvia said.

"What can I do for you?"

"Austin called me Saturday afternoon."

Finley was not surprised. "And?"

"It was about your news coverage at Sheldon."

Finley had wondered all weekend why the roar from corporate about the demonstration hadn't come sooner. Her answer was prepared. She spoke calmly. "The event was newsworthy. Coverage was warranted."

Sylvia's eyes narrowed over the bulges beneath them, and she looked ready to pounce across the desk. "Austin disagrees strongly, and so do I. Sheldon is one of our largest advertisers."

Finley crossed her arms decisively over her chest. "Sylvia, you know the rules—news and sales remain separate. Just because a client spends money with us, they will not get special treatment from this news department."

Sylvia spat out her response. "You may be playing a very dangerous game, Finley."

Finley glared at Sylvia. "What's that supposed to mean? Is this a threat?" The question was moot. She had already figured out the mechanics of Sheldon's relationship with Austin. They were another cog in the Morgan election wheel. "Sylvia," Finley continued, leaning forward, elbows on her desk. "How much further does it go? Is the mob connected? And what is Austin's involvement in all this?"

"That is not a matter for your concern. I just know that you have to call in your hounds. I assume you've taken Emily off the Cavaleri story?"

"I'm waiting for her to come back to Philadelphia. Then I'll make the decision whether or not there is a story."

"But you promised corporate to back off on that."

Finley shook her head. "Not true. I promised to take it under consideration. There's a big difference."

Sylvia pulled herself to standing and stormed from the room, snarling. "You will regret this, Finley Smith."

Thirty-eight

Monday afternoon

Finley clicked off her phone when Emily Sanders entered her office. "Am I interrupting?" the woman mouthed.

"No, it's okay. I was talking to Meadow. She is over the moon because our demonstration changed Sheldon's position about her mother."

"I saw it on television in Harrisburg," Emily said. "Looked like every station in Pennsylvania was there. It was huge. Loved seeing Chris on camera again. He looks great."

"Yes, they had a portable Teleprompter for him," Finley said, chuckling. "He was quite the evangelist for sick folks getting screwed by health insurance companies, wasn't he? His boss, Joseph Heaton, was beaming the whole time Chris was on air. They love him at Blue Care."

"So, Meadow's mom will get her transplant?"

"She's in the hospital as we speak having stem cells harvested. Next comes chemo and radiation. Her odds for remission go up seventy per cent with the stem cell transplant. The stats blew my mind."

"Will she make it to Meadow and Ben's wedding?"

"No doubt in my mind she'll be there. She'll be post-chemo by then and, hopefully, in remission."

"That's great, Finn. Arlene's such a sweetheart."

Finley nodded, smiling, then decided to get to business. "So, welcome back, star reporter. I haven't seen you in weeks."

Emily leaned back and stretched her arms over her head. "Tell me about it. I am so sick of motel beds that I don't care if I ever sleep in one again. Being in my own apartment is heaven."

Finley waited. "So, what have you got for me?"

Emily grabbed the large briefcase she had placed beside the chair. She began to pull tapes and papers from it. Finley could sense her excitement.

"I am ready to go on the air with a full series on Cavaleri Construction. The stories are written, interviews filmed and I 've got video of all the messes Cavaleri has made around the state. Fortunately, many of the people took pictures of the crummy work before the y had it repaired. And I got every one of them…on tape."

"Let's take a look."

Finley and Emily went in to the production room and closed the door. This was nothing that should be seen by others in the department, especially Rick Stone. Emily slid the first tape onto the player. The image on the screen was of a Sister of Mercy sitting at her desk. She wore a lapel microphone and squirmed nervously, but her dark eyes were determined

Emily addressed the camera, "This is Sister Mary Elaine of St. John's hospital in Pittston." The sister smiled into the camera. "She will tell you her experience with Cavaleri Construction when her hospital added a children's oncology wing to their existing building."

The camera panned to the sweet-faced nun. She cleared her throat.

"In 1984, we contracted with Mr. Cavaleri to do an addition to our hospital." The screen dissolved to an imposing grey building with a cross on top then back to Sister Mary in close up.

"Central Pennsylvania had experienced an increase in pediatric cancers," she said. "And there were no hospitals in the area equipped to treat them. So, after much prayer, we were able to secure a grant from the governor's office to start construction. But the grant had strings attached. Mr. Morgan was quite specific about what construction company had to do the work. Cavaleri Construction."

The camera cut back to Emily, "Tell us your experience with this project, Sister."

"The day we were to break ground, all the sisters were so excited about getting started. But to our dismay, the crew never showed up. When I called Mr. Cavaleri, he said they were running late on a job in Wilkes-Barre and would be there by the end of the week."

"And did he keep his word?"

"We didn't see a single workman at the hospital for over two months. I was pulling my hair out trying to make excuses to the Diocese and my mother superior. Since I couldn't get my calls to Mr. Cavaleri returned, I didn't know what to do." The memories were disturbing to the little nun, and her eyes glistened.

"When they finally started the work, the cement trucks destroyed our parking lot and the constant noise and noxious odors made many of our patients sicker than when they had come into the hospital. When we asked the crew for advanced notice on where they would be working in order to move patients, they refused."

"Was the finished result worth it?" Emily asked.

"Hardly," the nun said shaking her head. "The walls of the children's rooms were constructed with sub-standard materials." The screen dissolved to a picture of pink wallpaper peeling off a crumbling grey wall. "The floors of the operating rooms were so uneven that our surgeons complained constantly about instruments sliding off surgical trays."

"Did you contact Mr. Cavaleri about your dissatisfaction?"

"Repeatedly and often," the sister said, looking as though the memory could still make her cry. "Once he'd gotten his money, he seemed to evaporate. He was always in a meeting or at a site and never responded to any of my calls or letters."

The sister dabbed at her eyes with a tissue. "I'm sorry for getting emotional. But the truth is, I almost had a breakdown over this, and worse, nearly lost my faith in God and my fellow man."

Emily concluded the interview with a picture of the beautiful children's wing at St. John's hospital as it looks today, after another company had come in and rectified the shabby job by Cavaleri construction. "This story has a happy ending, although the project ended up nearly three million dollars over budget. I just thank God the work was corrected before there was a tragedy."

Emily removed the tape from the machine.

"Emily, that was strong," Finley said. "How many interviews do you have?"

"Five...enough for a five-day series. Besides the hospital, I have an apartment complex, an orphanage, a shopping plaza and a rehab center. And, believe me, every one of them is as powerful as the one you just saw. This Cavaleri guy is an equal opportunity bastard, Finn. He doesn't care who he hurts, and the governor is behind him all the way."

Finley was quiet for several moments. Emily jittered in her seat, waiting for an answer.

Finally, Finley spoke, "I just negotiated two million dollars in company stock by implying I'd lay off on this story."

"What?" Emily said.

"I said I implied it. I made no promises. I know how furious Austin will be if this airs so soon after the demonstration at Sheldon."

"But Finn, truth is the job of this department."

Finley held her breath, remembering Sister Mary Elaine's despair. Emily's eyes were hopeful, trusting. *That's how I used to be*, Finley thought. *Fresh out of school, my journalism degree clutched tight in my hand. Truth was the only option ever considered.*

Finley exhaled and straightened her shoulders. "You are absolutely right. Thank you for reminding me. We'll run your first story tonight in the six."

Thirty-nine

Tuesday morning

Sylvia was waiting in Finley's office and slammed the door. "Pull the rest of the Cavaleri series. Austin's orders—how could you be so stupid, especially after that goddam demonstration on Saturday? He called me at home last night demanding retractions."

"I can't retract a demonstration," Finley said. She'd anticipated this and had planned her response. "And it's too late on the Cavaleri story. Did you see the *Inquirer* this morning?" She held the paper up in the air.

Sylvia snatched it from her hands and scanned it until she found the headline. **WABN Alleges Corruption in the Governor's Office.**

"Oh, my God," Sylvia said, pacing around the office and smacking the paper in her hands. "Finley, do you have any idea what you're doing?"

"I know exactly what I'm doing. Airing a thoroughly-researched news story. There's not a doubt in my mind that Morgan is exchanging contracts for campaign donations. How can I retract the truth? And why does Austin care?"

"That's none of your business. He wants the Cavaleri series pulled." Finley said quietly. "I won't do it."

"Then you tell him," Sylvia threw the paper on Finley's desk and stormed from the office. "I'm out of this."

As Sylvia slammed Finley's door, her phone rang. It was Stephanie. "Finley, the switchboard hasn't stopped buzzing since I got here. Sylvia's refusing to take calls, so I'm trying to answer questions, but I can't keep up. I'm swamped here. People are hanging up before I can get to them. I need help."

Finley's secretary scoured the station and found a typist in the engineering department who could pitch in at the switchboard.

At eleven, Finley approached Stephanie's desk. "What's the feedback?"

"Solid support on the Cavaleri series," Stephanie answered, putting the next call on hold, "and outrage over the Sheldon demonstration. I had no idea how many people have been screwed by their health insurance companies. Meadow's mom is just the tip of a big iceberg."

The woman answering calls next to Stephanie rolled her eyes. "Yeah, I intend to go home and read my policy tonight. I've got three kids. A quarter of my income goes for health insurance. They'd better not mess with me if one of my kids gets sick." She paused, said, "One moment, please," into her mouthpiece, put the call on hold and continued. "My sister lives over in Pittsburgh and just called to say there's a crowd protesting at that bridge Cavaleri is supposed to repair."

Finley realized she could procrastinate no longer. *Time to bite the bullet, girl*, she thought, returned to her office to dial Austin Montgomery's number.

"How dare you air such a series without corporate clearance," he screamed as soon as he heard her voice.

"This series is probably the best-vetted and produced story I've seen since I came to WABN. It's Emmy quality. News has never required corporate clearance in the past. Mr. Prescott gave me full authority to broadcast any story, as long as it was thoroughly researched—and this one was."

"Mr. Prescott," he said sarcastically, "is no longer chairman of Prescott Broadcasting. I am. Things have changed."

"If you want me to resign, I'll do so immediately," she said. "However, the response to the Cavaleri story is enormous. My resignation might cause you a public relations problem, Austin. Are you sure that's what you want?"

He slammed the phone in her ear.

~ * ~

Marty walked into Finley's office just before the six o'clock news started. She was relieved to see him. With Meadow gone, Marty had become her station confidante and support system.

"How're you holding up?" he said. "The piranhas circling your raft?"

"And how. Demanding I pull the series on Cavaleri, but I won't do it. I'll quit first."

"Don't quit, Finley. I'm hearing rumors that the FCC is taking a look at Austin's shenanigans."

"The FCC?" she exclaimed. "What do you know?"

"Nothing definite—yet. When I'm sure, you'll be the first to know." He stood. "By the way," he continued, "anything new on Arlene? I haven't talked to Meadow since Saturday."

"They harvested her stem cells this morning. She'll begin chemo and radiation as soon as she's recovered from that. Meadow sounded optimistic."

"Great. Okay, kiddo, I'm out of here. Got a date with my wife. Keep the faith."

Keep the faith. She wondered how long she could do it. She flipped on the television set in her office to watch the six. Emily's second segment was airing.

"This is where the stairs collapsed after Cavaleri finished their renovations on my shopping center," a man said, pointing to a staircase. "Three people had to be taken to the hospital. Thank God none of the injuries were fatal, but the lawsuits nearly put us under. When I finally got hold of Vince Cavaleri, he told me I could pound salt." He raised his hands in frustration. "The governor knew about it, too. I wrote him a letter." He shook his head. "Never heard back. How he could contract with such scum is beyond me."

The governor's P.R. people had better start working overtime, Finley thought. *They're going to need a lot of perfume to cover the stink of this mess.*

~ * ~

Sylvia went to New York on Wednesday at Austin's demand. "I want to discuss Ms. Smith," he'd said on the phone. "I expect your cooperation."

"Of course, Austin," she'd answered. "I'll do whatever you say."

"I don't want to talk about this over the phone. Be here at eleven tomorrow."

She waited in the reception area for thirty minutes before the receptionist told her Austin would see her.

"We're very disappointed with your handling of the Finley Smith matter," he said as soon as she sat down. "You said you could manage her."

Is he going to fire me? Sylvia wondered, panicked. *My father would gloat.* She opened her mouth, but he interrupted her.

"Never mind," he snapped. "It's too late. The damage is done. It must be repaired."

Perfect, Sylvia thought. *He's not going to fire me.* Her confidence somewhat restored, she said, "You're right, Austin. It seems to me Finley has left us with only one recourse. We must wait a couple of months, though." She held up the *Inquirer* and showed him the headlines.

"Shit," he said. "That bitch is smart." He stared into Sylvia's eyes. "What kind of recourse are you talking about?"

"To make Finley go away. And Austin, somehow I think you might have the connections to make that happen."

Forty

August 12

Meadow waited anxiously in Dr. Howe's sunny office. As she looked around it, she thought, *This is the kind of office an oncologist should have. Warm, hopeful, bright.*

Arlene had endured ten weeks of intense chemotherapy, and the strain showed. She was thin and hollow eyed. Her fair skin appeared nearly transparent. Meadow had bought her mother a wig weeks earlier, but today her head was bald.

"Thanks, darling," she had said. "I know you mean well, but I'll save it for special occasions. It's cooler being bald. Hot as it is, that's a plus. This is who I am now, Meadow. I'm not ashamed."

She was right, Meadow thought. This August had broken decades-long heat records. She almost wished she could shave her head like her mother's.

She held her breath as she waited for Dr. Howe to speak. Finally, the doctor looked up from the reports on her desk and smiled. "I am very pleased with the results of your blood work and the most recent MRI, Arlene." Meadow exhaled. "You are progressing toward remission much more quickly than any of us anticipated. The tumors on your bones have shrunk dramatically."

When she heard her mother's sigh, Meadow realized Arlene had been holding her breath, too. Stan put his arm around his wife's shoulders and pulled her close to him. "Oh baby, thank God. I was scared to death."

Meadow's love for her parents swelled like a wave on a warm beach. The moisture from the wave moved into her eyes but she brushed it away. She had been the rock supporting them for the past two months, and she wasn't going to cry in front of them now.

"So, Dr. Howe, what's next?" Arlene asked.

"We'll continue with the chemotherapy for another month and then check to make sure your numbers are still holding up. If that's the case in September, all your doctors will decide if it's time to re-transplant your stem cells."

The doctor was a consummate professional, but Meadow spotted the happy twinkle behind her eyes. *Dr. Howe is genuinely surprised at mom's progress*, Meadow thought. *How marvelous that she cares so much. Just like Ben. He can't disconnect from a patient either, any more than he can stop breathing.*

Meadow, Arlene and Stan were silent on the elevator going down from the appointment. *Everyone's saying thank you prayers in their own way*, Meadow thought.

"Well, my girls, what do you say I buy you both the best lunch in Philadelphia?" Stan said as they walked out into the stifling summer heat

Arlene nodded enthusiastically, but Meadow said, "Love to, Dad, but I'm meeting Finley. I'll see you later at dinner. Ben's cooking brisket, remember?"

"How could I forget that? It's the best brisket I've ever tasted."

Arlene punched him in the arm. "So what's mine, chopped liver?"

"Now, Mom, I still like yours better," Meadow lied. "We'll see you at seven."

As she drove toward the station, her heart soared above the waves of heat rising from the pavement. After this scorcher of a summer, she looked forward to fall. Even more, she looked forward to December sixteenth when she would marry the love of her life.

She couldn't wait to see Finley again. They had both been too busy to spend much time together, and Meadow missed her. Since Finley broke the Cavaleri series two months earlier, she knew that Sylvia had made life at WABN hell for her, but Finley had remained firm. She was proud of her. Her friend had become a warrior. Though Meadow had always known Finley was strong, she hadn't realized how much iron lay behind the fragile beauty. She could tell that the loss of David still hurt Finley, but the battle at WABN had energized her.

Meadow chuckled as she recalled their dinner with Caroline and her future roommate three weeks earlier. The girl's name was Samantha, but Caroline called her Bugsy because of her all-consuming interest in insects.

"How can you *not* be interested in bugs?" Bugsy had asked them as they sat at Finley's table. "They're probably going to be the last surviving species on this planet. They are the most fascinating creatures on earth. When I'm a professor of entomology at some Ivy League school, I'll invite you to my book signings."

The skinny Bugsy, all arms and legs, had slightly protruding eyes. After the girls left to meet friends, Meadow and Finley laughed about how "bugsy" Bugsy looked. "She'll be perfect at her readings. People'll take one look at her and think of a fly," Meadow had choked out.

~ * ~

Meadow saw Finley waving her over as soon as she walked in the door to Joe's. "What's the news on your mom?" Finley asked as soon as she sat down.

"Better than I could have dreamed. They're actually talking about shortening her chemo and re-transplanting her stem cells next month. Mom and Dad are out celebrating as we speak."

Finley took her hand and squeezed it. "Have you told Ben yet?"

"Not yet. He has a packed day at the office. But I'm gonna stop on my way home and get a big bottle of Cristal. He's cooking a family dinner tonight, and this party needs to be a special celebration." She placed her napkin on her lap. "So, what's happening at work?"

Finley sipped her water. "Oh, the stew keeps on cooking. Sylvia watches every move I make." She chuckled. "Sometimes, I wish they'd fire me just so I can get away from her."

"They're scared to fire you," Meadow said.

"I suppose so. Afraid I'd spill even more beans on our esteemed governor. But if I didn't have Marty to unload to, I think I'd quit."

"God, I miss him," Meadow said. "I miss everyone, but mostly him and you."

"Believe me, everybody misses you, too. The sales manager Sylvia brought in from Pittsburgh is lame. A Nielsen bureaucrat without a creative thought in his mechanical little brain. Everyone calls him the Rick Stone of the sales department."

"That bad?" Meadow was pleased. Natural reaction, she thought, forgiving herself.

"Yep, except he's not as racist as Rick. He wouldn't dare show that with Marty around."

"Guess not." Meadow laughed.

"Forgot to tell you something," Finley said, lightly smacking her forehead. "Austin Montgomery is coming to town next week to have dinner with me. He called me out of the blue—nice as pie. I have no idea what he wants. Maybe he'll fire me."

"He doesn't have the guts."

"Probably not. Everyone is still buzzing about the stories on Cavaleri and Sheldon. Austin puzzles me, though. He was so sweet on the phone when he set up the evening." Finley shook her head. "You'd think we were buds."

"Where are you going?"

"Carlucci's, I think. I'm craving Tony's eggplant. It isn't fancy, but I don't need to impress Austin. I can scarcely stomach the man, so I may as well eat something I like."

~ * ~

Meadow sang along with the radio as she drove toward home. "Like a virgin," she crooned in an off-key voice. "Touched for the very first time." *Yeah, right,* she thought. *Some virgin. No woman could live with Ben Freedman and remain pure for long.* She was so happy with this kind, sexy man that she could scarcely remember the lonely nights before they met.

She pulled into the parking lot of Barbara's World of Wine and Spirits, got out of the car, humming all the way to the front door. *Better stop singing,* she thought. *Don't want to sour the wine.*

"Bottle of Cristal, Barb," she said to the woman smiling to her in greeting. "Actually, make that two bottles."

"Celebrating, Meadow?" Barbara asked, opening the refrigerator door to the fine wine case. "This stuff's pricey."

"You bet I'm celebrating. My mom just got great news from her doctor, and the world is a beautiful place. Hot, but beautiful. Nothing is too good for tonight.

Even so, Meadow jumped a little when she checked the slip from her credit card. "Wow, how do people afford to drink this stuff on a regular basis?"

Barbara laughed. "They don't, unless they're rock stars or Sylvester Stallone. He comes in and buys it when he's in town visiting family."

"Well, that's fitting because I feel like Rocky today. But no way I'll try to run up the library steps in this heat."

Forty-one

Friday, August 16

Finley dreaded this night. She was to meet Austin for their scheduled dinner and still couldn't figure out what he wanted. To make things more confusing, Sylvia was acting as though her nerves might come through her skin. Finley noticed her nails were bitten to nearly bleeding and that Sylvia constantly scratched her arms.

"Something wrong?" she asked when she left their meeting in the morning. Sylvia shook her head and brushed her off.

At six thirty, as Finley repaired her chewed-off lipstick, she was surprised to see Sylvia skulk into her office. "You still here?" Finley asked. "I thought you'd left an hour ago."

"I did but then remembered something," Sylvia stammered. "Is tonight your dinner with Austin?"

Finley nodded.

"Where are you meeting?"

"Carlucci's on Sixth. Nothing fancy but it's one of my favorites. I don't figure this dinner requires a grand setting." She paused, then decided to chance the question she was wondering about. "Sylvia, do you have any idea why he wants to see me?"

She shook her head.

Finley didn't believe her.

"Maybe just to catch up on how things are running in the news department," she said.

"I don't think so, Sylvia, and I think you know better. Is he going to fire me?"

"Not that I've been told, though I wouldn't blame him if he did. You've caused a lot of trouble with your stupid crusades." She punctuated the phrase with a twirl of her hand and sarcasm in her voice. "It's all so ridiculous. Why can't you let things alone? Prescott profits were on a steady rise until you started with your investigations. Now, some of our biggest clients are pulling their commercials."

Finley tossed the lipstick into her bag and snapped it closed. "Temporarily. An honest news will increase our ratings and our profits eventually. It's just a matter of time. Already, we're getting new advertisers—advertisers who aren't sucking at the governor for contracts." She stood to leave. "Must go."

Sylvia's shoulders drooped. She shook her head, turned and walked out.

Finley shrugged. *Sylvia looks awful Bet she's aged ten years since she arrived here. I don't know if it's the drinking, but she's doing a lot of that. I smell it on her first thing in the morning.* Surprised, she realized she pitied Sylvia. The sentiment was brief. *Come on, Finley,* she told herself. *This is the bitch who fired Meadow.*

She ran her a comb through her hair, glanced at her watch and closed the office door firmly. Her appointment with Austin was in less than half an hour.

~ * ~

She saw him sitting near the back of the restaurant. She whispered to Tony, "Someone's waiting for me," and pointed to Austin. "We'll catch up after dinner." He smiled and led her to the table.

"Finley, nice to see you," Austin said, rising. "Quite the little joint you chose."

He wants to embarrass me, she thought. "I think you'll find the food makes up for the lack of elegance," she said as she seated herself opposite him.

Austin pursed his lips. "It'll be all right. Italian is not my favorite cuisine, but I can probably get a steak, right?"

"Of course."

"Do they make a decent martini?"

Finley felt her face heat. "Actually, they don't serve anything but wine or beer. Would you rather somewhere else?"

Austin wrinkled his nose. "Oh no, no, never mind. A good Cabernet will suffice."

Tony came to take their order, and Austin's manner bordered on rude. He was condescending and dismissive. "What's your best Cabernet?" He said, never looking up.

Tony left the table and brought back a glass with a sample of the wine for Austin to taste. "Will this do?" he asked.

Austin sniffed, sipped, and finally answered. "I guess it will have to."

"I'm sure it's delicious," Finley said, touching Tony's arm. "Please bring us a bottle."

All this reminded Finley with great clarity how much she detested Austin. Tony was one of the most respected restaurateurs in the city, and Finley worried that Austin's attitude had hurt him. She would apologize later.

She sat quietly, trying to dispel her anger at the pompous fool sitting across the table from her.

He broke the silence. "So, I hope you have no more bombshells brewing in your news department."

"Bombshells?"

"Yes, like the one you set off when you attacked Cavaleri Construction."

"I didn't attack anyone. The stories were documented."

Tony returned to the table, uncorked the bottle of wine and poured two glasses.

Austin interrupted her, ignoring Tony. "You know that Governor Morgan had to cancel his contract for that bridge?"

"Yes, I heard. And that's a good thing. Cavaleri is a disaster and a mob business. Everyone in Philadelphia knows that." She watched for his reaction and saw only a twitch in his right eyelid. "Did you know it, too, Austin?"

Tony turned and left, nodding to Finley.

Austin glared at her, his expression one of utter malice. "You know, Finley, you really are a cunt," he hissed.

Finley jolted in her chair. "How dare you use such a word with me?" she said, crossing her hands on the table and leaning toward him, never taking her eyes from his "Fire me, Austin." She leaned closer, her lip curling. "Maybe by now the press has forgotten I was behind the Cavaleri series. Memories are short in this business. Or could it be you don't have the courage?"

He pushed back in his chair and looked down, trembling with fury. He took a long swig of his wine and poured another glass, composing himself. He did not apologize.

Tony placed a sizzling steak in front of him. "I hope this will be satisfactory, sir."

Austin dismissed him with a wave of his hand and picked up the steak knife.

Finley raised her fork, wishing she could plunge it into Austin's hand. "Thank you, Tony," she said. "The eggplant looks delicious, as always."

Austin cut into the perfectly rare piece of meat. "All right, Finley. Let's calm down."

She couldn't believe he was asking for calm after what he had said. "I'm not the one who called somebody a cunt."

"Oh, I was just joking. Don't be so sensitive." His voice had changed to a friendly jocularity. "After all, what's past is past. What matters now is the future." He put a piece of steak in his mouth and, though he seemed reluctant to admit it, said, "This is really quite good."

I hope you choke on it. "I'm glad it meets with your approval." Her tone betrayed her feelings. She was still furious. "But I must be honest with you. If a news story meets my vetting standards, I will air it." She took pleasure in the way his eyes bulged at her words and decided to continue. "Perhaps you're being too sensitive, Austin."

The first bite of the eggplant burned her mouth, and she cooled it with a sip of the wine.

Austin put down his knife and fork. "So, no matter what Prescott Broadcasting orders, you will continue to ignore our wishes?"

"I have no choice." It was time to play her trump card. "If the FCC learns that you are bending the news for advertisers, we'll lose our license. Reagan eliminated the Fairness Doctrine, but they still watch graft." She watched his reaction carefully. "Especially if there's a paper chain." His expression told her all she needed to know. There was a chain. "That could turn into an indictment. Transparency in TV is mandated by the feds and you know it." She paused, studying him closely. "It occurs to me, Austin that the ice under your feet just might be cracking."

He stared at her, eyes blazing, but no words came.

Finley's head started to throb. She wanted out of here. "I'm going to do my job."

The impasse between them loomed like a vast, deep canyon. He sees it, too, Finley thought. There's no way we can traverse it. Anger narrowed his pupils, but she would not break her stare. They had reached the point of no return.

Finley wiped her mouth with her napkin and stood. "I don't think we have anything more to talk about, Austin, so I'll say good night." She slipped into her jacket and turned away. Just before she got to the bar area, she looked back. Austin was hissing into a pay phone, one hand cupped around his mouth. Finley wondered for a moment who he had called. Maybe John Prescott?

Tony was behind the bar, drying a glass. A slight figure dressed in black darted away from him toward the front door. Finley veered toward Tony and sat down on a bar stool in front of him. "Tony, I'm really sorry he was rude to you. He has zero class."

"I'm used to rude, Finley. I didn't grow up on the South side of Philly expecting to be pampered. Would you like anything to drink?" he asked.

"No thanks, I've a killer of a headache." She glanced back and saw Austin on the phone again. *Who is he calling anyway? He seems frantic.*

Forget him. She turned back to Tony. "Business is quiet tonight."

"Yes, the crowd came in earlier." He finished wiping the glass and lifted it to hang over the bar. "And I'm closing early. Flying to Florence in the morning. Tuscany has the best olive crop in decades. I want to buy oil for the restaurant." He leaned closer to Finley and whispered. "Did you notice that woman who was sitting here?"

"I saw someone's back. Couldn't tell if it was a man or a woman. Whoever it was sure seemed in a hurry."

"I hope she's not driving. She seemed okay when she came in and demanded vodka. I told her we only serve beer and wine, so she ordered a glass of white. After I served her, I realized I shouldn't have. She was smashed. She got belligerent when I cut her off and suggested a cab." He rubbed his chin and stared toward the front door. "I always feel bad when people leave here sauced up like that. But she was well on her way before that glass of wine."

"I never thought about that side of your business, Tony. Part father confessor, part mean daddy, right?"

He smiled. "You're a good lady, Finley. I hope you get everything you deserve. Including Dr. David, if that's in your scheme of things."

So, he did know about the divorce. Of course, he knew. He heard all the gossip in town from his customers. She shook her head. "I don't know about that. I think that for now, my job has to take precedence. But we'll see."

She put her credit card on the bar. "Tell him it's my treat." She nodded toward Austin.

She signed the slip, then stood up. "Have a great trip."

Tony came around the bar, took her to the door and opened it. "Drive safe, pretty Finley."

"Thanks. I will." As she turned to leave, she glanced one last time at Austin. One hand was covering his eyes.

Forty-two

Sylvia staggered up the steps outside the restaurant. Driving rain slicked the streets of Philadelphia. The southside neighborhood around the restaurant was hazy under dim street lamps and looked deserted for as far as she could see.

What the hell was I thinking coming over here dressed like a goddam fugitive? That was stupid. Austin said I should stay home, but I wanted to see Finley get her comeuppance.

She had hit the vodka, neat, as soon as she got home from the station. Booze had battled reason and won, again. At some level, Sylvia was worried that, in spite of their plan, Austin might offer Finley her job to gain her cooperation. She didn't trust him. All he'd told her was that if Finley didn't play ball, something bad might happen to her. Sylvia figured a bomb in Finley's car or house. And that was fine with her. Austin had finally implied to her that he'd used the mob to pressure uncooperative business associates in the past.

He'd laughed. "You can't do business in Philadelphia with clean hands, Sylvia. It pays to have some well-connected friends, swarthy though they might be."

She was happy to see Finley get her comeuppance. She hated the woman in more ways than she could count. She'd seen Rick go to Finley's door first that night in New York. *Sloppy seconds, that's what I am. He'd rather have been with Finley, but she wouldn't let him in. I did.* She knew she couldn't compete with Finley in the looks department but had assumed the memory of that night at O'Hare would have drawn him to her first.

She laughed out loud. "Who cares?" she said to no one. "He won't like her so much after the blast does its number on her face."

Stupid, she thought. *Putting on this trench coat and covering my head with a black scarf and driving over here like some kind of James Bond-ette.* She giggled at her pun.

She stopped for a minute and huddled under a nearby awning to escape the chilling rain. Standing there, she dug her fist into her bag, searching for car keys. As her finger collided with something hard in the bottom of the bag, she felt her nail break. *Damn it. I hate these big purses.*

Then she remembered the look on Finley's face back in the restaurant, angry, confused and, perhaps, a little scared. For a moment, she felt guilty. *What could I do anyway? If I had warned Finley, I'd get fired. And what do I know for sure? Nothing. Nada!* Her hand finally connected with the key ring, and she tugged it out of the purse. Good, she thought. She chewed off the broken nail and started walking again.

Keys in hand, she began to wonder where the bomb was going to be planted. "Oh, screw it," she murmured. "She's a big girl—not my problem. Let her take care of herself."

As she stumbled down the dark sidewalk, Sylvia debated whether to find another bar or head home. Better make sure you can find your car first. She giggled again.

She had walked less than a block when the dark figure darted from behind the parked car. The presence scarcely registered until he grabbed her arm and pulled her into an alley.

"Well, Miss Smith," a muffled voice said from behind a mask. "Seems you've been causing some trouble. We need to fix that."

She tried to scream. His calloused hand clamped over her face.

"I'm not..." she said, the words strangled by the constant pressure on her mouth.

"I can't breathe," she tried to gasp. "I can't breathe."

They were the last words Sylvia spoke before the sharp pain of the needle pierced her neck.

~ * ~

When Sylvia didn't show up for work on Monday morning, nobody was particularly concerned. In truth, the staff at WABN was glad to have a respite. Her secretary said she may have forgotten an out-of-town meeting. After three days passed with no sign of her, people started asking questions. There was no one to call. She had no friends or family in Philadelphia that anyone knew of.

Rick Stone stopped Finley in the lobby on Wednesday. "Any idea where Sylvia is?"

"No. She didn't say she was taking time off."

"Maybe we should check her apartment," he said. "She gave me a key when I first arrived here. You know, just so I could keep an eye on things if she went out of town."

Finley pretended surprise and agreed to go there with him. When they opened the door, Finley felt she was violating Sylvia's privacy but knew she had no choice. The barren apartment revealed nothing. A half-empty bottle of Grey Goose vodka sat on the kitchen counter with an unwashed glass. No clothes seemed to be missing, and suitcases were thrown in a messy pile in the back of a closet. Their search produced no clue as to what had happened to her.

When Finley called Meadow that evening, she told her Sylvia seemed to have vanished into nowhere.

Meadow said, "Weird. She's a bitch, but she was always the type to show up. Oh well, enjoy the peace, Finn. It probably won't last long."

~ * ~

John Prescott called Finley. "Finley, we're concerned here about Sylvia. Do you think we should call the police?"

"I've been thinking the same thing, John. I don't know what else to do. There's no one to contact here. We checked her apartment, called her father, but he hadn't heard from her and didn't seem concerned." She didn't tell John that Michael Reynolds had asked her out.

After two weeks of police search and rescue, with pictures of Sylvia plastered over every newspaper in the state, the police reclassified Sylvia's case to search and recovery. "We're operating with zero clues, ma'am," the assigned detective told Finley. "No one saw her leave her apartment that night. We found her car, locked up, on Market Street."

In the third week after Sylvia's disappearance, Finley was surprised by a call from Tony Carlucci. "Hi, Finley—just got back from my trip to Tuscany."

Finley was puzzled. He had never called her before. "That's great, welcome home," she said.

"Could you come here this evening?" he said. "Dinner'll be on me."

"Why, Tony?"

"I need to talk to you about something," he said. "Something important."

She arrived at the restaurant at seven thirty. Tony poured two glasses of wine and sat down. He wasted no time in getting to the point of his invitation. "When I got back from Italy, I started looking through the back issues of the newspaper to catch up before recycling. Needed to know what was going on while I was away."

Finley nodded.

He continued, "Remember that night you were here with that stuffed shirt who hates Italian?"

"Yes. Austin Montgomery."

"How can anyone hate Italian?"

"Beats me, especially the way you make it. His loss."

"Yeah." His expression changed. "But anyway, when I got back, I started going through the newspapers before I recycled them. I happened to see a picture in the paper of a woman who disappeared that night. She worked at WABN, too."

"Yes, Sylvia Reynolds, the general manager. They still don't know what happened to her."

"Describe her," Tony said.

"Little, bottle-blonde hair, sharp features. No distinguishing marks or anything. Why?"

"Cause when I saw the picture, I made a connection."

"What kind connection?"

"Remember the woman sitting at the bar who ran out of here that night?"

Finley wrinkled her brow as she thought back. Then she saw the scene again, the small, dark figure darting toward the door just before she sat down to apologize to Tony. "Oh yes, I remember. The woman was really drunk and you were feeling guilty that you'd served her."

"Exactly. I didn't get a great look at her because of the scarf she kept pulling over her face, but that picture in the paper sort of reminded me of her. I'm wondering if I should call the cops."

"Oh, I don't think she would have come here, Tony." As she said the words, she remembered Sylvia's curiosity about where she was meeting Austin.

An eerie fear crept over her. She recalled Austin punching in numbers on the restaurant phone. What if? No, that can't be. Austin might have mob connections, but certainly he wouldn't resort to having someone killed. Would he?

Had she struck a nerve when she mentioned the FCC? Was that it? *No*, she told herself again. *You're letting your imagination go crazy. But what had happened to Sylvia? How could a grown woman disappear?* Then, the scariest thought of all hit her. *Did someone mistake Sylvia for me?*

"Tony," she said, hesitating for a second. "Do you know much about the mafia?"

"Are you kidding? Half the kids I grew up with are the muscle in this town."

"How do they make someone disappear?"

"Simple. Grab them, kill them with drugs, cut up the body and toss it in waterways across the state. Weigh each part down with cement so it'll sink. By the time anyone discovers it—if they ever do—the fish have done their job."

Forty-three

Friday, late in August

Caroline was asleep when Finley got home from Carlucci's. She dialed Meadow's phone. When Meadow answered, Finley's voice was shaking. "Meadow, I'm scared."

"What's the matter?"

She told her what Tony had said. "Maybe I'm going crazy, but I keep seeing Austin's face as he dialed and redialed that phone. First, he looked furious, then panicky, and then absolutely helpless." She took a breath and uttered her worst fear. "What if he was calling somebody to tell them I was leaving the restaurant—that they should grab me?"

"But, Finn, if that's true, why didn't they grab you?"

"Because I stopped to apologize to Tony. Because Sylvia left the restaurant first. Because maybe they mistook her for me. I don't know. I just don't know, but put together, it all makes some kind of sick sense."

"Finn, I'm coming over. You shouldn't be alone right now."

"Thank you, thank you. Hurry."

~ * ~

Meadow rang the doorbell twenty minutes later. A frightened voice said, "Who is it?"

"It's me, Finn. Open the door."

In spite of the stifling heat, Finley was dressed in the blue cashmere sweats, her arms crossed over her chest. Mascara ran in black streaks under her eyes. Meadow saw that her nail polish was chewed off.

"Where's Caroline?" Meadow asked.

"Sleeping. She doesn't know any of this."

"Good, let's keep it that way. Now, I'm gonna make us some tea. We'll sit down and talk this out. I'm not going home tonight. Ben says if we need him, he'll come over. What do you think?"

Finley shook her head. "No, as long as you're here, I'm okay."

Meadow put water on to boil and sliced a lemon from the refrigerator. When the kettle began to whistle, she took valerian tea down from the top shelf and put a bag in each of the two cups on the counter. When she returned to the living room, Finley was nestled on the couch covered by a blanket.

"Are you cold? It's ninety degrees out. Should I turn down the air?"

"It's just nerves. I always feel better with this blanket on me when I'm upset."

"Okay, sweetie. Let's go through this again. Tell me everything Tony said."

Finley was calm as she recited the story to Meadow right up until she got to the end, and then she broke down. "He said the fish would do their job."

Meadow shuddered. *Lord, I hated that bitch, but to end up like that. No one deserves that. And it could have been Finn.* She thought, but didn't say the words. *I think it was supposed to be Finn.* She pulled Finley into her arms and squeezed tight.

"Should we call the police, Finn?" she asked.

"I don't know. We don't have any real evidence. It's just conjecture. I'll let Tony decide what to do about that. I think he has connections with the police department, and he'll do what's right."

"So, what do we do?" Meadow asked.

Finley bobbed her tea bag up and down in her cup and then took a sip. Her eyes cleared and she stared into Meadow's. "I think it's time—actually long past time—that Marty and I put our plan into action. I'll call him and ask him to come here in the morning."

Meadow nodded and relaxed back on the couch. *Yes, Marty. He would make things better.*

"Okay," Marty said after he'd heard the entire story the next morning. "You're right. We have to get a move on." He stood and started to pace around Finley's living room. Caroline had gone to the gym with a friend, oblivious to the drama unfolding in her mother's life.

"But there's a problem I hadn't anticipated," he said. "I've talked to Joe Heaton and my other pals who bought stock all these years. The way I had it figured, with mine and theirs and yours, Finley, we'd have a controlling share. But I figured wrong. Austin did a big buy out last year. No matter how I work it, we're at only thirty-two per cent. That's not enough to vote Austin out."

"I've got some," Meadow interjected. "Maybe about two thousand shares."

"That's good, honey, but not enough," Marty said.

They ran through the roster of all the employees at WABN who might have stock but, in the end, knew they were still falling short.

Finley was quiet. She saw defeat on Marty's and Meadow's faces, and couldn't bear it. She had been so certain that with Marty's help, she could pull off a takeover. Now she knew that it was up to her alone, and she had to find a way. She might be putting her very life on the line. But she had no choice.

Forty-four

Mid-September

Caroline babbled incessantly on the beautiful fall day her mother and father drove her to college. September had cooled after the long, hot summer and Finley was happy to have time with David. Caroline was in the front seat as he drove, and Finley sat in back. As she watched the fall-hued countryside swirl by her window, she rehearsed the course of action she must take before the shareholders' meeting.

"Dad, are you sure you know the way?"

"Yes, Caroline, I definitely know the way. Once we get off Route 81, it's clearly marked. Plus I've got the GPS."

"I can't wait to get there and see our room. And I can't wait to see Bugsy. We're lucky to get a double. Lots of the kids I've talked to are in quads. I wish we'd gotten into a co-ed dorm, but we'll meet guys on campus at mixers and stuff."

He laughed. "Trust me, honey. You'll have no trouble meeting guys. You are the image of your mother. They'll swarm you."

His words broke through Finley's strategizing. So, he still found her attractive. Good—then why wouldn't he return her calls and requests for dinner? Much as she hated to say goodbye to Caroline, she looked forward to the ride back to Philadelphia to try to get some answers. After all she'd been through, she deserved clarity from David.

Bugsy was already in the room when they carted the first armfuls of things up the two flights of stairs. She greeted them. "Welcome to Chez Carobugs." She'd placed a sign naming the room over the door. The room was tiny, and Finley wondered where they'd put the carload of linens, the

TV, the computer and all Caroline's clothes. They would never fit.

Once the last load had been carried up the steps, Caroline turned to her parents. "Well, folks, guess you guys can take off."

"But honey, don't you want us to help you arrange things and, you know, hook up the computer and make your bed?"

"Nope, Mom. We want to do it on our own. Bugsy and I discussed it last week and decided it's best to cut the cord quick and clean. Her parents are already gone."

Finley looked at David. He shrugged his shoulders. "Sure you don't need any help, honey?" he asked.

Caroline shook her head in the way that both of them knew was final.

~ * ~

Finley began to cry softly as they started the drive back to Philadelphia. David reached over and took her hand. "It's okay, babe. Understandable, your baby bird has flown the nest, and it hurts. Makes me sad, too."

His hand felt strong and warm and she covered it with her other hand. "This feels so final. I know she'll be home for holidays and the summer. But this really is the beginning of her new life, isn't it?"

"Sure is. I know once I left for college, home was never home again for me. How about you?"

"Well, considering my mother, home was never home anyway, so I have no point of comparison. My life started when I left her."

"That I understand. Marion is a pretty cold fish."

"Yes, she is." *And I'm not.* Finley turned her body toward him. "David, why won't you give us a chance? I've changed. I have a battle to fight next month at corporate, but I hope I'll win it. Then I can write my own ticket. A ticket that includes you." There, she'd said it. She held her breath waiting for his reply.

He took his hand away. His jaw tensed. "When you took off for New York that Monday to negotiate your stock package, I gave up, Finn. Frankly, I was surprised at your guts. I see you as a big player in Prescott

Broadcasting. How's that going to give you time for me?"

"By demanding that time. I'll have the leverage to do that soon."

"Why don't I believe you, I wonder? Experience, I guess. I know you well. When the first big story comes along, you'll be off chasing it. And I won't matter. Sky's the limit for you, baby. Follow your bliss—but I don't think that bliss can include me."

"You don't love me anymore?"

"Did I say that?"

"No, but..."

"Loving a woman who's tied to a rocket ship of success won't work for me. That's final, Finley."

When they arrived at her house, she said, "Would you like a cup of coffee?"

"No thanks," he said and drove away.

Forty-five

October

Finley scoured through her desk until she found the old Rolodex. She hadn't called Regina Prescott Montgomery in years. In fact, she didn't remember that she had ever called Regina, but she knew she had her number somewhere.

She turned the pages to "M". Nothing there. Hmmm—oh, that's right—Regina never changed her name. She would still be under "P".

The voice was cultured, but distant and a bit wary. "Yes, I know who you are, Finley. I hear through the grapevine you're trying to put the governor out of office. Not a bad idea, but I can't imagine what you could want with me."

"Mrs. Prescott," Finley began.

"You may call me Regina."

Thank you. I have an important reason for calling."

"All right. What is it?"

"I'd rather not talk about it over the phone. Not to sound crazy, but my phone may be bugged. For all I know, yours might be, too."

Regina Prescott's laugh was an amused tinkling. "Oh my, how clandestine you sound. That's funny."

"Regina, things are happening that are in no way funny. That's why I need to see you."

Finley heard pages turning. What was Regina doing? Perhaps checking her appointment book?

Finley continued, "If this matter weren't so important, I wouldn't bother you."

Again, the bell-like chuckle. "I never doubted the matter's importance. You do not impress me as a trivial woman."

"Thank you."

"I've been looking in my appointment book and have some time next Thursday morning before the shareholders' meeting. You'll probably be in the city anyway that day. Would eleven work for you?"

"Yes, Regina. I will be in New York, and eleven is perfect. Thank you so much. Are you still on Park Avenue?"

"Oh no—I moved from there after Austin and I divorced. I'm in the East Village now." The chuckle turned bitter. "I wanted to get as far away from him as I could and still be in the city. I'm at five twenty-two Cornelia Street. Just take a taxi from the train station, all right?"

When she hung up, Finley stood and stretched her arms to the ceiling. Her neck had tightened and nerves threatened to take that tightness up to her head. She didn't want a headache now. There was too much to do. She inhaled slowly through her nose and held the breath, focusing it up into her forehead. As she exhaled the breath, the stars that had been forming behind her closed eyes faded into mists of spider webs. Relieved, she repeated the stretching and breathing exercise. I'm all right, she thought. I can do this. I can do whatever I have to do.

When Finley had relaxed from the call, she called Marty's number. After the first ring, though, she disconnected the call. No reason to get his hopes up.

Forty-six

The brownstone on Cornelia Street was elegant. *No wonder Regina lives here*, she thought. Stylish women perused menus in the windows of trendy restaurants lining the street. At any other time, Finley would have been interested in those menus, too. But not today. Breakfast had been coffee and a bagel on the train, and the food had settled like cement in her stomach as she anticipated this meeting.

She took one last breath and ascended the steps. When she rang the doorbell, chimes pealed through the carved wooden door. Finley looked through sheer curtains drawn back from sparkling windows and straightened her shoulders.

The door opened. A middle-aged woman in a blue dress stood there smiling. "Are you Ms. Smith?" she asked.

Finley nodded and extended her hand. "Yes, Finley. Finley Smith."

"I'm Priscilla—Regina's personal assistant."

The woman took her hand and led her in through the door. Finley looked around the foyer of the East Village town home of Regina Prescott. A thick Persian rug covered the dark mahogany floor. The weaving was worn just enough to testify to origins more than a century earlier. A wooden staircase spiraled out of the foyer to upstairs. The walls gleamed with muted silk wallpaper. A small chandelier hung from the second story down into the hall. It tinkled softly as the door closed. *Murano*, Finley thought. *Nothing else could have such delicate prisms*. They sparkled like diamonds and reflected lights across the walls of the foyer.

"Ms. Prescott is in the study," the woman said. "I'll take you there.

Tea has been prepared."

They passed a beautifully-appointed living room, a brick-walled kitchen gleaming with copper, and continued toward the back of the house. The woman paused before a closed wooden door and tapped lightly. "Regina, your guest is here."

A voice answered. "Show her in, Priscilla."

When the door opened, Finley was surprised to see a small room circled by book shelves. It was unlike the rest of the house—less elegant, warmer. As Finley stepped into the cozy space, she relaxed. *No one who inhabited this room could be as intimidating as Regina Prescott sounded on the phone. Austin would hate it.*

Regina rose from the velvet loveseat and gestured to the chair opposite it. She was as stately as Finley remembered: nearly six feet tall with silver hair pulled loosely into a chignon. Her trousers were linen, the color of flax. The sleeveless sweater exactly matched the emerald of her eyes. The heavy gold jewelry was simple and expensive. Finley wondered, as she had each time, she saw Regina, what such a magnificent woman could possibly have found appealing about Austin Montgomery.

The teapot on the coffee table was ceramic and the color of sunshine. Matching cups and saucers encircled it. Priscilla brought a plate of tea cakes from a side table and placed them next to linen napkins. "Shall I pour?" she asked.

"Yes, thank you," Finley said.

Lemon slices, sugar and cream were offered and the cakes passed.

"How is your husband, Finley? I believe his name was David."

"You have a good memory."

"Yes, I remember meeting him at a meeting in The Bahamas— charming man."

"Yes, he was—is a charming man. Unfortunately, we're now divorced."

"I'm sorry to hear that."

"So am I. It was my fault—I neglected him because of my career. He was right to leave me."

"Is there a chance he'll change his mind?"

"I doubt it, but I intend to try. We took our daughter to college last month. I haven't seen him since."

"I wish you well with him. Men like that are hard to find. My first husband was that kind—a real gentleman." Her eyes were sad as she sipped her tea. When she put it down, she said, "Perhaps it's time for you to tell me the purpose of this visit."

"Yes, Mrs. Prescott. It is time."

"Regina, please."

Finley placed her cup on the saucer, crossed her ankles and leaned forward. "Regina, I need your help to save Prescott Broadcasting."

Regina laughed softly. "Now, isn't that a bit dramatic? Save Prescott Broadcasting? At the last board meeting, reports indicated the company is doing very well."

"Who prepared those reports?" Finley asked.

Regina looked surprised. "Well, I don't know exactly. I suppose Austin did."

"Did the reports indicate any interest from the FCC about the company's association with Governor Morgan?"

Regina put down her cup. "The FCC?"

"Yes. Rumor has it they're taking a long, hard look at the company. I learned just yesterday that an aide from the governor's office sent an anonymous report to the feds. It implies that the governor's taken bribes from corporations in return for favored status on bids. WABN is mentioned as the TV station where some of that money has been funneled in return for soft reporting."

Regina squeezed lemon into her tea and raised her eyes. "Is there more?"

"Sylvia Reynolds, our general manager, has gone missing for nearly a month," Finley said.

"She has? I didn't know."

"Yes, and the circumstances associated with the night she disappeared are suspicious," Finley continued. "Not to alarm you unduly, but I have reason to suspect that she may have been the victim of a mob hit." Finley straightened. "And that I was the intended target."

"Go on."

"I met Austin for dinner at an Italian restaurant in Philadelphia. It was at his request. Our conversation became extremely argumentative. He actually called me the 'c' word."

"Surprise, surprise," Regina Prescott said.

"Excuse me?" Finley said.

"Conversations with Austin often seem to end that way. He used that word for me many times during our marriage. He's a pig, you know."

Finley nodded and continued. "There was a woman at the bar that night. I didn't get a look at her, but Tony Carlucci, the owner of the restaurant, says that she resembled pictures of Sylvia he saw in the papers. She left just before I did. I would have been the one out that door except that I stopped to apologize to Tony for Austin's rudeness."

Regina smiled. "You took Austin to an Italian restaurant? How amusing. He hates Italian food."

"He made that quite clear," Finley continued. "When I stopped to speak to Tony, I watched Austin punching numbers into a pay phone. He looked frantic. He covered the phone with his hand, but it was clear he was desperate."

"And you suspect?"

"I suspect that Austin called his mob connection and told them that I was on my way out of the restaurant—to grab me. But by stopping to apologize to Tony for Austin's rudeness, I ruined his plan. Sylvia left before me. I think that Sylvia may have—" Finley's words choked in her throat. She couldn't say them.

"You think that Austin's 'friends' may have grabbed the wrong woman?" Regina said.

"Exactly." Finley said.

"I'm not totally surprised at this," Regina said. "I left Austin to guard my money. He's in debt up to his neck. He just can't stay away from the roulette tables in Atlantic City. That could account for your suspicion."

Finley relaxed, nearly causing her to tip her tea cup. She steadied it and continued. "Tony Carlucci has informed the police in Philadelphia about what he saw that night."

"I see."

"Regina," Finley said. "I need to ask. Why did your father let the company fall into Austin's hands?"

"Oh, Dad was approaching eighty. He was tired, trusted my judgment in choosing a husband." She laughed bitterly. "Austin fooled us both. His resume looked marvelous. Educated at Princeton, jobs in Big Pharma. Dad and I were completely taken in by him. My first husband had died two years earlier. I was lonely." She looked deep into her tea cup. "It was the biggest mistake I ever made."

"Are you interested in fixing that mistake?" Finley said.

Regina looked up, green eyes staring into Finley's. "You want my stock. Is that it?"

Startled at her direct question, Finley paused. "Yes, I imagine that you have enough to put us in a controlling situation. You need to do this for your father and for yourself. WABN will lose their license if the FCC learns the extent of Austin's graft. You do have a large share of the stock, don't you?"

"Oh, my dear, of course I do. Besides what my father has set aside for me, there's what I got when Austin and I divorced."

Finley nodded. Of course, she remembered.

"You must have read the stories. They were plastered over every television trade journal. One of the reasons they were so juicy was that I refused alimony in lieu of Prescott stock. My financial adviser tells me I have thirty-eight per cent of all the outstanding shares."

Forty-six

October, the Shareholders meeting

The street outside Prescott Broadcasting's headquarters was teeming with traffic as the cab pulled up to it. The October day was unseasonably warm and people were anxious to take advantage of the great city before winter grabbed her by the throat. Leaves crunched under Finley's feet. She looked up at the trees and saw some stubborn stalwarts still clinging to the branches as if bragging about their stunning crimson and yellow hues.

It reminded her of the fall day she had first met David, but she shoved the memory away. She hadn't heard from him since they took Caroline to school. His last words to her had put a funeral pall over her hopes of a life with him and, though it still hurt, she had no choice but to accept his decision.

Steeling her resolve, she stepped up onto the sidewalk where Marty Sax waited for her. "Okay, pal, this is it," she said to him.

"Sure is," he said. "Good luck, Finley. I'm sorry I couldn't deliver on the stock."

"That's okay. Plan B may just work out."

"Plan B? What's that?"

"You'll see." *All this time, I've depended on Marty to pull this off. Because I didn't trust myself enough. Those days are over.*

When they walked into the boardroom, Marty headed for the old man seated near the head of the big table. He pulled Finley with him. "John, good to see you."

"You, too, Marty. You don't change."

"You look good, John."

John Prescott dismissed the compliment with a wave of his hand. "Don't bullshit a bullshitter, Marty. I look exactly like what I am—a very old man." He turned to Finley. "Sorry for the language, Finley."

"Not to worry, Mr. Prescott. And I don't think you look old. I'd call it distinguished."

Finley excused herself and walked toward the large carafe of coffee on the side table. She nodded to Regina Prescott as she passed her chair. As she took a cup, a familiar smell assaulted her senses. It was cologne. Without turning her head, she said, "Hi Rick."

"How'd you know it was me, Finley?"

"Your cologne. I can always smell it a block away."

He took her words as a compliment. "Thanks, Finley. Yes, I've been complimented on it often. It's Fragonard."

"Hmmm, certainly distinctive."

He moved in closer. She hardly wanted to inhale. "Finn, any news on Sylvia?"

It was the first time he had mentioned Sylvia since their unproductive search of the apartment. *What a callous man he is. He was probably only asking so he'd have an answer in case someone asked him about Sylvia.*

"Nothing. I spoke to the missing person's unit yesterday. They are now implying this is a case that will not be solved.

"Mystifying," he said and walked away toward a redhead who was tugging at his sleeve.

Austin Montgomery entered the board room. He was smiling. Impeccable, as always. He hardly missed a beat when he saw Finley, just nodded cordially. She turned her head.

"Welcome everyone," he began. "All of you have coffee?"

Murmurs of assent buzzed around the room.

"Very well then, let's get started?"

Ten seats circled the conference table. All occupied. Twenty or thirty more chairs were arranged in a semi-circle around the room. Finley and Marty seated themselves. Marty put down his briefcase on the floor next to him. "That's a relief," he muttered to Finley. "This thing is heavy."

Austin spoke, "Well, fall is well under way. From the looks of advances, our prime schedule will deliver record ratings in the November Nielsen. The network has been promoting the new programs in billboards all over the country, and they appear to be winning their time periods in most cases."

Words of approval circulated through the room.

Austin flipped the switch in his hand and the sixty-inch wall screen came alive with the Prescott Broadcasting animated logo. Another flip o f the switch and the screen dissolved to a new one with two lines, one in red and one in yellow. "The yellow line represents year-to-date revenues for last year. The red line is year to date this year. As you can see, revenues are up for most of this year."

"Austin," said a grey-haired woman seated at the board table. "What happened in May? There, the revenue line slips below last year?"

Without taking a beat, Austin answered, "We replaced a long-time anchor at our flagship station, WABN. We anticipated a t emporary dip in revenues until the new anchor, Rick Stone, catches hold in the market. " He turned, "Rick, stand up, won't you?"

Rick stood, smiling, and waved confidently to the board. "Overnights look good now, folks. Just a temporary glitch. Happens all the time. Right, Finley?"

Finley didn't respond.

Austin spoke again, "The pretty lady in the red suit is Finley Smith, news director at WABN. She's a crackerjack, and I'm certain we can count on her to bring those ratings back in line, right, Finley?"

"Actually," Finley stood and approached the large screen. "If you look at the marked pitch upward right here," she pointed to the sharp incline in the red line. "You'll see the results of one of my reporter's investigations into the graft suspected in the Pennsylvania governor's office. During a series we ran on Governor Morgan's association with a company called Cavaleri Construction, our ratings went through the roof. Local advertisers jumped all over our news, although we lost some revenues from HMOs and pharmaceuticals."

"Why would you lose money from those industries?" the grey-haired woman asked.

Finley crossed her arms. "Perhaps Mr. Montgomery would like to answer that question, ma'am."

For the first time, Austin's confident face began to shine with the beginnings of perspiration. "Spending was down all over the country for insurance and pharmaceuticals during that period. It wasn't just WABN."

Marty stood, "Excuse me, Austin. No disrespect intended, but I happen to have Nielsen's report on industry spending on stations nationwide for that period of time." He opened the book in his hand. "Here's what it says, 'Insurance and pharmaceutical companies continued to spend record amounts on television during the summer and fall seasons. With automobile advertising down, these two industries kept TV revenues steady across the nation.'" He snapped the Nielsen report closed.

The grey-haired woman and the other board members stared at Austin, waiting for an explanation that did not come.

"I have every confidence that WABN will bounce back to the top of the ratings chart once the November book comes out. We'll have advances on that in two weeks," Austin said. "This is nothing to worry about, and I suggest we move on now. New business, anyone?"

Finley remained standing. "Mr. Sax has a proposal he would like to present to the board."

Austin looked startled but recovered quickly. "Very well."

Marty got to his feet. "Because of irregularities coming from our corporate offices, I move that Austin Montgomery be replaced as chairman of Prescott Broadcasting."

Austin's face turned ashen under the tan. "Irregularities?"

"Yes sir," Marty continued. "Our news department uncovered stories of graft in the Governor's office. You, sir, did everything in your power to keep them off the news. Do you deny that?"

"Absolutely. Of course, I deny that. You have no proof of such a thing." He laughed at Marty's allegation.

"Actually, we do," Finley interjected. "Phone calls, letters, and a man named Tony Carlucci's account of the conversation between Austin and me at his restaurant."

Austin looked incredulous. "That's ridiculous. Some greasy spoon Italian waiter gossiping about what he overheard in a restaurant. Who'd believe that?"

"The Philadelphia police department believes it, Austin," Finley continued. "And they think that the woman Tony saw leave his restaurant that night might be Sylvia Reynolds who, as you know, has been missing for six weeks and is now presumed dead."

Austin smacked his hands down on the boardroom table. "Can you believe this?" His voice rose to manic pitch. "Have you ever heard such crackpot accusations?" He began to laugh and looked around the table. "They're asking you to trust an Italian waiter in Philadelphia over me." He scanned the faces of the shareholders obviously hoping for looks of affirmation. Finley saw only confusion.

Marty's calm voice spoke again. "For a second time, I move that Austin Montgomery be removed as chairman of Prescott Broadcasting."

"How dare you, Mr. Sax?" Austin sneered. "You're an over-the-hill salesman at a television station. I know you have stock in this corporation, but not even close to enough to pull off getting rid of me."

"You're absolutely right, Austin," Finley said quietly. "Even with the stock I negotiated in what you thought was my agreement to squelch the stories on Morgan, we came up short. Combining all our certificates, we did not have majority control."

"Well then, I guess it's time we adjourn," Austin said.

"Not quite," Regina Prescott said from her seat at the table.

Forty-eight

Regina stood. Every head in the conference room swiveled to watch as her narrow right hand reached into the large Birkin purse on the floor by her feet. She retrieved a sheath of papers and put them on the conference table in front of her. She fanned the papers, scanning them carefully. When she seemed satisfied, she lifted them, put them under her arm and carried them to the place in front of Marty Sax where the stock certificates lay on the table.

Austin stared at his ex-wife, hatred and fear blazing his eyes. She smiled, then took her papers and laid them gently on top of Marty's. "There, Mr. Sax. That should do it." She turned back to look at Austin once again, then returned to her chair.

The room fell deadly still as each person watched Austin, waiting to see what his reaction would be. He didn't speak.

"There's one more thing," Finley said. She stood and walked to the door of the conference room, opened it, and said, "Come in, please."

When the tall, brown-haired man entered the room, murmurs of confusion emanated around it. Finley said, "I'd like to introduce James Browning from the FCC. He has a few questions for you, Austin."

Austin reddened, then sputtered out the words, "You can't prove a thing, Finley. All you have is hearsay and you know it."

"On the contrary, Austin. I saved our phone conversations and your letters." She picked up a paper from in front of her. "And this is a signed testimonial from Tony Carlucci about what he heard in his restaurant. You remember Tony, the one you insulted?"

"You say I insulted the man, Finley? Then why should anyone believe what he swears to. Obviously, he has an axe to grind."

"Your problem, Austin, is that you underestimate people—especially people like Tony. He's highly respected in the city of Philadelphia, and the police department there found his statement completely credible."

"I do not believe that a waiter—or your recorded phone calls are enough to incriminate me." He stood as if to leave. "This is ridiculous and insulting. I'll tender my resignation as chairman, effective now. But I still say you have nothing to incriminate me."

"Again, Austin," Finley stopped him. "You underestimate people. You really need to work on that. You'll have plenty of time." She reached into her briefcase and pulled out a small tape. "You forget that a good reporter is always prepared for the big interview. And I'm a very good reporter. I never go anywhere without my tape recorder. I had it with me that night when you ordered me to stop the investigation on the governor." She held up the tape.

James Browning approached Austin. "Mr. Montgomery, we have reports leaked directly from one of the governor's aides. You will need to come to Washington with me now. The Federal Communications Department has questions for you. I suggest you call your lawyer and ask him or her to accompany us."

Austin's face blanched. A tic started in the lid of his left eye. Suddenly, time and sound dissolved into slow motion. Austin stood as if to follow Browning out of the room. Then, he stopped, his face contorted. He stooped to pick up his briefcase. He retrieved a small revolver.

Men shrunk into their chairs. The grey-haired woman screamed and slapped her hand over her mouth. Hands gripped the leather of their arm rests. Finley watched, her eyes glazed with terror.

He pointed the gun at Regina. John Prescott gasped and tried to rise from his chair.

Before John could reach his daughter, Regina stood. She turned her back on Austin, then looked back over her shoulder. "You don't have the courage, Austin. We both know that." Smiling, she started to leave the room.

Austin's eyes went wild.

Now I know what insanity looks like, Finley thought.

Before anyone could say another word, he put the gun into his mouth.

"Don't do it," someone screamed. James Browning ran to where Austin stood and lunged toward him, trying to tackle him. Before Browning hit, Austin pulled the trigger. The explosion resounded off the walls of the conference room in what seemed to be the same second those walls were covered over with bloodied white hair, bone fragments and brain matter.

Just before Austin's eyes clouded over and closed, Finley saw an expression of utter surprise.

His body lurched backward and jackknifed over the leather chair before landing on the floor in a pool of blood.

As screams rang through the conference room. Regina Prescott walked to where her father was standing and put her arms around him. "It's okay, Daddy. Now everything will be okay."

James Browning went into official mode. He ordered everyone to stay seated and called 911. "Please send an ambulance immediately to Prescott Broadcasting's headquarters on Madison. There's been a suicide. We won't touch the body until someone gets here." He hung up.

Finley sat stunned next to Marty, the tape still in her hand.

"He didn't know," she said dully. "I never pushed the record button."

Forty-nine

After the police placed the body on a gurney and took it away, they asked each person to adjourn to John's office to be interviewed individually. White-faced men and women followed the interrogator in a line from the conference room and sat, looking deadened, in chairs outside the office. Yellow tape marked it off as a crime scene and everyone was instructed to stay away from it until the investigation was completed.

John Prescott was the first to be questioned.

When he came out, he was shaking visibly and sat next to Regina and Finley.

"They asked me if I suspected Austin was of a suicidal nature. I told them I had no idea he was capable of such a thing but that I was becoming suspicious about his business dealings. I told them many people were. Austin had secrets in his life that he shared with no one." The old man shook his head. "His secrets would ultimately destroy my company."

Regina said, "I told them that I knew a bit about the men—the assignations he arranged with them. I told them it was never clear which were his gambling contacts and which were his, um, personal friends."

She turned to Finley. "I figured out his password at the bank when we were still married and routinely checked his account after the divorce." She shook her head in disbelief. "I couldn't believe he never changed that password. Anyway, there were big withdrawals and checks to casinos. Thank God we didn't share accounts. Some second sense warned me not to do that when I married him."

Her father put his arm around her. "Sweetheart, why didn't you tell me?"

"It was my decision to marry him, Daddy, and mine to divorce him.

I didn't want you worried about it. It was foolish that I kept the money problems from you, though, because they were going to impact the corporation. I had no idea how deeply, though." She sighed. "When Finley came along with the idea of taking the company away from him, I thought that would solve everything. I had no idea he'd do what he did."

Finley and Marty were waiting to be called into the room. "No, neither did I," Finley said. "It's awful it had to happen this way, but honestly, with the company he was keeping, I guess it was inevitable. We still don't know what happened to Sylvia, but if Austin owed money to the mob, he would have ended up the same way."

Marty clenched his fists. "This feels like some old movie or something. Not real. I never thought in my lifetime that I'd see anyone take his own life. I just can't wrap my head around what I saw." He took a deep breath. "Anyone we need to inform? Did he have family?"

"No one," Regina said. "Except for a dog and his housekeeper, Zee. We probably should call her and let her know he won't be coming home. She knows his lawyer's name and we should call there, too."

"Who wants to make that call?" John said.

No one spoke. The silence was unnerving.

"Very well, I'll do it," John said, pulling himself to his feet. He picked up the phone, dialed and waited for the connection. "Hello, is this Zee?"

He looked confused. "I can't understand her. She thinks I'm someone called Sal and keeps screaming at me in a foreign language. Here, Finley," he said, handing the phone to her.

Finley took it from his hands. "Zee?" She listened for a moment. "My name is Finley Smith. Austin was my boss, too. I'm here at his office."

She listened as the woman started telling her about the dog peeing on the rug and that Mr. Montgomery should come home early.

Finley interrupted, "Zee," she said, taking a deep breath. "There's been a terrible accident at Austin's office. We need to know the name and number of his lawyer. Can you help us?"

Again, she listened, then spoke. "Zee, I'm sorry to have to tell you this over the phone, but Austin has died."

Finley held the phone from her ear to escape the wailing that assailed her ear. Everyone in the room could hear it. It was accompanied by the sound of a dog barking loudly. Finally, the moaning calmed. Finley heard her say, "Shhhh, Genghis, hush. You'll be all right. I'll take care of you." The woman, clearly fighting to gain control, asked Finley to hold while she found the number of the lawyer. After giving it to her, she started to sob again and hung up.

"How strange," Finley quietly murmured to Marty. "Someone actually did cry for Austin. I would have bet against that."

Fifty

"How're you doing, champ?" Marty asked Finley as they careened past the lush Pennsylvania foliage on the train ride back to Philadelphia.

"Not sure. I feel numb. I think this would be called post-traumatic stress syndrome. The whole takeover thing wore me down, and then seeing what happened with Austin." She shivered.

Marty put his arm around her shoulders and started massaging her arm. "It's gonna be okay in time, Finley. You just need to take some time to get over this."

She felt him shudder beside her.

"Maybe I have some PTSD, too. Trying to pretend I didn't see what I did see, you know?"

She nodded.

They sat quietly together, huddled for warmth and comfort like soldiers in a foxhole.

"I can't go back to the station tomorrow," she said

"Yes, take a day or two off, Finn. God knows you deserve it."

"More than a couple of days. I must take enough time to assimilate all that's happened and try to figure out which way to go from here on out."

"I understand, Finley. God knows I understand."

She continued to stare silently out the window of the train, and then spoke. "John and Regina approached me about taking over as chairman."

He swiveled his body to face her. "That's wonderful. You'd be great in that position. Help the company heal from all the awful stuff Austin was doing."

"I didn't accept."

"Did you say no?"

"No, I just told them I needed time to work things out. They were kind."

"Just know that whenever you need a sounding board or a shoulder, I'll be there for you."

"Thanks, Marty. You'll be the first person I'll call. Or maybe second. I need to talk to Meadow."

"Does she know what happened today?"

"Yes, I called her while you were being questioned. She couldn't believe it. She'll be waiting at the train station."

"Good, just take your time, Finley. Take all the time you need. The healing will come."

"I suggested they appoint Meadow as general manager at WABN. They seemed agreeable to that."

"Good idea," Marty said.

"I also mentioned that I felt you would be invaluable as a kind of watchdog board member, and said you should be reimbursed for such a position with stock."

She turned and was happy to see him smile. "Good plan, Finley. Thank you. I'm going to be retiring within the year, and this'd give me something to do without the daily grind. What was their reaction?"

Finley squeezed his hand. "I'd say it's a done deal, Marty."

Finley saw Meadow as soon as she stepped down onto the platform. Meadow ran to them and opened her arms to hold both close to her. "My dear, dear friends."

Finley felt the steel of her spine begin to soften as she sobbed out the details of the story to Meadow. "Oh God, Meadow. It was so awful. There was blood everywhere and Austin just looked so surprised when he pulled that trigger."

"Let it out, Finn. Let go."

"But, Meadow, you don't know—I told him I had recorded our conversation that night. It was a lie. I lied to him and he killed himself over my lie. I'm responsible for his death."

"You were playing hard-ball. You had to play that way," Marty said. "You bluffed—not lied. There's a difference."

"How's there a difference?"

"Obviously, you haven't played much poker, have you?"

"Never."

"See—that's why you women keep hitting that glass ceiling. You weren't taught the rules of the game."

Meadow stepped back to study his face. "This is Marty the mensch, justifying lying?"

Marty looked exasperated. "Jesus, Meadow. I'm just trying to give you two a business lesson you need to learn. Men get it. Whether it's on a golf course, in a poker game or, sometimes, in a board room like this morning, a little bluffing is acceptable. Austin should have known that."

"Obviously, he didn't," Finley said, numbly.

"He was so damn guilty he couldn't think straight," Marty answered. "That's another part of the game—you don't do stuff that makes you really have to lie. Austin's whole life was a lie."

Finley shook her head. "Not a game I think I can learn."

Marty pulled her close for a hug. "Quite honestly, I don't want you to learn it. Maybe you women will figure out some new rules. Us guys are slow learners, but be patient with us. We'll get it eventually." He released her. "I'm going home. I need Barbara."

"I'm coming with you, Finley," Meadow said. "I'll spend the night and as long as you need me."

Finley looked into the worried face of her dearest friend and shook her head. "No. I need to be alone."

Meadow started to protest, but Finley continued, her voice stronger. "Really, Meadow. I know you love me like a sister and I feel the same about you, but this time I have to decompress alone."

~ * ~

Finley didn't leave her house for the next ten days, except to run to the grocery store or library. She answered no phone calls, except from Caroline and Meadow.

Nightmares woke her screaming each night at three o'clock. She'd jerk up from her pillow trembling as she saw his eyes, the bloody white hair, the bone fragments on the wall behind him. A sleep medication prescription helped some, but she still woke drenched in sweat and shaking with the memory.

To escape the nightmares, she bought a book on meditation and began practicing it each morning. Her times at peace lengthened until she could stay focused on something as simple as a number or vowel for half an hour. After these sessions, she always felt better—calmer and more in control.

One night, instead of the nightmare, she dreamed of something she had avoided thinking about her entire adult life—the death of her father. She could see her eight-year-old self as though in a movie and found herself admiring the pretty, spunky child her mother called "impossible." Now, unlike during the time she was really eight, Finley could realize that any child would be impossible for her mother. Her mother was a child herself— a social climbing, vain, immature female who saw the pretty eight-year-old as no more than competition.

It was her father who gave her any stability or love she knew as a child. A family-practice doctor with his office part of his home—he always had time for her, relished teaching her things and gloried in her every accomplishment, no matter how small.

While her mother lectured her about the need to be popular, her father stressed the importance of good grades and ethical behavior. "Be careful how you treat people on the way up, Finley. You're going to go places, girl. I can tell that already. Whatever you do, don't sell yourself just for money. Money comes and goes, but integrity lasts."

He'd hoped she'd be a writer. "Boy oh boy, Finley, this is good stuff," he'd said when she showed him her first poem. So, she wrote more poems and then stories about her dolls and a neighborhood dog she adored. Her mother wouldn't let a dog in the house, so Finley adopted Freckles who lived next door and pretended he belonged to her.

On her ninth birthday, she won an essay contest over every kid in her school. She ran home holding the certificate carefully, lest it might get wrinkled before he got to see it. She was so happy and so excited to show him that she didn't even stop for a quick swing on the playground with her friends.

She ran into his office and was surprised to find no patients in the waiting room. His nurse, Sarah, came out of the examining room and softly pulled the door closed behind her.

"Sarah, where's Daddy? I have to show him something. He's gonna be proud of me." Finley said, waving the certificate gaily in the air.

That's when Finley noticed that Sarah had red eyes.

"Honey, come sit with me. I need to tell you something. Your mother isn't here, and she said I should tell you."

"Tell me what?"

Sarah took Finley onto her lap in a way that made Finley uncomfortable. She was nine years old—too old to sit on a lap—especially her dad's nurse's lap. She wiggled around until she was seated on the couch next to Sarah.

"Where's Daddy, Sarah? I need to show him this. I won the school essay contest. He told me I could do it, and I did. Where is he?"

Sarah opened her mouth to speak and seemed unable to form words.

"Where is he?" Finley repeated, getting upset.

"He was just sitting there talking to a mother about her little boy. Nothing strenuous at all. And, honey, all of a sudden, he fell forward."

Finley began to understand what the nurse was telling her and started to scream, "But I need to show him my certificate. I need to see him."

Finley never saw her father again. Her mother felt it best though Finley begged to look at him one last time. She heard whispered terms like "aortic aneurism" and "only forty-seven years old" at the funeral but no one explained to her why she couldn't have seen him one last time.

Finley thought her mother enjoyed the funeral. She took great care in shopping for just the right black dress and pearls and clearly relished being the center of attention in the funeral home.

He wasn't buried like other dead people she'd heard about. He was cremated and his ashes sat in a fancy urn on the mantel of their house. One night, after her mother was asleep, Finley snuck down the stairs and took a chair to stand on. She opened the urn and shoved the tightly folded certificate into it, then replaced the cover. "See Daddy, you were right. I really can write."

When Finley wakened from the dream about her eight-year-old self, she felt a tremendous weight had been lifted from her. Her head was clear, and so was her conscience. For years, her mother had insinuated that Finley's poor behavior might have caused her father's death. But now, as a grown woman, Finley recognized that, in her father's eyes, she never did anything poorly. She shone like a goddess. If there was one relationship in her life around which she had no regrets, it was the one with her father.

That's when Finley began to heal from the trauma of the past two weeks. When she looked in the mirror, she saw a beautiful woman with healthy skin and a strong body and she acknowledged that, just as she hadn't caused her father's death, neither had she caused Austin Montgomery's.

Each time her phone rang, she was always disappointed the caller wasn't David. Surely, he must have heard about what happened in New York. She supposed he just didn't care anymore. And that bothered her because she felt that if David would give this new Finley a chance, he'd really like her.

She did yoga with tapes she'd found at the library and eventually, the tightness around her heart began to loosen. Novels, dusty from their long neglect on her bedside stand, were read. *Why did I stop reading? I always loved novels.* She cooked hearty meals of fish, steak and vegetables and devoured them hungrily as she watched the WABN news. A frozen berry pie was cooked and gone in two days. When Finley finally stepped on her bathroom scale, she was relieved and surprised to see her weight was down from before the New York trip.

One night after she flipped the remote for the news, the realization hit her. Emily was doing a great job. The thought pleased her even as it gnawed away at her self-esteem. *Everyone is replaceable*, she grumbled to no one but herself.

On the eighth day of her self-imposed exile, she settled in front of her television set with a glass of wine, a plate of grilled salmon and a Caesar salad. She took the first bite of the fish when Rick Stone came on the screen.

"Ladies and gentlemen, I have an announcement. I will be leaving WABN after this broadcast. While I've enjoyed my evenings with you, an opportunity has come up for me that I cannot pass up. I have accepted a position as press secretary to Republican Congressman Jonathan Marcus, and will begin to work from his Harrisburg office next week."

Finley choked. Marcus? He's a Jew—the only right-wing Jew Finley knew about. Oh my God, Rick must have been hard up to agree to work for Marcus.

When her phone rang, she checked the number and picked it up.

"Meadow," she said, hardly taking a breath. "Did you see the news?"

"Yes, isn't that a blast? That racist bastard is going to work for Marcus. Marty had told me that John Prescott gave him his walking papers right after the shareholders' meeting. He called me again this morning. They're having a going-away party for him and Marjorie. Let's go, Finn. We need to gloat."

Finley smiled. The time off had worked. She was ready for a party. "Wouldn't miss it for the world."

~ * ~

Finley drove up to the Hilton Hotel and gave her keys to the doorman. She took the ticket and tucked it into the tiny evening purse.

Winter was closing in on Philadelphia and Finley had pulled out a blue velvet cocktail dress to wear tonight. She made sure to choose something with a high neck. She couldn't bear the thought of Rick Stone ogling her cleavage. She wanted to have a good time and see her friends from the station.

Stephanie spotted her as soon as she walked into the grand ballroom. Stephanie's hug and scent were as wonderful as Finley remembered and it felt good to be back in her friend's arms.

"Didn't realize how much I've missed you, Stephanie. You look terrific and you smell even better."

"You, too, baby. Absolutely beautiful and more rested than I've seen you since before Sylvia came to town. Say hello to Anthony."

The huge man enveloped Finley in an embrace. Yes, it was good to be back.

Meadow and Ben were next. Arms entwined around each other's waists, they insisted she sit with them for dinner.

"Getting excited for the wedding?" she asked them.

"More than excited," Meadow exclaimed looking up at Ben with a grin.

These two are headed for forever, Finley thought. *But who knows? Everyone would have sworn David and I were, too*.

"There may be some surprises there for you."

"Surprises? What are you talking about?"

"If she told you, it wouldn't be a surprise any more, now would it?" Ben said, smiling and bending to kiss Finley's cheek.

She shook her head, puzzled. What kind of surprise could they have planned for her at their wedding?

As cocktails were served before the banquet, Finley basked in the warmth of old friends. It was good to be back with these people, the people who had been her co-workers for the past ten years. She felt the pain of what had happened in New York recede to the back of her soul. She had done what had to be done for these people, and they were worth it.

Chris Andrews whispered in her ear. "They asked me to come back, Finn, but shit, I don't want to do it. They love me at Blue Care. It's a sweetheart place to work and Joe Heaton is a great guy."

"I don't blame you, Chris. It's great you made the break when you did." Made the break. Is that what she should do as well? Is this her time?

Surprised, you saw Regina Prescott walking toward her. "Finley, wonderful to see you again."

"Delighted to see you again, too, Regina. Didn't realize you knew Rick."

"I don't, really. But my father and I have agreed that I'll take a more active place in the company from now on. This seemed a good place to start. Plus, I wanted to see you."

"Thank you, Regina. I am so happy to hear you're going to be involved in Prescott. I always believed you had more talent than Austin." She bowed her head. "God rest his soul." Then she looked up and laughed. "Seriously, you'll be a great addition."

"Thank you. I hope you're right. Daddy wanted me to ask you if you've considered our offer of chairmanship."

Finley had thought about the offer often during her retreat into herself. It was everything she had worked for and more. It would mean a move to New York but, with Caroline out of the house, that wasn't out of the question. The power to run an ethical news in three markets was enticing. But how important was it in her present scheme of life?

"I'm sorry, Regina, but I haven't decided yet. It's not right to hold this up for you and John, but I'm just not ready to make the commitment yet. Can you give me a little more time?"

Regina's kind smile told her all she needed to know. "Of course, we understand. All the work you did on the takeover and then to wat ch what Austin did? Your mind must still be a jumble."

Finley nodded gratefully. "I promise you a decision by mid-December. Is that okay?"

"That's perfectly okay, Finley. I'll tell my father."

As Regina walked away, Finley smelled the familiar scent and without turning said, "Hi Rick."

He laughed. "Nice you remember, Finn. Must have made quite an impression on you during our time together, right?"

"Quite an impression." *If only he knew.*

"So, what do you think about my new job?"

"I think you'll be perfect for it." He had no idea this was not a compliment.

"Yeah, well I just couldn't pass it up, y'know. I'm hoping it'll be a gateway into a political career of my own."

Oh my God. What a frightening prospect. Rick Stone as a right-wing Senator or Congressman. And he's just slick enough to pull it off.

"You know," he continued moving and leaning in conspiratorially. "I'll be just down the road in Harrisburg. Maybe we can get together once in a while. I'm sure we'll both be spending time in New York. It'd be fun to catch up." He put his hand on Finley's shoulder, and she cringed away.

Just then, Marjorie Stone appeared at his side. "Hello, Finley. Good to see you."

"You, too, Marge. Found a house in Harrisburg yet?"

Finley watched as the woman looked up at her husband. For the first time, the look was not one of adoration. "Yes, but it's not like our place here in Philly. It's a kind of blue-collar town, you know?"

Finley nodded. "I'm sure you'll love it once you get acquainted."

"I certainly hope so."

When Marjorie left to say hello to Regina Prescott, Finley turned back to Rick. "We won't be getting together, Rick. I know about you and Sylvia. I saw you go in her room that night in New York. And frankly, your lack of concern over her disappearance clarifies for me what I already suspected—that you're the kind of person I never want to lay eyes on again." She smiled up at him. "Good luck now."

He sputtered something about, "You are mistaken. I was never in her room."

Finley turned and walked away. *Liar.*

At dinner, Finley sat between Meadow and Marty, and each time an accolade for Rick came from the dais, Marty nudged her with his elbow, and Meadow hit her with her knee. "Quit it, you two, I'll be black and blue by the time this joke is over."

"When are you coming back to the station, Finley?" Emily Sanders asked Finley put on her coat to leave.

"I'm trying to decide that, Emily. I've been offered a position in New York, but I'm not sure I'll take it. I will say this—you seem to be doing just fine without me. It even makes me jealous."

"I was taught by the master, Finley. You're my hero, you know."

Finley was touched by the sincerity in Emily's voice. "Thank you. I can't say how much that means to me. Watching the news go on without me, smooth as silk, I have wondered if I was needed at all."

"You'll always be needed by me. If you decide to step away from WABN, I'll understand. But I hope and pray you'll always be a phone call away for me."

The two women gazed deep into each other's eyes. "I always will, Emily. That's a promise."

When Finley arrived at home, flushed from the warmth of her friends' welcome, she checked her mail basket for the first time since Austin's suicide.

Over one hundred letters. The number astounded and dismayed her and the customary discipline forced her to begin to answer them. Finley used to pride herself on answering every letter within one business day, and now they had piled in like this without even a look or regret.

She scanned them, trashing the obvious junk mail which made up the bulk of the pile. She looked for one from David but, sadly, realized she didn't see his name. There were political entreaties for cash, catalogues trying to sell her furniture she didn't need, even a cure for erectile dysfunction. The last one forced a grin to Finley's face. They really should check their target a bit better.

As she neared the bottom of the basket, she saw the return address for *Time Magazine*. *Don't they know I already subscribe?* Finley wondered as she clicked it onto the screen.

It was not a solicitation or even a survey. It was a letter from Matt Parker, managing editor, requesting a meeting. *Hmmm,* she thought. *What could Matt want with me?* They had met at trade conferences, and he seemed a cordial, intelligent guy. He had impressed her with his casual humor and lack of pretense—especially for a man in a position of such importance.

When she responded, she apologized for the lateness of her reply and said she'd be happy to meet with him any time. Her schedule was clear. She took it to the mailbox and forgot about it.

Five days later, he wrote again asking her to come to the city the following week.

Fifty-one

Last week in November

Finley studied the elevator roster of the gorgeous Rockefeller Center building until she found what she was looking for. *Time/Life* offices.

Just before the elevator door closed, a man rushed on to it. She recognized Joe Klein. "Mr. Klein, excuse me, my name is Finley Smith. I just want to tell you how much I enjoy your columns. I never miss one."

"Thanks, Finley. I know your name from somewhere," he rubbed his chin trying to remember.

"WABN-TV in Philadelphia?"

A light went on in his eyes. "Of course, weren't you the news director who blew the whistle on Morgan?"

She nodded.

"Great job," he said extending his hand.

Matt Parker's office was as unassuming as the man himself. His desk was cluttered with papers and pictures of a smiling wife and children. Matt's shirt sleeves were rolled up to his elbows. He smiled as he uncoiled his lanky frame to greet her.

"Finley, great to see you. Have a seat."

"Thanks, Matt. It's been a while. How's Diane?"

"Good. Asked me to give you her best."

Finley was beginning to feel uncomfortable. Here she was sitting in the office of the managing editor of *Time Magazine* and hadn't a clue as to why she was here.

"Why did you ask for this meeting, Matt?"

He paused only momentarily. "To offer you a job." The statement was as simple as it was earthshaking.

Finley was stunned into silence. She had written for a small, regional magazine in Philadelphia before starting out in television and loved the work. But she had never considered getting involved in a magazine the size and scope of *Time*.

"You look surprised and that surprises me. You're an excellent writer, and that's what *Time* looks for. I've read your pieces through the years."

Finley felt her heart expand in her chest at his compliment. He'd read her work.

"Look," he continued. "I've heard about what happened at the Prescott shareholders' meeting. My condolences, by the way."

Finley nodded, still shocked to silence.

"I've always admired your work. Even when you wrote for that monthly before you started in TV. I thought of trying to lure you away from Prescott in the past but didn't think the timing was right. I'm hoping it might be now."

"Forgive my shock, Matt. I didn't anticipate this—haven't even considered writing for *Time*. But, my God, what an honor."

"Well, sometimes a change of pace is just the ticket, you know? I started out as a sports writer in Columbus. You just never know what's going to open up."

A writer, Finley thought. Writing was always her first love—even before she got into television. As a reporter, she'd insisted on writing her own stories and her editor never changed a word—unless he was scared of offending someone.

"Are you interested?" Matt asked.

"Tell me what you have in mind."

"We'd call it Finn's Final Word. It would be the last article in each issue. I'd want you to pick a topical issue from the preceding week and dig as deep into it as possible. Really look at it from every perspective and come up with your conclusion. No slants. Just pure news gathering with an intelligent summation. Interested?"

~ * ~

As her train raced back to Philadelphia, Finley's mind hurtled faster than the locomotive. The deal was sweet. A column a week on any subject that piqued her interest. Probably a leaning toward the political and never fluff issues. But not soft issues. Matters of importance—no fluff. Since he took over as publisher, Matt Parker had maintained the legend that was *Time Magazine* and had turned it into an even more relevant publication in today's troubled world. He would never accept what some editors expected from women columnists. He demanded substance and didn't have a chauvinistic bone in his body.

When she'd asked about a move to New York, Matt had said it wouldn't be mandatory. "You can write from anywhere. There may be occasional TV appearances on cable shows, especially during political seasons, and then you'd need to come to the city. Otherwise, stay in Philadelphia if you wish."

And the money was enough. Not as much as she'd earn as chairman of Prescott Broadcasting, but money had never been her motivating factor in making a career decision.

She'd told Matt she'd let him know within one week. She wanted time to sort things out and see how it all felt. But right now, right this minute, sitting on this train headed back to Philadelphia, it felt very, very good.

Fifty-two

December 15

Caroline had arrived the night before for winter break with one mission in mind. "Mom, I need a dress for Meadow's wedding. I have absolutely nothing to wear."

Though Caroline had plenty of suitable outfits, Finley grabbed onto the chance to take her daughter shopping. "Great—Wannamaker's, here we come."

She tried on dress after dress, all of them flattering. "I've put on five pounds, Mom. I'm a tank."

"You were skinny when you went to college. Now you're perfect. It's the freshman five. I put on ten pounds my freshman year. Just watch it from here on out."

Finally, she pulled a lavender sheath over her head and the deal was sealed. "Yep, Mom, this is it. I can wear it to formal parties at school, too, so it's not extravagant."

Finley checked the price tag. Two-hundred and seventy-five dollars. "Well, it's less than mine cost for the wedding, so okay, we'll splurge."

They gathered up their parcels and walked out onto the snowy Philadelphia streets looking for a place to have lunch.

"Mom, do you like sushi?"

"Yes, it's okay."

"Let's check out the Sushi Shack. It's right over there on the corner."

When they had settled into their booth and ordered their food and hot tea, Caroline got down to business. "I loved your article in *Time Magazine*, Mom. I'm kind of a celebrity on campus having a mom who's a famous writer."

"I'd hardly say 'famous.' I've only had one published so far. But I've got some great ideas for future weeks, so maybe your celebrityhood can continue."

Caroline put lemon into her tea. "Now that you're around so much, maybe you and Daddy can?" She didn't finish the statement.

More wasn't needed. Finley knew exactly what she was driving at.

"That was part of the reason I took the job, but he hasn't made any move to approach me, so I think he's not interested anymore."

"Bet he is. I know he isn't dating anyone."

"How do you know that?"

"I asked him, and you know him, he always tells the truth."

Finley smiled. "Yes, I know."

"Well, for what it's worth, I think you should make the call. It's nearly nineteen eighty-seven for heaven's sake. Women should be the aggressors these days."

"Is that right, Caroline? I haven't noticed you calling any boys—not that you need to. They seem to surround you constantly."

"If one of them didn't call me and I wanted to see him, I would make the move, trust me."

"I'll just bet you would."

Caroline was turning into a stunning young woman. Finley was proud of her good looks and, more so, of her good grades as a freshman. "Thanks for the compliment about the article, honey. I'm pretty proud of my terrific daughter, too."

"Well, let's go," Caroline said. "We've got to dress for the rehearsal dinner. And I want to look smashing. Meadow's son is pretty hot, don't you think? Should I call him Mikey?"

Fifty-three

December 16, late afternoon

Snow dusted the streets of Philadelphia, turning the city into a sparkling fairy tale. Holiday songs resounded through the stores and good cheer filled the air.

Still, Meadow Marx was a nervous wreck. "Oh my God, Finley, what am I doing? You know as well as I do that marriages don't last. What was I thinking?"

Finley watched as Meadow paced around the hotel room they'd rented to dress in for the wedding wearing nothing but a strapless bra, frilly panties and a garter pulled so high it nearly met her bikini wax. Everything was white, and Meadow would have been white, too, Finley was certain, were it not for the tanning booth she'd stood naked in the day before.

"Let's escape, Finn. I've got the tickets to Fiji. If we don't show up at the Temple, they'll figure things out pretty fast."

Finley lay back on the king-sized bed she'd shared with Meadow the night before. They'd had a last hurrah of a slumber party as single women. Emily had come, along with Stephanie and Jenny and even Caroline. Wine was served, with caviar, chocolate and popcorn. Finley was relieved when Caroline asked for a coke.

"You've got the jitters, Meadow. That's all. It's understandable, but you don't really want to go to Fiji with me. You want to go with Ben. Remember?"

"I hardly know him. You said that when we first started this thing. And you were right. I hardly know him."

"You do know him. And you love him. Just like your mother loves your dad and his folks love each other. Which, by the way, is terrific. Ben's parents fit in with yours like long-lost friends, and that nephew who's going to carry the ring is adorable."

Meadow flung herself onto the pillow next to Finley and laughed nervously. "Of course, I love him. That's never been a question. And, yeah, his family is great. I lucked out on them. I'm just not so sure I should be marrying him, or anyone else. I've got a station to manage, you know."

"And you're going to do a brilliant job at it, too. Everyone says so."

"How can you be so sure? Maybe I'll turn out as nasty as Sylvia. Oh, sorry. I shouldn't speak ill of the dead. You do think she's dead, don't you? Cause I'd have to kill her if she came back and wanted this job now."

"I think she's dead all right. And it still gives me the willies when I think it was supposed to be me."

"Now don't start thinking about that, Finley. Go meditate or something."

Finley giggled. "Ommmmm."

"Why can't you spiritually evolved freaks speak English?" Meadow said, starting to giggle herself.

A knock at the door silenced them instantly. "Who is it?" Meadow asked.

"It's your mother, that's who. Let me in."

Finley ran to the door and opened it. Arlene stood before her in a long periwinkle blue lace dress and full makeup. She looked beautiful, and the grey crew cut only enhanced her glamour.

"You should wear your hair that short always, Arlene—I mean even after it grows in."

"I just might. I never realized how much time I took blow drying until now. Wash and wear is the way to go." She walked to the bed. "Get up, Meadow. You only have ninety minutes and the hairdresser and makeup person are in the lobby waiting to come up here. Marla's in the hall." Marla was Ben's Mom.

"Oh, Mother," Meadow wailed. "I'm so scared."

"Well, get unscared—fast. And thanks for calling me mother. Ben's chomping at the bit."

"He is?" Meadow asked, her eyes turning starry.

"Yes, he says I was crazy to ask him not to see you for seven days before the ceremony. He hardly made it through one night." Arlene whacked her daughter on the frilly lace panties and said, "Move."

~ * ~

At Ben Freedman's apartment, his soon-to-be father-in-law adjusted the black bow tie over the white pleated shirt while his father, Bill, looked on. "There—that looks good, Ben. Those things are a pain in the butt to get right. I'd rather the clip-on variety myself."

"Yeah, well, Meadow insisted. And you should know better than anyone that when that woman insists, there's no changing her mind."

Stan shook his head. "Oh, yes. Absolutely. Meadow has always had a strong will. I'd say 'bull headed', but Arlene calls it a strong will. You're taking on quite a woman, Ben. Hope you know that."

Ben grinned and gave the tie one final tweak. "I can handle her."

"He can handle anything, Stan. Always could, even as a kid," Bill said.

"Even with her big new job?"

"Especially with her big new job. Now that's she's G.M., she needs a soft place to fall more than ever—and that's what I give her." He turned and looked deep into Stan's eyes. "That's what I'll always give her, Dad."

Stan's eyes misted. "I know that, son, and I can never tell you what that means to me and Arlene—to know that our girl will have the kind of love in her life that we've had together." His shoulders slumped. "I just hope I have my girl with me a lot longer."

"All her numbers look good, Stan. I watch them right along with her oncologist. I wish I could promise you a cure, but that isn't possible. I can promise you, though, that this remission looks like it's going to stick."

Stan straightened up. "And that's good enough—yes, good enough."

"Are you two finished with your girly stuff?" Bill asked. "If I'm not mistaken, we have a wedding in an hour and a half. Maybe we should get our rears in gear?"

Fifty-four

Evening, December 16

Temple Emmanuel glowed with the lights of candles as Finley entered its vestibule. It was to be a small wedding—Meadow and Ben wanted intimacy, a family-and-close-friends ceremony. The attendees were already assembled, sitting down near the front of the temple. There were approximately fifty people there, and Finley recognized many of them. Chris Andrews, Emily Sanders, Stephanie and her sister, Jenny, Marty and Barbara, of course, and a scattering of Marx and Freedman family members and—David. Finley couldn't believe her eyes. Meadow had not told her she had invited him, and when she looked at her, Meadow simply smiled and said, "I figured it'd be okay."

A violin and flute started to play "Always" which was the signal for the wedding party to assemble. Meadow had wanted "The Bridal March," but Ben told her he refused to have music by an anti-Semite like Wagner played at his wedding.

"He was Hitler's favorite composer, Meadow," he'd said when Finley feted them at a shower at her home a month before the wedding. So, "Always" was the selection. No one could complain about Irving Berlin.

The chuppah was set up on its four poles in front of the altar covered in white roses. When Meadow saw it, she cringed against Finley's side. "Oh God, it's official."

But then Ben joined the assembled people waiting to walk down the aisle. Finley felt Meadow relax, nearly melt against her side.

Finley heard him whisper, "You are beautiful, my love."

"Oh, yes," Meadow whispered to Finley. "That's right. I'd

forgotten how much I love him. It's fine."

The Rabbi walked to the front of the chuppah and Ben took Meadow's hand. Her parents stood beside her and Ben's next to him and they proceeded down the aisle toward the chuppah. chosen Meadow's son, Michael, as his best man. The somber young man followed his mother and grandparents down the aisle. Then, it was Finley's turn. She saw David turn and catch her eye. He smiled.

When they all arrived at the chuppah, Meadow took her parents' hands and circled the chuppah seven times. Finley had been surprised that she chose to honor this ancient tradition, but Meadow had embraced the rituals of her religion for this most important day of her life. It was her first Jewish wedding. When Meadow had married before, it was before a judge.

After the seven circles, Meadow joined Ben under the chuppah. The Rabbi began the ceremony of the vows and exchanging of rings and then gave them each a small glass of wine to drink. As Meadow lifted it to her lips, Finley was stunned at the adoration she saw in her friend's eyes as they looked up at Ben.

It was time for the ritual of the seven blessings. The parents each read a blessing, Meadow's son read one, and Finley read the final blessing.

The Rabbi read the Ketubah, the Jewish wedding contract, in Hebrew, and Ben and Meadow signed it.

A glass was placed on the floor in the center of the chuppah and after Ben smashed it with his foot, the temple resonated with cries of "Mazel Tov!"

Finley thought she had never seen a couple as jubilant as Meadow and Ben. Their faces were aglow with joy as they embraced and walked down the aisle to the waiting limousine.

Finley followed down the aisle, avoiding David's eyes.

~ * ~

"Beautiful ceremony, wasn't it?" Marty said as he poured Finley a glass of wine at Klancy's Kosher Kitchen.

"Nicest one I've ever seen," she agreed.

"They're nuts about each other."

"That's why it was so lovely, Marty. That's the secret to a great wedding."

Stephanie and Anthony came up and hugged Finley. "Wow, girl, you look amazing in that dress," Stephanie said.

"That's for sure," Anthony echoed, averting his eyes from Finley's neckline.

"How're things at WABN?" Finley asked.

"Good—almost as good as if you were still there. Emily's doing a great job as news director. By the way, she gives you all the credit, Finley. Says you taught her everything she knows."

"That's nice to hear," Finley said. "But she was a quick study. Sharp from the very beginning."

"Of course, with Meadow as G.M., there's never a dull minute around there. That girl has more ideas than an encyclopedia has stats."

"How's the new anchorman?" Finley asked. She had watched him on television and liked everything she saw. Nice looking, but real—craggy even—and obviously understanding everything he said. This guy was no news reader.

"Dynamite, I'd say," Stephanie confirmed her observations. "We get calls every day about how much people like him, most of them from young women. But, seriously, he's a really good guy. Treats everyone well."

"Good. I'm glad to hear that."

Arlene put her arm around Finley's waist. "Thank you for all your help on the wedding, sweetie. Meadow's so lucky to have you as her friend."

Barbara joined the two of them. "Just like you're lucky to have me, right, Arlene?"

Arlene laughed, "Right, Barbara." She turned to Finley. "If I didn't have this one to get me out of the house and away from Stan once in a while, I'm afraid I'd murder him. He treats me like I might break. I keep telling him I'm not fragile and to back off, but he just can't help himself."

Finley smiled. "I think that's called love, Arlene."

"Yes, I know, but you know, I need my space once in a while."

Finley understood perfectly. She had worried that working from her home on columns for the magazine might leave her lonely, feeling isolated. Nothing could be further from the truth. She enjoyed the autonomy, the freedom from panty hose and heels and the ability to write on any subject she chose. So far, her columns had been well received. There was even talk of a Pulitzer for the one she wrote on the genital mutilation of young women in Africa.

Suddenly, Ben appeared in their midst. "Arlene, you owe me a dance. You promised it the night Meadow and I got engaged. Remember?"

The circle was forming on the small dance floor and the music struck up the hora. Stan walked up to Finley. "Dance, Finley?" he said.

"I don't know how to do the hora, Stan," she said.

"It's easy—I'll teach you."

Suddenly, Finley found herself twirling around the floor and learning the intricate steps as though she had been born to the dance. The music informed her feet and she was able to pick up the progressions easily. It was fun and fast and breathtaking, and Finley realized she had never enjoyed a dance so much.

When she whirled to a stop, catching her breath, David stood before her, smiling.

"May I have a dance?" he said.

Her heart stopped. He looked so very handsome and tall and, she laughed at her next thought: *Hot.*

"What's funny, Finn?"

"Oh, just that I think Caroline is wearing off on me. I'm becoming absolutely adolescent in my thinking. But it's so much fun having her around now."

"Yes, it is. She's grown up a lot, hasn't she?"

Finley nodded. "David, now that I've caught my breath, I'd love a dance."

The orchestra started to play "For All We Know" and Finley slid effortlessly into David's arms. *We fit together as well as the first time he held me. He feels wonderful and smells better. His practice must be going well. This suit is soft as cashmere.*

"Nice dress, Finley," he said looking down at her appreciatively. He did not avert his eyes from her cleavage.

"Thanks. I love it. I got it the same day I bought that blue cashmere jumpsuit. Remember it?"

Did he blush? Maybe just a little. "I remember it well."

Fifty-five

December 16, midnight

When they pulled in front of the house, David asked if he could come in. She hesitated. All that time after Sylvia went missing, and he never contacted her. What did he want with her now?

But the anticipation of another lonely night won over reason, and she agreed.

As they settled in their customary places over cups of decaf, David said, "Finn, I've been thinking a lot about you lately. I think I made a mistake when I wouldn't give us another chance because you took that trip to New York."

Her face reddened with sudden anger. That seemed a thousand years ago. So much had happened to her since that train ride. She hardly felt like the same woman who had gone to the city, negotiated the stock deal and then bluffed Austin into desperation at the shareholders' meeting.

"David, so much water has gone under the bridge since then. Why the sudden change of heart?"

"When Caroline and I had dinner last week, she told me all the stuff you went through. I honestly didn't know. Had I understood that your very life was in jeopardy, I'd have been here." He shook his head sadly and she thought she detected tears in his eyes. "I'd have been here."

"I can hardly believe that. I thought everyone knew—about Sylvia's disappearance—that was supposed to be me, by the way. About that horrific board meeting. About my refusing the chairmanship of the company. I thought everybody knew—most especially you, David."

"After you took that trip to New York, I buried my head in my work,

Finn. Hardly picked up a newspaper. I was trying to escape you and everything you mean to me. When Caroline told me you had been in danger, I could have slit my wrists."

Was he telling the truth? Of course, he was. David didn't lie. He wasn't capable of deception. He really hadn't known.

"So, what are you saying, David?"

"Just that I want another chance. With you, for us. Is it too late?"

Finley sat silently staring into her cup. Should she take a chance on him again? Finally, she spoke. "I would have said it was too late. I was so hurt when you didn't call me after the board meeting, but now I'm so confused." Maybe he really didn't know.

He moved toward her on the loveseat and put his hands on her bare shoulders. "One chance, Finn?"

His hands on her skin reverberated with memories. His hands never failed to excite her. As they moved to her breasts, she stopped him. "Easy, David. Not so fast. I can't wrap my head around this. I'd given up on you."

He smiled that smile that always melted her heart. "That was a mistake, sweetheart."

She pulled away from him and stared deep into his eyes. Her mind was whirring with the realization that he still loved her. She knew she'd never stopped loving him. Her life was in better control now that she was writing from home, but what if she allowed herself to get consumed by a job again? Then she relaxed, knowing that would not happen because she would not make the same mistake twice.

She reached for his hand. "I'll give us one year to prove that we won't make the same mistakes as before," Finley said. "I need to prove it to myself, too. I couldn't bear losing you again."

"One year? Fine. That's fair. But could we begin that year tonight, my love?"

Fifty-six

One Year Later

Tony Carlucci set the bottle of wine on the table in front of the four of them. *"Buon appetito!"* he said. "This bottle's on the house. I'll be back to take your orders shortly."

Finley stood to embrace Tony before he left the table. "Thank you, Tony—for everything."

"Honest to God, Finn—it just keeps getting better," Meadow said, squeezing Ben's arm. "To get any happier, I'd have to be twins."

"Lord," Finley said feigning fear. "Please don't even think that. I can hardly handle one of you," A laugh teased the sides of her mouth. "How are things going with your mom?"

"So far, so good," Ben answered. "Her numbers remain good, so we have reason to think positive."

"How about Caroline and Mikey? They're still seeing each other. Oh, Finn, wouldn't it be great if they ended up together? Then we'd be in-laws."

"Yeah, and I couldn't hope for a better guy for Caroline than your son, but they're so young."

"You're going to Marty's retirement party next month, aren't you?" Meadow asked.

Finley nodded. "Wouldn't miss it for the world. It'll be good to see everyone at the station again. How's it going there?"

"Good," Meadow said. "Emily is doing a great job as news director. You trained her well. Though you know I'd rather it be you."

"Not going to happen, sweetie," Finley said. "I've done my TV time. Plus, I really love writing. Most of the time, I can do it from home, and the occasional trips to the city are fun. This works a lot better for my life now."

David slipped his arm around Finley. "We have some things to celebrate, too, guys," he said.

Ben jumped at the bait. "Like what?"

"Well, it's been a year—the year Finn made me wait and prove to her that we could make it stick this time." He turned to Finley. "So, what do you think, love? Did I make the cut?"

She nestled her head onto his shoulder. "Oh, I'd say you more than made the cut, Dr. Smith. I'd say you've made it clear that we can go the distance now. We both had to grow up a bit and I needed to get some priorities in order. I think I've done that now."

Meadow clapped her hands together. "So, we have a wedding coming up, do we? I'm the bridesmaid, right, Finn? Or I guess it's bridesmatron now that I'm an old married lady."

"Yes, Meadow. You'll stand by my side when I say my vows to this gorgeous man. We'll grow old and doddery together."

"Speak for yourself, Finn. Before I think about 'doddery,' I'll have an appointment at the best plastic surgeon in Philly," Meadow said.

Ben looked alarmed. "Not a chance, Meadow. I mean it. You look great and always will to me. I don't want a phony-looking broad as my wife."

"Just testing, love," Meadow said, kissing Ben on the cheek. "Just testing."

She picked up the bottle of wine. "So, what do you say? Shall we have a toast to forever?"

She poured the wine into David's and Ben's glasses, then tipped it over Finley's. Finley covered her glass with her hand. "None for me, thanks."

Meadow's eyes widened.

Finley looked up at David. His eyes crinkled, and he nodded his assent.

"You guessed it. I can tell by the look. Yes, I'm due in eight months. And we can't wait. With Caroline, I was so young and obsessed with a career that I almost felt she was an inconvenience." She turned to David. "Don't ever tell her I said that."

He shook his head.

"Oh, but this time, I'm so happy I could burst." Her eyes changed from sparkling to concerned as she turned to Ben. "Do you think my age could be a problem?"

Ben shook his head. "Probably not, Finn. Lots of women are putting off babies till they're your age. You can have a test later on if you're concerned."

"I don't think so. Even if there was a problem, I wouldn't do anything to end this pregnancy. So why bother, right?"

He nodded. "Well, we'll keep a close monitor on you anyway." He smacked his forehead. "Hey, here I am acting like your obstetrician. I'm sorry, Finn. I shouldn't have assumed anything like that."

Finn reached for his hand and squeezed. "Do you really think I'd trust this baby to anyone else? Of course you'll be my doctor. I'll call your office tomorrow for an appointment. I've taken three pregnancy tests, so I'm pretty sure you can't surprise me."

"Any idea if it's a boy or a girl?" Meadow asked, leaning across the table to kiss Finley on the cheek.

"No, not yet. And frankly, we don't care." Finley turned to David. "Whatever it is, this baby is a celebration of our second chance. I take it as God's sign that we're doing the right thing. I love it already."

"What about your work?" Meadow asked.

"I do most of that from home now anyway." She laughed softly. "Oh, forgot to tell you something else. Stephanie and Anthony are expecting at just about the same time. We've already talked and will share baby-sitting when the other needs it."

"By the way, love," Meadow said. "Plans are being drawn up to open a daycare center at WABN. We just can't afford to lose people when we've spent so much on training. I've had an extensive study done, and it'll end up saving us a ton of money in the long run."

David signaled to Tony. "Tony, could you bring a glass of pom and soda for Finley? And then, sit for a moment and share a toast with us."

Tony returned in minutes with Finley's drink. He sat down and accepted a glass of wine. "So, to what do we toast?" he said.

"To love, Tony, to love," Meadow said. "And to Finley and David's remarriage."

Tony stood. Finley saw a shimmer of tears in his eyes. "I am so happy to hear this. You two should never have parted," he said.

Finley said, "Tony, you make the toast."

"*Centi anni di salute e felicita*," he said.

"*Mazel Tov*," Meadow answered.

They clicked their glasses and drank.

About the Author

Before becoming a novelist, Jeanne Charters was Vice President of Marketing for Viacom Television and owner of Charters Marketing, an award-winning broadcast advertising agency. During her time in broadcast, she observed prevailing pressure on News Directors to slant the news to favor certain politicians and corporations. *Yellow* is meant as a cautionary tale about what can happen when greed and corruption invade the airways.

Also by the Author
at
Rogue Phoenix Press

Lace Curtain

Nellie is the daughter of Shanty-Irish parents, now risen to Lace Curtain middle class. Will Nellie possess the wisdom and perseverance of her mother, Mary Boland? Or will she succumb to sexual attraction and convention and wed a scoundrel?

Neo is the son of African slaves, now one of the richest black sons in America. Will Neo break free from the white supremacy mindset in America? Or die at the end of a rope?

Will a return to Ireland change the course of each of their lives?

Prologue

Shanty Gold—The Final Chapter

Boston, 1857

Sunlight streams through sparkling stained-glass windows and dances off flickering altar candles. The wooden pews gleam, and I'm glad I brought Shannon and Molly with me last night to polish them. The scent of wax from the wood and the vinegar we used on the windows meld with the ancient smell of incense. Truth be told, this fragrance is more pleasing to me than perfume.

As I wait in the vestibule for the organist to start the music, I yearn to see my Daniel. Every moment away from him is torture now and, even when we're together, I can't get enough of him. But when I get too close, my spine still stiffens in fear. Please, God, help me this night.

Kathleen's daughters, Shannon and Molly, look pretty as the Gainsborough oil painting we saw last year at the Boston Museum. Wearing their yellow Easter dresses with a single daisy peeping out from behind their left ears, they are beauties. Their wild-flower bouquets are tied with white ribbons that cascade down the front of their dresses.

My short veil is fastened to a wreath of daisies. When I turn my head, the veil brushes my shoulders, reminding me I am, indeed, about to become a bride this day.

I worried over wearing the white dress since some here have heard what happened to me on the ship, but when I mentioned this to Tommy, he shushed me. "What happened to you was rape, Mary, pure and simple. Besides, more non-virgins than virgins have marched down that aisle in white. I know all their secrets. They've poured stories over me bar for twenty years now." He laughed, then squared my shoulders toward his. "Let there be one word of criticism, and that person will have me to deal with." His words were a relief to me.

When the organ peals its first note, Daniel and Kam walk to the foot of the altar. They stand, flanking Father Ruzzo. I can scarcely tear my glance from Daniel. His navy suit nearly matches his eyes, which are devouring me from the altar. His look almost makes me blush. The white shirt we bought last week is stiff with starch. I've not seen the navy-blue cravat, and I wager from its perfection that Kam had a hand in tying it.

Kam's all in black, except for the white shirt that gleams against his mahogany skin. These two are, without a doubt, the handsomest men in Boston. My heart bursts with pride that soon, one of them will be my husband, and the other my forever brother.

Molly is the first to step on the long white runner, followed by Shannon. In the pews, heads turn and mouths murmur in appreciation.

My focus is so fastened on Daniel that I'm startled when Tommy takes my arm and says, "Let's go, Mary." His eyes are misty. I lean down to kiss him on the cheek. I know he misses Kathleen this day. I float down the aisle toward Daniel, never taking my gaze from him. When I see pomade in his hair. I grin, knowing that must have gone against his grain. Daniel is a man of reality—not artifice.

Father Ruzzo says, "Who gives this woman?" and Tommy and the girls whisper together, "We do." Tommy kisses me on the cheek and puts my hand into Daniel's.

Our Nuptial Mass begins. After the Kyrie and Gloria, it's time for our vows. "Daniel Kelly, will you take this woman to be your wife?"

"I will, Father." He squeezes my hand tight.

"Mary Boland, will you take this man to be your husband?"

"I will, Father." I squeeze back.

"Then, by the powers vested in me by the state of Massachusetts and by Almighty God, I now pronounce that Daniel Kelly and Mary Boland are husband and wife."

When Daniel gives me that first kiss as his wife, the entire congregation jumps to their feet and cheers. Ah, the Irish are such emotional saps, saints be praised.

~ * ~

Back at the pub, Tommy plays his fiddle while Shannon sings the old Irish song, *The Rose of Tralee*:

She was lovely and fair, as the rose of the summer. Yet 'twas not her beauty alone that won me. Oh no, 'twas the truth in her eyes ever dawning, that made me love Mary, the Rose of Tralee!

All of us know the legend behind the words of the song—how beautiful Mary O'Connor, a poor kitchen maid, caught the eye of William Pembroke Mulchenock, a wealthy land owner and poet. They fell in love, and he swore to marry her when he sailed back from his travels, only to find that she had died just prior to his return. Years later, he was buried at her side in Tralee.

The song, combined with a liberal drinking of spirits puts many at the party into a romantic mood. Couples sway on the tiny dance floor and their kisses grow more passionate. As the day fades toward evening, clouds and thunder roll in over Boston, adding mystery to the magical mood of the night.

Suddenly, a fiddle strikes up a reel, and Tommy yells, "A dance from the bride and groom before they take their leave."

Daniel takes me round the waist and says, "It's time to finish that dance you refused me St. Patrick's Day a few years back, Mrs. Kelly." He whirls me expertly around the floor as everyone claps and cheers from the sidelines.

"I'd forgotten you were such a dancer, Daniel," I exclaim.

"The best in my village."

"So was I, my love. So was I."

His eyes never leave mine as we dance and twirl, surrounded by our friends. When the dance is ended, he pulls me toward him for a deep, long kiss. The crowd cheers, but I can scarce hear them above the beating of my own heart.

It is time to say our farewells and to begin our life as husband and wife. Tommy's arms feel as though they never want to let go, but finally, they do. I stand before Kam and smile up into his eyes. He whispers, "Be happy, my sister," and kisses me on the cheek.

~ * ~

Daniel helps me into his wagon, hefts up my small chest and then brings the reins down on the horse's back. I look back at our friends outside O'Halloran's, their hands waving farewell.

The streets of South Boston are nearly deserted now, and I lay my head on his shoulder remembering back on our wonderful wedding day. But now I must think of the wedding night.

At our door, he asks me to stay in the wagon. Then, he hefts my chest up and out of the wagon and carries it in the front door. Returning, he helps me down from the wagon and lifts me into his arms as though I weigh no more than a tiny child. I bury my face in his warm neck, and he carries me into the house. When my feet touch down in our living room, a fire is lit in the hearth. The evening has turned chilly, and I welcome its warmth. "Who set the wood?" I ask.

"Kam. You didn't notice that he disappeared from the party?"

I shake my head.

"It was while we had our dance."

"Ah, of course. He would do that, wouldn't he?" Standing there with my new husband, I am assailed by confusion. What am I supposed to do now?

As if reading my mind, he says, "Mary, love. Why don't you go into the bedroom and make yourself more comfortable?" I feel my face redden, then scold myself. It's not as if I've never been touched by a man. That thought brings a stinging pain to my temples. *Stop it, Mary. This is Daniel. It'll be different.* But then, my breath catches, and the other voice says, *but will it?*

I close the door behind me to take off my wedding dress, then realize I can't reach the tiny buttons down its back. "Oh, shite."

At the sound of my voice, he's there behind me, his fingers slowly trailing down my spine. Halfway, he stops and lifts my hair and then lowers his lips to my neck. I shiver, and he chuckles and nips me lightly. I tremble but do not know if it's from excitement or terror. His mouth comes down now on the other side of my neck and suckles gently. The trembling goes to my toes. I've never felt this way. Is it normal? Sensations course from my neck to my breasts and then down to that place I've protected from any man since that awful time eight years past. These feelings frighten me to my very soul.

"All right, you're undone," he says, lifting his lips away from me. "Do you want me to wait in the other room?"

I nod, knowing my face blazes red as my hair.

A single candle flickers on the dresser. After removing the dress, shoes, stockings, and chemise, I stand naked and shivering in the center of the bedroom. I open the lid of the small chest, take out the white lace nightgown and slip it over my head. Then, I pull the pins from my hair and shake it free. Daniel's shaving mirror sits next to the candle, and when I look at myself, the image startles me. The gránna Mary Boland is gone. Mary Kelly looks like the Celtic goddess Da said I am. My hair blazes like fire and my cheeks glow pink with anticipation. I take a deep breath and open the door.

His gasp tells me all I need to know. "Oh Mary, I feel like the luckiest man in the world to have you for my wife. You are so beautiful." Tears rush to my eyes. He kisses them away as he takes me into his arms. "Come, *Mo chroi*, sit with me before the fire a bit."

There is no rushing, no roughness, no force. He is slow and gentle and so loving that I begin to respond to him—but only *begin*. Fear battles passion in my mind and body. When his hand brushes my breast, the tingle of pleasure becomes terror as Seamus's face flashes before my eyes.

He lifts me from the couch and carries me to our bed. As he lays me down gently, so gently, my trembling suddenly turns to deep, convulsive sobs. I try to stop them, but fear becomes a cavern that threatens to swallow me into it. Daniel rises up onto his elbows and looks into my eyes. "Easy, love." Then he kisses me and covers my body with Kathleen's quilt. He holds me there, whispering how much he loves me until I fall asleep.

Somewhere, in the core of the night, I waken and look at the man sleeping beside me. Moonlight falls on his bare shoulders. His full lips are parted and softly breathing. His lashes fall onto his cheeks and his face gleams in the light from our bedroom window. When images of Seamus or Jack flash above him, I look more closely. It is Daniel, my beautiful husband. The husband I adore and need to kiss right now.

When I lower my lips to his, his eyes open. "It's all right, Mary. I can wait."

"Ah but, Daniel, I don't think I can—not another moment."

I sleep barely a wink the rest of this night.

Chapter One
October 10, 1870

Boston Massachusetts

Sister Sarah reminds me of a penguin as she stands erasing the blackboard, all black and white and round. She's two big jiggly balls stacked on top of each other with a smaller one on top. Every bit of her is covered in black veils. When she turns around, the white wimple goes right up to her chin and down to her eyes and pinches. I wonder if it hurts. The worst of it? I know that underneath that top round veil, she's bald as an egg.

When Monsignor asks which girls in our class want to be Sisters, I never raise my hand. Sometimes, that gets me in trouble. Of one thing I'm certain, I will *never* let anyone shave my black hair off. It took too long to grow it this long.

"Nellie Kelly, stop daydreaming." Sister hollers.

"Yes, Sister," I answer, glad she can't read my thoughts.

My mother scolds me if I say bad things about Sister. She says I'm too smart to talk such skilamalink about poor Sister, but is it all right to think it? After all, I can't help what I think.

No question about it, Sister in her long, black habit, bobbing from foot to foot at the board, is the image of a penguin. Not that I've ever seen a real penguin, just pictures of them. Oh, and those penguins didn't have rosary beads wrapped around their middle. Sister must have two or three of them around her. One would never reach.

I can't let her catch me staring at her again, so I gaze down at my paper, pretending to pray to The Father, Son, and the Holy Ghost. Actually, I finished my quiz fifteen minutes ago. So here I sit, watching the clock and pretending to check my paper again while the other girls hunch over their tests like crows over dead rats.

Religion *is* dead in a way, especially its language, Latin. I loathe all the stuff about crucifixion and suffering and blood. The most boring part of being a Catholic is having to memorize all the prayers. And the Commandments. Nothing but rules, rules, rules. Wish the Church would come up with some new ideas. Perhaps I'm a terrible girl, thinking these thoughts, but I do think them. Don't tell Sister Sarah or Mother, though.

Hiding my face with my hand, I sneak my eyes over to the window. The sun glaring through the wavy panes sure doesn't warm things up much. They must be trying to save money on coal again.

My stomach rumbles, wanting lunch.

Hurry up, time. Hurry up. Hurry up.

At last, Sister glances at the round wall clock and clucks. She reaches under her desk to bring up the big copper bell and clangs it three times.

I shake my pen into the inkwell and wipe it on the rag in my desk. That black ink is impossible to remove if it gets under your fingernails. My mother made me soak my hands in a nasty mix of vinegar and ammonia last time that happened. You should have seen my fingers. For a week, they looked like the peeling varnish on the pews at church.

"Everyone, put on your shawls. It's chilly out." Sister declares.

It's pretty chilly in here, too. I can almost see my breath.

Brigid, Kate, and Lizbeth, the three first graders in the front of the classroom, stand and file out. Lizbeth pulls her shawl around her shoulders, then looks back at me and smiles, her big blue eyes shy yet mischievous. I cross my eyes and stick out my tongue at her. She laughs.

Lizbeth's my favorite and she knows it. If I had a little sister, I'd want her to be just like Lizbeth. I don't have a sister, and wish I did. I'd even take a brother.

The four second graders start out next, then the third, fourth, fifth, sixth, and seventh graders. The room empties so fast you'd think someone had set off the fire alarm. Finally, it's our turn. The eighth graders. After eight years in this one room, it's hard to believe I'll be leaving it come summer. In a way I'll miss St. Augustine's, but I do wish it was bigger. At Boys' Academy where all the rich Protestant boys go, every grade has its own classroom. Sean O'Halloran goes there, though I don't think he's rich. I can't understand that. Sean's as Catholic as I am.

"Just one minute, ladies," Sister pauses. "I've graded your arithmetic tests." She holds the papers up in the air and bustles back to us, turning sideways so as not to smack her wide hips on the desks. My stomach clenches a little. I need to keep my marks up so I can get into Girls High next year. Mother and Da are counting on me. Arithmetic is hard. I'm never sure how I did in it.

Sister's round face betrays no expression as she hands me my paper, but I spot the word '*EXCELLENT*' scrawled at the top. My one hundred percent is right under the A.M.D.G. we always print. Sister has explained it's Latin from St. Ignatius and means "For the greater honor and glory of God."

I catch a glimpse of the paper under mine. It's Fiona Doggett's and it's covered with red X-marks. *Oh, no.* Sister doesn't look up as she hands Fiona her paper. I shove my test into my book bag, hoping Fiona didn't see it. She'd be jealous, and a jealous Fiona is meaner than a cat hung on a clothesline in the rain. When Fiona's mad, her eyes narrow into slits of blazing red fire. She's scary. When Fiona's scary, all the store-bought dresses in the world can't turn her pretty, and she has most of them. Actually, Fiona's not very pretty even when she's happy.

Once out of the classroom, I race past the brown wood walls of the hallway and glance out the window to the St. Augustine Chapel graveyard.

My schoolmates have grandparents buried there. My father's parents are, too, but my mother's mother died in Ireland and her father's ashes disappeared somewhere. He was murdered by some old mobster here in Boston before I was born. We visit my father's parents' graves every Sunday after church.

Outside, cold air blasts my face like a slap of ice. My eyes water instantly. Before the tears freeze on my cheeks, I brush them away. Good heavens, it's frigid. Heavens, this is only October! What will February bring? I pull my shawl tight around my shoulders.

I run for the swing Father Ruzzo hung on the oak tree. Jumping on it, I start pumping right away. As I swing out from under the tree, the sun, a warming fire, hits my face. As I pump harder, the air pulls my hair into my mouth, but I spit it out. My breath pours out in a foggy mist as I soar higher and higher. The rope starts doing that topsy-stomach stall that happens just before flying back down.

Sister's yelled at me about swinging so high, but I can't stop doing it. How am I ever going to be a trapeze performer if I can't get used to heights? I'm still not sure if I want to be a teacher or fly on a trapeze in the circus. I lay back on the swing and extend my arms and legs out to the side, balancing perfectly. My skirt flutters above my knees, showing the lace on my pantalettes, but I don't care. These girls have seen pantalettes before.

I'm flying. I'm flying. Higher and higher. I bet no one in this school has ever flown this high before. Opening my eyes, I see people on Dorchester Street way beyond the fence. I want to shout to them. "Look at me. Look at me! I'm flying." Higher, higher, higher.

Suddenly, Sister Sarah roars out the door yelling, "Nellie, get off that swing. One of these days, you'll break your neck, I swan. And pull that skirt down."

Darn. Who told?

Sister shivers and rushes back inside, her chubby bottom wiggling, two battling piglets under the black skirt of her habit. It makes me giggle out loud.

She slams the door. I pump twice more and ready for the jump. It must be timed perfectly or I'll land face first in the dirt like that time in sixth grade. The scabs lasted a month. My mother scolded me even as she plastered my puss with some foul-smelling ointment she got from Uncle

Neo. The girls called me Smelly Nellie.

There will be no such mistakes this time. When the swing hits its highest point, I soar. Arching, then rounding my back, I pull my arms back next to my ears. I point the heels of my boots down. Suspended in the air, I pretend I'm the trapeze lady I saw in a poster from the Dan Costello Circus. When I hit the dirt in a hard-heeled landing, I am only two feet from the wire fence.

A new record. Brilliant. What a day. First, the A+ in arithmetic and now a record landing. Life is perfect.

Right then, a cloud passes over the sun and my shoulders tremble with the chill.

Skipping to stay warm, I join the other girls at the wooden table. As I unwrap my cheese sandwich, I look up and realize Fiona, her eyes narrow, is staring at me, eyes blazing. I hadn't noticed her sitting there or would have sat on the grass.

Actually, Fiona always looks mad about something lately, except when that disgusting Orville Mattison's around. She told us girls Orville said her brown eyes were his sparkly diamonds in the sunlight. Ever since he said that, she flutters her eyes all over the place on sunny days, but not today, not with that cloud.

Fiona likes Orville, and that confounds me. Most boys stink of dirty socks and rotten underwear. The stinkiest of them all is Orville Mattison. Really. It's true.

Last winter, when Fiona and I were still friends, we had a snowball fight with Orville and some kids. I flopped down on my back and started making an angel. That pig, Orville, jumped on top of me and put his hands on my chest. I kneed him so hard he screamed as if I'd stabbed him. He climbed off me, in a hurry. He stunk that day, and still does.

I uncap my jug of water and take a swig.

"Did little Miss Kelly get a perfect paper again?" Fiona spits sarcastically.

"Not sure," I lie, taking a bite of my sandwich.

"Oh, right." She laughs, but it's not a happy laugh. It's a laugh squeezed through an angry throat, with not a bit of belly in it. "You might be the teacher's pet, Nellie, but you don't know everything. There's things we all know that you don't." Her raspy voice is as ugly as her tight-grinned face.

What does she mean by that? What things? I think for a second that I should just ignore her and walk away, but my curiosity gets the best of me. I bite. "Like what?"

The other girls grow quiet and seem to be holding their breaths. My sandwich sticks in my throat. Fiona's secrets are never happy ones. I grab my jug of water again.

Fiona sits back, brushing a crumb of bread from her uniform. "Oh, just an itty-bitty secret everyone knows but you." She fluffs out her hair.

A crow caws as another cloud passes over the sun.

I swallow too fast and hiccough. "What secret?"

"Oh, nothing." She grins and whispers something to Annie O'Hara.

"Fiona, tell me right now or I'll tell Sister."

Her eyes bug out. "Oh, no!" Her mouth twists. "All right, if you insist. What you don't know is that your mother was the whore of the Pilgrim's Dandy, that coffin ship, when she came over from Ireland. Everybody else knows." The hiss of her words bounces off the brick walls of the school house, a devil's echo. She rises from the table and pats her skirt down over her bustled rump.

The playground freezes into a tintype. There's no sound until a second grader leaps off one end of the teeter totter, bouncing the other-end girl to her backside. The one who lands wails, "Sister Sarah."

Her cry sounds as if it comes through a cotton fog, but I don't take my eyes off Fiona.

What did she say? My mother? The whore of a ship? That's crazy.

"Take it back," I snarl. "You're lying."

"Am not. My mother told me." She turns away as though this is the end of our conversation.

I grab her by the shoulder and whirl her back to face me. "Your mother's a liar, too."

"Nuh-uh," Fiona shakes her head, "my mother was on that ship, and she knows."

There's Banshee blood on my mother's side of the family and she's always warning me not to lose my temper lest I unleash a Banshee inside me, but this time I can't help it. I ball up my fist and hit Fiona square in the snoot. She squeals like a pig stuck for roasting. Blood spurts from her nose and down the front of her blue silk uniform.

Suddenly, Sister Sarah is between us, pinching our arms with fingers strong as a blacksmith's vice. "Stop that, you two brawling street urchins. I won't have you fouling the air of St. Augustine's with a donnybrook."

"She started it," Fiona whines, tears streaming down her face as she tucks her curls back into their topknot and wipes the blood off her face with her shawl.

"I don't care who started it," Sister yells. "I'm the one who'll finish it." She grabs me by the ear. "Nellie Kelly, in my office." She jams a finger into Fiona's collar bone. "I'll deal with you later."

My heart hurts from Fiona's lie, and I blink back tears. She used to be my best friend. I loved sleeping at her mansion on Beacon Hill and eating crust-less sandwiches cut in perfect little triangles by her maid. Her closet was a fairyland, packed tight with beautiful dresses. I'd die for such dresses. It was wonderful being Fiona's friend. Since last year, though, she hates me.

"Sit, Miss Kelly." Sister points to the leather chair opposite her desk. I fidget into it, pulling at the tight buttons on the seat. Her office is warm, and I feel perspiration pop out on my forehead. My eyes fix on the crucifix on Sister's chest. She settles in, huffs, and crosses her arms. "Now, Miss Kelly. What's this all about?"

What can I say? If I tell the truth, I'll be punished for repeating a bad word, whore. If I lie, Jesus on Sister's crucifix might start bleeding right down the front of her habit as a sign of my sinfulness. I've heard that sometimes Jesus does things like that for punishment.

"I asked what this is all about," Sister repeats.

I can't sit here quiet all day. She might take out her ruler and pound my hands like Sister Annunciata did to Maeve O'Grady's last year after she caught Maeve smooching some kid from Boy's Academy. After that, they shipped the old nun back to Ireland.

"I'm sorry, Sister," I mumble.

"Sorry for what?"

"For fighting with Fiona."

"Look, Miss Kelly. You can stall 'til the cows come home, but you're not leaving this office 'til I know what the fight was about." Her brogue is thick now, a sure sign she's mad.

I suck in a deep breath and admit, "Fiona said something bad about my mother."

"About Mary Kelly?" She gasps, her eyes round as two blue marbles. "Who could say anything bad about Mary? She's a saint, she is, a saint."

I dig my nails into the wooden arms of the chair. People are always saying my mother is a saint. They should only see the way that saint rubs up against my da, nibbling on his ear. It's embarrassing. I slump down in the chair.

"What exactly did Fiona say?"

The 'saint' comment made me so mad I don't even care if I shock Sister now, so I say it. "That my mother was the whore of the ship she came over from Ireland on."

The chubby face flames above the white wimple. She sputters something in Irish I can't understand and catches her wire-rimmed glasses just before they fall off the tip of her nose. For a minute, I think she's going to climb over the desk and smack me one, but she stays squatted there, like a little black-and-white hen. "This is a matter for Monsignor Varley."

Panic floods over me worse than the Charles after a storm. *No. Monsignor'll go to my house. My mother and da'll think he's visiting because of me getting good grades or something. My mother will make black-currant scones like he's the President or Pope or something. Then Monsignor'll tell them I hit Fiona. My da'll be so mad. My mother might cry. Think, Nellie, think.*

Taking in a deep breath, I say, "Sister, can't we handle this another way?" I clasp my hands into a steeple.

She doesn't answer.

I say a quick prayer to St. Jude. He always works. "What if I ask my mother to come here for a meeting with *you*?"

She pushes her spectacles up again. One eyebrow rises, and the other flattens, then she smiles. I think my idea makes her feel special, perhaps nearly as important as Monsignor. If that thought wasn't so funny, I'd feel sorry for her. Nuns beg for money at the Beacon Hill mansions; monsignors are wined and dined in those same houses.

She finally speaks. "Very well, Nellie. Tell your mother to be here tomorrow after school, and you with her. We'll settle this between us."

Good. My mother will say Fiona lied, and that'll settle it. Then, Fiona'll be the one in trouble. I won't have to watch my da's face when Monsignor says bad things about me. "All right, Sister. I'll tell her."

"Now, tell Fiona Doggett to get herself in here. Tomorrow afternoon, you get to confession, girl."

Oh, no. I hate confession.

VISIT OUR WEBSITE
FOR THE FULL INVENTORY
OF QUALITY BOOKS:

http://www.roguephoenixpress.com

Rogue Phoenix Press

Representing Excellence in Publishing

*Quality trade paperbacks and downloads
in multiple formats,
in genres ranging from historical to contemporary romance,
mystery and science fiction.
Visit the website then bookmark it.
We add new titles each month!*

www.ingramcontent.com/pod-product-compliance
Lightning Source LLC
Chambersburg PA
CBHW051416170626
46809CB00006B/2190